SAVING SOFIA

THE RUSSO SISTERS, BOOK 1

LINDA SEED

GET A LINDA SEED SHORT STORY FREE

To my husband, John

BY LINDA SEED

The Main Street Merchants
Moonstone Beach
Like That Endless Cambria Sky
Nearly Wild
Fire and Glass

The Delaneys of Cambria
A Long, Cool Rain
The Promise of Lightning
Loving the Storm
Searching for Sunshine

The Russo Sisters
Saving Sofia
First Crush

1

———————

S ofia Russo liked to tell people she lived in a whorehouse. It was true, after all—even if the whores in question had long since moved on.

One thing hadn't changed since the days, a hundred and fifty years before, when her house had been an establishment of prostitution: it was now, as then, occupied entirely by women preoccupied with the subject of men.

"All I said is that I'm lonely," Sofia told her sisters as the four of them bustled around in the kitchen on a sunny August morning, getting ready for work. "I didn't ask to be psychoanalyzed."

Martina, the youngest of the sisters, was spreading almond butter on a slice of whole wheat toast, her dyed auburn hair piled on top of her head in a precarious updo. "And all *I* said is that you wouldn't be lonely if you'd stop dumping every guy you go out with."

"I liked Steven." Benny—short for Benedetta—extended her index finger to emphasize her point. She held a mug of coffee in her other hand. "He was hot. Those abs ..."

"Why were you looking at Steven's abs?" Sofia demanded.

"Oh, please." The oldest sister, Bianca, rolled her eyes as she stood at the kitchen counter slicing fruit on a wooden cutting board.

"We all looked. The man took his shirt off so often you'd think he was allergic to cotton."

That was true. Steven had enjoyed showing off his body, which had been one of the reasons she'd broken up with him. He hadn't just displayed his abs to her sisters—he'd displayed them to everyone who came into visual range.

When he was doing yard work? No shirt. Housework? No shirt. Of course he'd worn no shirt at the beach, but you'd have expected him to put one on at the taco truck, say, or at Soto's Market.

Steven's abs had been viewed more times than *The Wizard of Oz*.

She sighed. They really *had* been nice.

"What about Greg?" Martina asked. "What was wrong with him?"

"Forgot her birthday," Benny reminded her.

"Jason ... what was his last name?" Bianca tried.

"Elliot. Jason Elliot," Martina filled in. "Liked shellfish."

"I'm *allergic* to shellfish," Sofia pointed out. "Was I supposed to just *ignore* it when he ate lobster in front of me? Was I supposed to just *die*?"

"The point is," Bianca said, putting her coffee mug in the sink and filling a plastic container with the fruit she'd prepared, "You might be a little ... what's the word?"

"Picky," Martina offered.

"Self-defeating," Benny put in.

"Can't I complain that I'm lonely without getting a lecture about what's wrong with me?" Sofia asked.

"We offer that as a bonus service, at no extra charge," Bianca said sweetly. "I've gotta go. I have the Donaldson triplets at eight."

Bianca, a pediatrician, was dressed professionally in black slacks, a white button-down shirt, and low-heeled pumps. Her dark, glossy hair had been smoothed with a straightening iron, and it lay to her shoulders in a shiny bob.

Briefcase in hand, she grabbed the container of fruit and headed for the door.

"It's your turn to cook!" Martina called after her.

"I remember!" Bianca called, then shut the door behind her.

Sofia glared at her younger sister. "It's *your* turn to cook."

Martina shrugged. "If she can't remember whose night it is, she deserves what she gets."

UNLIKE BIANCA, Sofia didn't need to do much to get ready for her day. Her wardrobe didn't matter because she wore a wetsuit to work. There was no point in wearing makeup because it would just smear and run the first time she went underwater. And obviously, any effort to do something with her hair would be a waste of time.

All she had to do was brush her teeth, put on a pair of jeans, a T-shirt, and a pair of boots, and run a brush through her long, dark hair, and she was ready to leave the house. It was one of the perks of leading kayak tours at San Simeon Cove.

She probably should have used some of the time she saved on primping to clean her room, she thought, looking around her cluttered, chaotic space.

The house, a big log cabin with an ocean view, had belonged to her parents, who had bought the place ten years before. With their girls grown, they had treated the house as their baby. It had originally been two side-by-side log cabins on adjoining lots, each in such desperate disrepair that they were on the verge of falling down. The cabins had originally been houses of prostitution in a neighborhood that, at the time, was full of them—giving Cambria's Happy Hill neighborhood its name.

Aldo and Carmela had worked with an architect and a contractor to merge the two structures into one. Then they had painstakingly restored and improved it until the house had become so cozy, so quirky and charming, that it had been featured in a Central Coast design magazine.

The idea had been for them to live out their golden years in the house, welcoming their eventual grandchildren into this haven that was so much a part of them, so intimately theirs.

But then, there'd been the cancer diagnosis. Carmela was at stage four by the time the disease was discovered. She'd died just a few months later, and Aldo had followed shortly after in a car accident—vehicle vs. tree—that no one was certain was truly accidental.

In the wake of that one-two punch, the four women had inherited the house. None of them had wanted to sell it, given how much their parents had loved it. And none of them had been able to agree on who should live there.

After a couple of months of bickering, Martina had pointed out that there were four of them and four bedrooms.

The solution was obvious.

Sofia's room had white wood paneling, an oak floor the color of caramel, a stone fireplace, and a big window facing the ocean. There was still some grumbling from the others that she'd scored the prime bedroom, with both the fireplace and the view, but the room assignments had been chosen randomly, so here she was.

The least she could do was take care of the room better than she had been, but she couldn't bring herself to do it. This room had belonged to her parents—it wasn't supposed to be hers. If she were to make it her own—if she were to take pride in the space and truly enjoy its comforts—she'd be admitting that her parents weren't coming back. She wasn't ready for that. Not yet.

And right now, there wasn't time to think about it, because she was running late. She grabbed a duffel bag containing her wetsuit, a towel, a bar of soap, and travel sized bottles of shampoo and conditioner. Then she went outside, climbed onto her bike—a Triumph Tiger—put on her helmet, and headed toward Highway 1.

She had a tour group at nine, and she didn't want to keep them waiting.

～

PATRICK THOUGHT, not for the first time, that he might be making a mistake.

He'd never been kayaking. He had no interest in kayaking. He was terrified of the water. And he couldn't swim.

But he had to meet Sofia Russo, and if that meant risking death by drowning, then so be it. Besides, wasn't that what life jackets were for?

"You sure you want to do this, man? You look a little green." Patrick's friend Ramon was peering at him with concern as they got out of Ramon's truck in the San Simeon Cove parking lot.

"Uh … yes. Let's just … yes. I can do this." Patrick nodded his head firmly to reinforce his positive self-talk.

"At least put on some sunscreen." Ramon tossed him a tube of SPF 50. "If you don't drown, you're gonna fry to a little smoking crisp."

Patrick accepted the tube and went to work on the few areas of his body that weren't covered by his board shorts and rash guard. With his white-blond hair, pale blue eyes, and skin that freckled at the mere suggestion of sun, he would be courting melanoma if he didn't slather himself in the stuff.

With that done, the two of them looked over to where Sofia, her curves deliciously encased in a wetsuit, was pulling kayaks off of a stack in preparation for the tour. A few tourists in bathing suits were gathered around her.

"I've got to hand it to you, Patrick." Ramon slapped him on the back hard enough to make him stumble forward. "You're putting yourself out there. You're going to get shot down like a duck during hunting season, but at least you're going for it." Ramon started off toward Sofia and the kayaks, and Patrick followed him.

2

———————

The whole ill-conceived kayaking plan had come about earlier this week after Patrick had stopped in at Jitters, a coffee place on Main Street in Cambria, to grab a large latte for his drive to work in San Luis Obispo.

He'd walked in the door and had been struck senseless by the sight of the woman ordering at the counter.

Five-foot-eight, probably. Thick, dark hair that flowed down her back in waves. Skin that spoke of Mediterranean climates and sun-baked cobblestone streets. Long, smooth legs in very short shorts. Eyes the color of espresso. A body that sloped and curved in all the right places.

He couldn't move. He couldn't think. He forgot why he'd come into the shop.

"Excuse me. Excuse me, please."

He moved aside with a start, realizing he was blocking the entrance. A couple of tourists pushed past him, shooting him annoyed looks.

He was still standing there when the woman—no, the *goddess*—walked past him with her coffee cup in her hand and headed out the door.

Once she was out of his immediate vicinity, he was able to breathe again. He walked to the counter, managed to order his drink, then asked Connor, the guy behind the counter, "Who ... um ... who was that?"

"Which *who* are you referring to?" Connor took Patrick's money and put it into the register.

"The dark-haired woman who just left. Tall. Very ..." He cleared his throat. "... Very pretty."

"Oh, her? That's Sofia Russo."

Sofia Russo. Even the name was like music. Lost in his reverie, he didn't notice that Connor was handing him his change.

"Dude?" Connor wiggled the coins a little.

"Oh. Sorry." Patrick took the change, dropped it into the tip jar, and headed toward the door. Before he got more than a couple of steps away, he turned back. "Um ... Connor? Do you know anything about her?"

"Not nearly as much as I'd like to." He wiggled his eyebrows. "But I do know that she leads kayak tours out of San Simeon Cove."

"Kayak tours." Patrick let the information sink in.

"Dude. You're way out of your league," Connor observed. "I asked her out once, and she teed off on me like it was the fourth hole at Augusta." He shook his head at what seemed like a fond memory.

Connor was probably right. Patrick was probably headed off on a fool's quest. But how would he know if he didn't try?

So here he was, strapping on a life jacket and hoping he wouldn't get eaten by a shark. People did get eaten by sharks, didn't they? That was a real thing that happened sometimes, not just in movies.

"Everybody ready?" Sofia asked the group—seven people, most of them looking far more enthusiastic than Patrick. "Terrific," she said, in response to the mostly affirmative answers. "Come on down, and I'll show you how to launch."

The kayaks were already laid out near the waterline, each with its own paddle. Sofia stood with her back to the waves, addressing the group, a teacher in front of her eager students.

The procedure was simple enough: They were to drag their kayak as close to the water as possible without it actually floating. Then they'd get in, keeping the bow perpendicular to the waterline.

Using their oar on one side and their free hand on the other, they were to shove the boat forward until they had enough water under them to paddle. Then, keeping the bow pointed straight oceanward, they were to paddle hard through the breaking waves until they were out into the calmer water.

"Don't worry, this is extremely low surf," she said. Because the beach was sheltered within a cove, the waves came barely to an adult's waist. "You shouldn't have any problems getting through the breakers. I'm going to go last, so I can help anyone who needs it. Once you're out there, just stay in the group and wait for me."

It seemed simple enough. Patrick watched while one person after another followed the procedure Sofia had laid out, shoving their little vessels toward the water and then paddling beyond the waves, letting out the occasional whoop of exhilaration.

Soon, there was no one left except Ramon, Patrick, and Sofia.

"You got this?" Ramon looked concerned at the naked fear on Patrick's face.

"Uh ... yeah. Sure. I've got it."

"Okay. Remember, if things go sour, don't go toward the bright light." Ramon stepped forward to take his turn.

He got out there with no trouble, which wasn't surprising, considering that he was much more outdoorsy than Patrick. He liked to jog and ski and probably wrestle alligators. It was why Patrick had asked him to come along.

Ramon had made it look easy. Surely Patrick could do this.

"You're up," Sofia said, giving Patrick a smile that almost made him forget his fear, or even why he'd come. "Nothing to it."

"Okay. Right. Nothing to it," he repeated, trying to convince himself.

He pulled his kayak toward the water, the way she'd told him to do. He climbed in, grabbed his paddle, and began pushing the boat toward the water. So far so good. But things started going sideways—literally—as soon as he had a little bit of ocean water under him. The kayak had barely lifted off the sand before the bow started moving to the left, positioning the kayak parallel to, rather than perpendicular to, the waterline.

A wave—thankfully, just a small one—smacked into the kayak, knocking it onto its side so that Patrick was lying in the wet sand, a glob of it in his left ear.

"Whoopsy daisy!" Sofia shoved both him and the boat upright again. Up to her shins in the water, she grabbed the bow and pulled it straight, then gave it a yank into the water and got deftly out of the way.

"Paddle!" she yelled to him. "Paddle hard!"

He did, gamely trying to power past the child-size breakers, reassuring himself that he was up to the challenge. The rest of the group sat in their kayaks about fifty yards away, yelling encouragement.

"You've got it! You've got it!" Ramon hollered.

For a moment, he truly believed that he did. He got over a wave, his kayak still pointing true. He paddled manfully, rising with the swell of the surf, his heart full of thrill and pride. Why had he been so worried? What had there been to fear? He was doing it, truly doing it, just a man and the sea, like Hemingway and like so many self-actualized men before him.

Patrick imagined this as the beginning of a new, more outdoorsy period in his life. He'd fish. He'd hike. He'd ... climb a mountain, maybe. What would stop him?

He was still fantasizing about the better, future him when the kayak began to turn sideways again with a wave—small but mighty—coming at him. He paddled furiously, trying to right his tiny boat before it was too late.

"Straighten the bow!" Sofia yelled from shore.

He'd just about convinced himself that he had it when the wave smacked into him, lifting him up and depositing him head-down into the water, the kayak on top of him. His head slammed into the side of his oar, and the world swirled to black.

"OH, SHIT!" Sofia rushed out into the water after him. She had never lost a tourist—not yet, anyway. But there was a first time for everything.

She wouldn't have thought a full-grown adult could drown while wearing a life jacket in less than a foot of water, but the guy seemed determined to do just that.

He wasn't getting up—wasn't moving at all, in fact. She grabbed his life jacket and used it to drag him out of the water and onto the sand. The guy was heavier than he looked, but a surge of horror and adrenaline gave Sofia near supernatural powers.

Was he conscious? He didn't seem to be. She leaned her cheek down over his nose and mouth and felt the whisper of steady breathing on her skin.

A middle-aged guy in madras shorts and a straw hat had come over to see if he could help, and he was now calling 911 on his cell phone. Her kayakers were paddling back in to assess the situation.

The guy on the sand had a pulse, and he was breathing, so there was no need for CPR. Still, she'd feel a hell of a lot better when the ambulance got here.

"Sir?" She spoke loudly in the hopes that it might rouse him to consciousness. "Sir!"

The guy's friend had made it to shore. He hauled his kayak onto the sand and ran over, looking scared.

"What's his name?" Sofia asked.

"Patrick. Patrick Connelly."

"Patrick!" Sofia yelled at the man on the sand. "Patrick! Can you hear me?"

Patrick woke up certain that he was dead. He had to be, because there was an angel standing over him.

Sofia was so beautiful with the sun behind her, creating a golden halo around her head. Those eyes, and her lips ...

But he couldn't actually be dead, because his head was killing him. He had to assume that when someone was dead, pain ceased. But then, there was the whole Judeo-Christian concept of Hell and eternal suffering, so maybe—

"He's awake!" Ramon announced, and some of the others whooped and cheered.

"Oh, thank God." Sofia made the sign of the cross over her wetsuit-clad body.

That body.

It was something to be thankful for, indeed.

3

____

Patrick tried to protest that an ambulance ride to the hospital was unnecessary, but the paramedics persuaded him to go along with it. He'd lost consciousness—however briefly—and that wasn't something to take lightly.

It was better to be safe than to ignore a traumatic brain injury.

So he let them strap him onto a gurney and load him into the back of the ambulance while he tried to look brave for Sofia's benefit. It was bad enough that she'd seen him get creamed by a wave not much taller than a toddler; he didn't need her to think he would fall apart at the first hint of pain.

"I'm sure it's nothing," he said to one of the paramedics, speaking loudly and clearly so that Sofia might hear him from where she stood outside the rig.

"Yeah, well, you never know," said the paramedic, an older guy with a balding head and a slight paunch. "One time I responded to a call for a guy who hit his head on a doorframe. No blood, no bump, no LOC—nothing."

Patrick surmised that *LOC* meant *loss of consciousness*, a piece of information he'd gleaned from watching medical TV shows. "So, what happened?" he asked.

"Buddy of mine at the hospital said the guy came in two days later with a brain hemorrhage. Died in the ER." He shook his head. "You don't mess with a head injury."

Patrick decided that a trip to the hospital wasn't such a bad idea after all.

SOFIA WASN'T sure what to do, as this had never happened to her before. Patrick Connolly was the first of her clients ever to be hauled off in an ambulance under her watch.

On one hand, she felt responsible for him. She'd been the one to put him in danger, after all, and had also been the one who'd likely saved his life. On the other hand, she had six other paying clients—five, after Patrick's friend opted to follow the ambulance in his truck—who hadn't had their tour.

Everybody was gathered on the beach, looking to her for guidance. She was shaken by what had happened, and she was worried about Patrick. He'd seemed so vulnerable lying there on the sand, his life in Sofia's hands.

She opted to compensate her clients—rain checks for two of them and refunds for the rest—gather up her stuff, and head to the hospital in Templeton to make sure Patrick was okay.

She didn't know if he had any family or anyone other than the guy he'd come with. He was her responsibility. And even if he hadn't been, she couldn't relax or concentrate on anything until she knew he was okay.

PATRICK WENT THROUGH A CT SCAN, a physical exam, endless questioning about what day it was and whether he knew his name, and several bouts of waiting so interminable that he almost wished his condition were worse just to move things along.

During one of the waits, after the CT scan but before anyone had told him the results, a nurse poked her head through a break in the curtain that had been drawn around his bed for privacy.

"That girl is still out there waiting," she said, as though they'd already discussed this and Patrick was supposed to know who she was talking about. "Do you want me to send her back?"

"What girl?" Ramon had wandered off to the cafeteria, and Patrick couldn't imagine who else might have come. His sister? She wouldn't have been able to make it here from Michigan by now, even if someone had called her. His mother? Surely she would have been described as a woman rather than a girl.

"Long, dark hair. Tall. Pretty. Says she's the one who pulled you out of the water. Is she your girlfriend?"

Sofia was here?

A riot of conflicting emotions swirled inside him. He was delighted that she'd cared enough to come and also that she was, even now, in his immediate vicinity. But the delight was overwhelmed by his state of humiliation. He'd proven himself to be disastrously inadequate at kayaking. And he was currently lying in a hospital bed wearing a thin paper gown that, should he stand up, would show a three-inch strip of his boxer shorts.

He was still pondering what to tell the nurse about Sofia when Ramon came back, his hands full of Doritos, Snickers bars, and Ho Hos from the vending machine.

"Hey, Patrick, your kayak babe is out there in the waiting room. You want me to get her, bring her back here? This is your big chance to play the sympathy card. Because, and I say this with all due respect, that's the only way you're gonna get anywhere with her."

Ramon might be right. It might take a head injury and a near drowning for her to view him as anything other than a client. But he couldn't let her come back here. He couldn't lose whatever masculine dignity he had left.

"Can you get rid of her for me?" he asked.

"Get rid of her?" Ramon looked at him like he was crazy. "What for?"

Patrick put all of his cards on the metaphorical table. "Look at me.

Look at this hospital gown. The nurse called me sweetie and offered to help me walk to the toilet. This is not how I want Sofia to see me."

Ramon considered that. "You have a point."

"Can you just ... just thank her for coming and tell her I'm okay? Tell her everything's under control. Then send her home or back to the beach or ... somewhere. Anywhere."

"All right. I'm on it." Ramon parted the curtain and turned back toward Patrick. "Before I go, you want some Ho Hos?"

ALL SHE COULD THINK WAS that maybe he was angry, somehow blaming her for causing the accident. Did he think she was negligent? Was he planning to sue?

He'd signed a release of liability before she'd taken him onto the water—all of her clients did—so that would be some protection. But that kind of thing was never one hundred percent. He could argue that the terms of the release hadn't been made clear. He could argue that she'd failed to perform on her end of things. He could claim that her equipment was faulty, that the life jacket had failed ...

None of that would be fair, but when had life gotten a reputation for fairness?

She was worried about all of that, yes. But that wasn't the only thing on her mind as she rode her bike home from the hospital, having failed to see or speak to Patrick. She was concerned that he might really be hurt. She'd have felt so much better if she'd been able to see for herself that he was recovering from his accident.

Sofia got home earlier than usual, just after noon, because she'd called everyone and canceled her afternoon tour. Martina, who worked from home as an interior designer, was making a cup of tea in the kitchen when Sofia came in, dumping her things on the sofa.

"What are you doing here?" she asked. "I thought you were taking a group out this afternoon."

"I was. I canceled." She plopped down onto a barstool at the kitchen island, suddenly exhausted.

"You did? But—"

"One of the guys in the morning group almost died, and I went to the hospital to make sure he was okay. So, that happened."

"That's awful." Martina's eyes were wide. "Let me make you a cup of tea."

Martina should have been British instead of Italian. The woman thought anything could be cured with a hot cup of tea. Sofia had less confidence in tea's curative powers, but it was nice to have someone fussing over her.

She covered her face with her hands, let out a moan, then scrubbed at her eyelids with her fingertips. "He wasn't even past the breakers. A two-foot wave dumped him upside down, and splat." She shook her head in disbelief. "He was lying there like he was dead. I thought he was dead."

Martina deposited a steaming mug of tea in front of her sister. "Is he okay?"

"I think so. I pulled him out of the water, and some guy on the beach called 911. He was conscious by the time they took him away. I followed him to the hospital, just to make sure, but his friend sent me away."

Martina was leaning on her elbows on the island. "He sent you away?"

"Yes. Which makes me wonder if I'm about to get sued and we're all about to be living in a cardboard box."

"Oh, I doubt it." Martina, always the most optimistic of the sisters, waved away the idea. "After all, you're the one who rescued him."

Sofia sipped her tea. It did make her feel a little better.

"I hope he's okay." She held the mug in both of her hands for comfort. "He was ... cute."

"Really," Martina said. "How cute?"

Sofia pondered the question. "You know how some guys just seem like any other guy, and then something happens and you can see exactly what they must have been like when they were five, or ten, and it makes you want to bring them home and stroke their forehead and make it all better?"

"Yeah." Martina's voice was dreamy.

Sofia pointed a finger gun at her. "He was exactly that kind of cute."

"Well ... sounds like he needs someone to make it all better. Maybe you'll still get your chance."

4

As it turned out, Patrick did have a concussion, but it was mild, and his brain wasn't bleeding—though there was some debate as to whether his brain had been functioning properly in the first place, given that he'd gone kayaking with no water skills whatsoever.

They'd kept him in the hospital overnight for observation, then sent him home with a headache, a bump on the top of his head, and a much more significant wound to his manly pride.

Ramon drove him home because he'd arrived by ambulance and didn't have his car. The fact that it was Saturday added insult to literal injury—he didn't even have an excuse to cancel his classes.

He said goodbye to Ramon, let himself into the one-bedroom guesthouse he rented in Cambria's Leimert neighborhood, and went into the tiny bathroom to take a long, hot shower.

Staying in the hospital overnight could make a person feel grimy enough, but Patrick had never had a chance to get clean after his close encounter with the sand at San Simeon. His hair still had grit in it, and he shampooed it gingerly, taking care to avoid the painful bump on his head.

He'd just come out of the shower, his hair still wet, a towel still wrapped around his waist, when his cell phone rang. He picked up the phone from the coffee table and checked the screen: an unknown number with a local area code.

He didn't know who he'd expected, but it certainly wasn't Sofia Russo. As soon as she identified herself, he felt a giddy surge of adrenaline.

She was saying something, but the buzz of nerves in his brain blocked part of it out, and all he heard was, "... to make sure you're okay."

"Oh. Uh ... that's nice of you." For some reason, that was all he could get out.

"So, are you?"

"Am I what?"

"Are you okay?"

He reminded himself to take a deep breath and quiet his mind. Then he focused on the simple, attainable goal of being coherent.

"Yes. I'm fine, thanks. A little bit of a headache, but they say that's to be expected. They kept me at the hospital overnight, but I'm home now."

There. That wasn't so hard.

"Good. I'm glad."

He wondered for a moment how she'd gotten his number, then he realized that was a stupid question—he'd given it to her when he'd signed up for the kayak tour. He just never thought she'd use it.

"Ah ... thank you, by the way. For saving my life. I don't exactly remember it, but that's what they told me. That you pulled me out of the water. So ... thank you." He was babbling. Damn it.

"You're welcome. I'm trained in CPR, and I thought I was going to have to use it."

For a moment, he imagined her pressing her mouth to his, blowing life back into his lungs, the intimacy of that, the two of them breathing as one. Did they still teach mouth-to-mouth as part of CPR? He seemed to remember that they'd phased it out. Still ...

"Patrick?"

He'd wandered off into a reverie. Maybe it was the concussion.

"Sorry. I'm here. I hope I didn't put you to too much trouble, with the almost dying and everything."

"No trouble at all." He could hear the smile in her voice.

"I owe you," he said.

"No, you don't. But still ... maybe you'll have a chance to make it up to me sometime."

As awkward and nervous as he was, he still recognized that as an invitation. She was leaving the door open to ... what? Dinner? A coffee date? A tip for her excellent service as a kayak guide and impromptu lifeguard?

It was only after the call was over that he mentally kicked himself for not asking her out.

He sat down on the bed, still in his towel, and flopped onto his back, staring at the ceiling. Was that what she'd meant? Was she open to him asking her out?

If he did go out with her, he'd be so outclassed that it would be like trying to perform open heart surgery while blindfolded and wearing mittens.

Still, a man who was afraid of risk was a man who was afraid of life.

He could do this. He just needed time to work his way up to it.

On Monday, he met Ramon at a coffee kiosk on the Cal Poly San Luis Obispo campus before teaching his first class—a survey of Western literature before the eighteenth century—to debrief him about Sofia's call. Ramon, an associate professor in the math department, rarely allowed himself to be scheduled for any classes before ten a.m., so he had time to counsel Patrick in the ways of women.

"These were her words: 'Maybe you'll have a chance to make it up to me sometime.' I'm quoting exactly." Patrick added sugar and cream to his coffee, then fitted the plastic lid on the cup. He turned to Ramon. "What do you think that means?"

"It means you're hopeless." Ramon, who had never progressed

past seventh grade in his food choices, was holding an iced, blended drink piled with whipped cream. "She wanted you to ask her out, and you dropped the ball."

"I didn't drop the ball," Patrick protested. "There was no ball."

"Oh, there was a ball," Ramon insisted. "And you bobbled it. You could be doing the touchdown dance right now, but instead, you're asking me for relationship advice."

Patrick had the sickening feeling that Ramon was right. She'd given him an opening, and he hadn't taken it. What if he never got such a chance again?

"So ... what do I do now?"

"Call her back and ask her out," Ramon suggested. "Obviously."

Patrick sipped his coffee for fortification. "I'm not sure I'm ready for that."

"Oh, you're not. Believe me. But you should do it anyway."

"I don't know. Maybe ... what if I tried kayaking again? You know ... just to spend some more time around her first."

"You're too scared to ask her out, but you're not too scared to do something that almost killed you the last time you tried it?"

Patrick frowned. "Well ... it sounds foolish when you put it that way."

Ramon raised one eyebrow. "There might be a reason for that."

HE WAS INFATUATED, but he wasn't stupid. He waited a couple of weeks before signing up for kayaking again. He let the bump on his head heal and made sure he wasn't suffering any lingering effects from the concussion.

When he was pretty sure he was okay, he went to her website and signed up for a Saturday tour. He'd have asked Ramon to go with him again, but he didn't want to be told that he was being reckless and foolhardy. He already knew that.

In the days leading up to Saturday, he was nervous about his physical safety. Drowning in the ocean was not part of his life plan.

But the idea of seeing Sofia again balanced out the fear. The risk to his body would be worth it if he could talk to her a little. Look into those dark, limitless eyes. My God, she might even have occasion to touch him—preferably not in the context of a tourniquet or chest compressions.

One could always hope.

~

WHEN SOFIA CHECKED her website and saw that Patrick Connolly had signed up for her tour again, she didn't know whether to be pleased or horrified. Given how the last time had gone, she wondered if she should call him and suggest other forms of outdoor recreation—like sunbathing.

On the other hand, with his fair coloring, that might be just as dangerous.

"I can't believe it," she told Benny when she saw his name. "I seriously cannot believe it."

Sofia was seated at the kitchen table with her laptop at around ten a.m., the golden morning sun flooding the room. Benny was rooting around in the refrigerator, her butt sticking out in Sofia's direction.

"You can't believe what? That somebody ate the last yogurt? Neither can I, my friend. Neither can I."

"Not the yogurt," Sofia said. "I can't believe Patrick Connolly signed up for the tour again."

Benny straightened and closed the refrigerator door, a cheese stick and a bottle of Coke in her hands in lieu of the yogurt. "Wait. Is he the guy who wiped out and nearly drowned?"

"That's the guy."

"Oh, man." Benny had just come in from a run, and she was wearing a pair of running shorts and a tank top, both damp with sweat. Her hair, the same dark color as Sofia's, was gathered into two stubby pigtails, her bangs skimming the middle of her forehead. "Either he really wants to learn to kayak, or he's got it bad."

"He's got what bad?" Sofia asked.

"Oh, come on. You can't tell me he'd be the first guy to sign up for kayaking because of the way you look in a wetsuit."

Sofia considered that. "Well … maybe not. But that's not it."

"Really. How do you know?"

"Because I gave him a chance to ask me out. Said he could find a way to repay me for saving his life. And he just … didn't do anything with it."

Benny shrugged. "Maybe he's shy."

That was possible. He certainly wasn't smooth with women. And he wasn't classically handsome, though he did have this … thing. This thing that made Sofia want to take him home with her, either to go to bed with him or just to make him a nice, home-cooked meal.

She wasn't sure about the nature of the thing, but it was there. The thing. Whatever it was.

"He could be shy," she admitted. "Or maybe he just really wants to learn to kayak."

"Either way, you've got to give the guy points for persistence."

5

On Saturday, Patrick drove to San Simeon telling himself not to think about the fear. Fear was just a thought, just a feeling. If he didn't allow himself to think it or feel it, then it wouldn't be real.

Of course, the danger he was putting himself in—that was real.

He'd taken some steps to mitigate the risks. He'd gone on YouTube to learn how to launch a kayak. He'd paid particular attention to keeping the bow straight, since that seemed to be where he'd gone wrong before.

And he'd done a little praying. He wasn't particularly religious, but it couldn't hurt.

By the time he parked his car and headed toward the place on the sand where Sofia was setting up her equipment, he felt as ready as he would ever be.

He was less ready to talk to Sofia, but if he could refuse to feel fear about kayaking, he could refuse to feel fear about that, too.

She was leaning down over a kayak, doing some unidentifiable thing to the inside of it, when he approached. She was facing away from him, giving him a view of her wetsuit-clad behind that almost made his knees weak. The other tour participants were standing around watching, chatting among themselves.

When she straightened up, turned around, and noticed him, she gave him a languid half smile that made him think of how she might look at him after sex, should he ever be that fortunate.

"Patrick," she said. "Are you sure you want to do this?"

"Absolutely." He tried to sound more confident than he felt. "Yes. Absolutely." And he *was* sure he wanted to do it. He'd surrendered a certain part of his manhood when he'd crashed into the sand two weeks before. The only way to get it back was to show her that he could do this and that he wasn't afraid.

Even if it turned out that he couldn't do it, and he was afraid.

"Well, all right, then." She rooted around in her pile of equipment and brought out a helmet. "I think you should wear this." She tossed it to him, and he caught it.

"Ah. Right. Good thinking." Between the helmet and the life jacket, what could possibly go wrong?

Sofia had to admit that the guy had grit. After what happened last time, most people would never go into the water again. But he was gamely giving it another try, even though he was plainly scared shitless.

"All right," she told him when the others had launched and it was time for him to go. "I'm going to hold onto the stern and keep you straight until you're past the first line of breakers. Once I let go, don't let yourself get turned sideways. If you start to go to the side, use your paddle to get straightened out again. Once you're past the surf line, you should be good. Are you ready?"

His mouth was too dry for him to speak, so he just nodded.

"Okay. Here we go."

She pushed him and the kayak forward, and Patrick used his hand and his paddle the way she and YouTube had taught him. When the first child-sized wave hit him, she was still behind him keeping the kayak straight. He paddled hard, moving forward, keeping the bow as straight as he could.

A second, larger wave headed toward him, and Sofia let go. This was the moment that would decide everything. Either he would keep the kayak straight and get past the wave line to join the others, or he wouldn't. There was more at stake than his paddling skills. He wanted her to see him as competent. He wanted her to see him as brave.

He wanted her to see him as a man.

The wave hit—admittedly, it was a small one, but it seemed colossal to him—and the kayak started to turn sideways. He used his paddle to fight the turn, pulling hard, using his weight and the balance of his body to turn the bow into the wave. He put his full strength, his full concentration, his full focus into the task, willing himself and the little vessel that held him to remain true.

When he emerged, still upright and still relatively dry, on the other side of the wave, he let out a whoop of pure joy. He could hear Sofia somewhere back there cheering for him. He paddled out to the others, triumphant.

None of the others in the tour group understood what a big moment it was for him, but Sofia did, and that was enough. He felt a surge of powerful, crystalline adrenaline, and for that moment, he felt like he could do anything.

Sofia was so delighted with Patrick, not only for what he'd accomplished but also for the courage it had taken to even attempt it, that she couldn't help herself. When the tour was done and everyone was on dry land, the kayaks sitting empty on the sand, she jumped into his arms and embraced him.

"You did it! You really did it!" She let him go and stood at arm's length, still holding onto his shoulders. "I'm damned proud of you, Patrick."

He was smiling and blushing, his eyes down, not meeting hers. And, holy crap, if that wasn't cute. So, yeah, he was shy, then. There was a sweetness in him that pulled at her, intrigued her.

So, she would give him another opportunity and see if, this time, he would take it.

"We should celebrate," she said. "Let me buy you a drink. I have another tour at two o'clock, but I'll be back on the beach by three thirty. Meet me here?"

There was the blush again, the smile. And the incredibly cute, shy stammer. "Uh ... that's ... I'd like that."

She gave his shoulders a squeeze and let go of him. She turned and walked away from him, and if she put a little extra sashay into her walk, well, a girl had to use whatever tools she had at her disposal.

PATRICK WENT HOME, showered, and tried to make sense of all that had happened. He'd done it—he'd actually done it. And then, good God, she'd asked him out. If there was any way today's adventure could have gone better, he couldn't think what it would be.

Perhaps if he'd found sunken treasure during the tour ...

As he dressed, he started to doubt himself. What if she hadn't actually asked him out on a date? What if she genuinely just wanted to buy him a drink to congratulate him on his kayaking success, and nothing more? What if she routinely bought drinks for participants of her tour—whether male or female? What if he was reading this all wrong?

Because he had few skills for interpreting the motivations of women, he called Ramon.

"I went kayaking again, and it went well—no paramedics required —and Sofia said she wanted to take me out for a drink. What does that mean?" He was sitting on the sofa in his tiny house, scrubbed clean and smelling of soap and shampoo.

"It means she has no taste in men," Ramon responded.

"But ... what does it *mean*? Is this an actual date? Or is she just saying, *I'm glad you didn't die?* Or ..."

"You know, I'm beginning to see why you don't get more action with women."

"Ramon ..."

"Just go with it," he said. "Go out, have the drink. Relax. And see what happens."

~

Patrick spent more time than necessary, probably, on deciding what to wear. He wanted to look nice, but he didn't want to look *too* nice, given the fact that he would be picking Sofia up directly from the beach. Clearly, this would be a casual thing.

He opted for jeans and a button-down shirt that someone had once said looked good with his eyes.

It occurred to him that she might be getting into his car, so he tidied it up, clearing out a stack of student papers that were waiting to be graded, then gave the interior a pass with the small hand-held vacuum he kept in the trunk.

Having assessed his hair (combed), his breath (fresh), and his wallet (present and accounted for—he'd forgotten it on a date once, and would never make that mistake again), he got into his car and headed for San Simeon.

When he got there, he spotted Sofia, parked the car, and walked over to her. She had just come back from her tour and was saying goodbye to the group—five middle-aged men who all seemed to know each other. Everyone was smiling and chatting animatedly. It seemed like they'd had a good time.

When Sofia saw him, she gave him a dazzling smile that made his palms sweat. He waved casually. At least, he hoped he'd done it casually.

"I'll just be a few minutes," she told him. "I need to lock up the kayaks and get dressed, and I'll be good to go."

"Take your time."

She'd already stacked all of the kayaks in a spot near the parking lot, and now she used a locking cable to secure them. With that done, she picked up a duffel bag and carried it to the outdoor shower just off the parking lot.

What happened next would forever be burned into his memory, to be replayed in happy daydreams and reveries for months to come.

Sofia stripped off her wetsuit, revealing a tiny red bikini underneath. Then she turned on the shower and began to lather up with a bar of soap she'd produced from her bag.

He tried not to stare as she soaped up her long legs, her strong, supple arms, her tanned, toned midriff, and the luscious expanse of cleavage that was barely covered by the bikini top. She shampooed and conditioned, the afternoon sun glistening off the water on her body and in her hair.

By the time she was done, he realized that an embarrassing situation had ... well ... *arisen*. He was sitting on a large piece of driftwood, and he was in no position to stand up.

He tried thinking of his mother, his taxes, and various household chores, and that helped some. But then she did something that overwhelmed all of his best efforts to calm himself down: she wrapped a big beach towel around herself, reached under it, and dropped first the bikini bottoms and then the top to the ground.

She rooted around in the duffel bag and somehow managed to put on first a bra and panties and then a T-shirt and jeans without exposing anything between her knees and her shoulders.

Patrick was fascinated. What kind of special woman-magic was this? And how could he be expected to control his body's response to it?

She removed the towel now that she was fully dressed, and she used it to rub as much water as she could from her hair. She slipped into a pair of ankle-high boots she'd taken from the duffel and turned to him as though she hadn't just left him utterly and irrevocably devastated.

"Okay, all set. You ready to go?"

"I ... uh ... I think I'll just sit here and enjoy the view for a minute. If that's okay."

"Sure." She came over and sat next to him. The day was somewhat cool, and he was glad he'd brought a sweater because it gave him something to put in his lap.

"Pretty day, isn't it?" she said.

"Gorgeous," he responded.

6

———————

He'd wondered earlier whether they would take her car or his. They took his, because she didn't have one, and he couldn't quite see himself getting on the back of her motorcycle. The morning's kayak adventure was all the danger he could face for one day.

As he drove north toward Ragged Point with Sofia in the passenger seat, it occurred to him that his nervousness, combined with the winding two-lane road leading into Big Sur, could be less than optimal, safety-wise. With that in mind, he took a few deep, calming breaths and put the idea of Sofia in a bikini out of his thoughts.

The drive took about twenty minutes, and that gave them time to chat a little. He already knew what she did for a living, but she had no idea about him. He told her that he taught English at Cal Poly San Luis Obispo, that he wrote a little, and that he liked his work—both the challenge of it and the satisfaction of opening people's eyes to the value of literature.

He could have filled in more detail—where he'd gone to school, for example, and his publishing credits—but he didn't want to sound like he was reciting his résumé.

Plus, he found that he was always more comfortable learning about someone else than he was talking about himself.

"So, the kayaking," he said as he drove. The Piedras Blancas lighthouse pointed its stubby white finger into the blue sky as though it were making a particularly salient point. "How did you get into that?"

"I used to live in Ventura. You could rent a kayak at the harbor for twelve dollars an hour. I fell in love with it—being out there on the water all by myself, the quiet. Just me and the sky and the ocean, everything else so far away, so ... irrelevant. Then, when I moved to Cambria, I bought my own kayak and started launching out of San Simeon. A guy down there had the tour business, and I got to know him a little. He wanted to retire, and my sisters and I had gotten some money from our parents' estate, so I bought the business from him."

He shot her a quick glance, not wanting to take his eyes off the road for too long. "Oh. How did your parents die?"

"Her, cancer. Him, car accident. My sisters didn't approve of the kayak business. They still don't. It isn't very profitable, but it's enough to cover my expenses, and I like the lifestyle."

It didn't escape his notice that she'd immediately changed the subject from her parents. It wasn't something he wanted to push right now, when they were just getting to know each other.

"Why don't they approve?" he asked instead.

"It's 'not a real job.' " She put air quotes around the words *not a real job*. "My oldest sister's a pediatrician, and the other two are a marine biologist and an interior designer." She shrugged. "I'm the underachiever."

He took all of that in. "Do they live near you?"

She gave him a half grin. "I'd consider the next room to be near me, so yes. We share a house."

He blinked. "All ... what ... four of you?"

"All four of us. We inherited our parents' house, and Bianca, Benny, and Martina all wanted to live there."

She'd conspicuously left herself out of the sentence.

"And you? You wanted that, too?"

"I wanted ..." She hesitated. "I guess I just didn't want to be left out."

~

They'd been chatting less than an hour, and already, Sofia had mentioned or alluded to her parents' deaths three times. That was three times too many for her taste, especially with someone she barely knew. She didn't even like to talk about them with her sisters.

When Aldo and Carmela had died, Sofia had taken the pain and the grief and sealed them inside a box that she tried never to open. She hadn't shed any tears, and she hadn't fallen apart. She'd just closed the box and put it away. She wasn't about to open it now.

It was time to turn to a lighter subject.

"Do you get up here to Big Sur much?" she asked. They were settled in at the Ragged Point Inn wine bar, her with a glass of chardonnay and him with a pinot noir.

"I've made the drive on Highway 1 to Carmel a couple of times. Other than that, no. I keep telling myself I need to explore the area more, but I never seem to get around to it."

She wanted to know how he'd come to live in Cambria, and he told her he'd moved to the Central Coast a couple of years before to take the associate professorship at Cal Poly. He'd lived in San Luis Obispo at first, to be close to his job, but he'd visited Cambria one weekend and had decided to relocate as soon as he saw the peaceful, quaint beauty of the town.

"San Luis Obispo is nice. I like it, I really do. But Cambria is special," he said.

"It really is."

If they had nothing else in common, he thought, at least they had that. It was something to build on.

~

When they'd finished their wine, they walked down the path that led to the dramatic, rugged cliffs of Big Sur, with the surf pounding against the rocks far below.

He wanted to hold her hand as they walked, but he wasn't sure this was a date, and if it wasn't, any hand-holding would be unwelcome and inappropriate. To resist the urge, he kept his hands in his pockets, where they couldn't offend anyone.

They stood at the railing overlooking a steep and treacherous path to the water.

"You want to try it?" She gestured toward the path.

A sign at the trailhead warned of possible injury or death and asserted that the inn could not be held responsible should someone be maimed.

"Ah ... would it be okay if we didn't? You've already had to rescue me once. If it happened again, I don't think my self-esteem could take it."

She laughed and put her hand on his shoulder. "Sensible. Fine, we'll stay up here."

He wanted to be a gentleman. He wanted to focus on her as a person and not on how much he wanted to kiss her. But her hand on his shoulder, just sitting there as though it were made to touch his body, made it damned hard to think about anything else.

She was saying something about his job—about teaching—but he wasn't hearing more than every third word. She deserved better than that. She deserved to have his full attention. So, despite the fear that he might be making a serious misstep, he decided to be completely honest.

"Ah ... Sofia. I really want to kiss you. I understand that you might not want me to kiss you, and if that's the case, I fully respect that. Of course. But I just thought I'd put it out there, because I'm distracted by wanting to kiss you, and you've probably *noticed* I'm distracted, so—"

And then her lips were on his and he wasn't distracted anymore. In fact, his attention was focused with laserlike intensity on the way her mouth felt and tasted.

He was glad he hadn't died at the beach or going down the trail, because he never would have experienced this.

SOFIA HADN'T BEEN PLANNING to kiss Patrick. In fact, she'd planned to keep her hands and her lips—and every other part of her—to herself for the duration of the date.

But he'd charmed her with his pronouncement about kissing and distraction and wanting. He was just so damned cute, and his yearning was so ... *palpable*. She was kissing him before she'd even known she was going to.

And then, once the kissing was actually happening, he didn't seem cute after all. He seemed so much more than cute.

It had started out simple and chaste, a mere touch of her lips to his. But in an instant, she was pressing herself against him, her body melting into his, her mouth devouring his.

Had she really thought he was shy? He didn't seem that way now. He kissed like a man who knew how.

She could have lost herself in that kiss for days, weeks. In fact, it was only a few moments before he pulled away and rested his forehead gently against hers.

"Wow," he said.

"Yeah." She would have said more, but she seemed to have lost any eloquence she might otherwise have had.

"Thank you for that." His voice was a little ragged. "For kissing me, I mean."

"It's part of the service," she whispered. "If you almost die on my tour, you get a kiss."

He smiled, and it was more than the curve of his mouth; he smiled with his eyes, too, in a way that made Sofia feel all warm and soft.

"I'll have to do it again soon, then," he said.

LATER, when he dropped her off in San Simeon so she could retrieve her bike, she didn't want him to leave. That was new. Lately, it seemed like she couldn't wait for her dates to be over.

She mounted the bike, put on her helmet, and rode home.

When she came in the front door, her sisters were gathered around the kitchen island sharing a pizza. They looked up as a unit when she came in.

"You're late," Benny said.

"I didn't know I had a curfew, Mom." Sofia hung her helmet on a hook by the door.

"You know what I mean, smartass. You're usually home sooner, that's all. Didn't your last tour end at three thirty?"

"Yep." She didn't offer any information. Instead, she went over to inspect the pizza. Vegetarian, for Martina. To Sofia's mind, no self-respecting pizza would be caught dead without pepperoni, or at least some Italian sausage. Still, she reached over Bianca and grabbed a slice. She'd thought about extending her outing with Patrick to include dinner, but that seemed like a lot for their first date. He'd been so nervous, she shuddered to think how he might have suffered if she'd kept him to herself any longer. The thought made her grin.

"You seem ... different." Martina looked at her carefully, scrutinizing her with a thoughtful expression.

"I'm not. What I am is hungry." She sat on an empty stool and took a bite of pizza so she wouldn't have to talk.

"Hmm," Bianca said. "What aren't you telling us?"

Sofia sighed and put her pizza down on a paper plate. "You guys are relentless. I had a good day, that's all. Remember the guy who almost died? Well, he came back today, and he kayaked, and it went really well, and I was proud of him. So we went for a drink after." She shrugged. "That's all. No big deal."

The other three exchanged looks while Sofia pretended not to notice. Bianca's eyebrows rose. "You went for a drink with him?"

"Yeah. So what?"

"To congratulate him on not dying," Martina clarified.

"Well, that and the fact that he really got the hang of it this time. I mean, it was brave of him to try again! That's all I'm saying."

And that, literally, was all she was going to say. She picked up her plate, added another slice to it, then took her food into her bedroom and closed the door to get some peace and privacy.

She didn't know why she was being so secretive about Patrick. Maybe it was because her sisters tended to hound her about every man she got involved with. Maybe it was because Patrick wasn't like the guys she usually dated, and she knew her sisters would grill her about it. Or maybe it was because today had felt ... different. Special.

She didn't want to share that with anyone—not yet.

She wanted to keep it for herself a little while longer before letting the rest of the world in.

7

———————

Patrick wasn't sure what to make of everything that had happened. Was it really possible that she'd kissed him? And, if so, was it possible—was it anywhere within the boundaries of rational thought—that she'd felt the same way he'd felt when she did it?

He wasn't completely inexperienced with women. He dated. On occasion, it even went well. But he'd observed other men over the years, and he knew he wasn't like them—at least, he wasn't like the ones who usually thrived in the areas of love and romance.

For one thing, he didn't look the way he should, from the standpoint of conventional attractiveness. He was too pale. His skin tended to freckle. His eyelashes were so light in color that they almost appeared to be absent. And his features were too angular: his nose was too narrow, and his lips weren't as full as one might consider optimal.

His body was okay, he supposed. He did get a fair amount of exercise. But he didn't have the definition that some other men had. He was too thin.

He was too much of some things, and not enough of others.

Much of the time, these things didn't bother him. He was an academic, after all—not a bodybuilder or an underwear model. But logic told him that Sofia, looking the way she looked, could date anyone she wanted.

It was hard not to wonder whether he was enough.

Some of these issues came up when he saw Ramon at the college on Monday.

They were sitting in Patrick's office with Ramon in the visitor's chair, his feet up on the desk. The office was tidy, with the books neatly shelved according to category and the student papers either carefully filed or stacked precisely on one corner of the desk.

Patrick wanted to ask Ramon to take his shoes off the desk, but it seemed imprudent to make demands of someone whose advice you wanted. Ramon was no expert on women, but he was married, so that had to count for something.

"How'd it go with Sofia?" Ramon asked, as though on cue.

"Well ... now that you mention it ... there *was* something I ... You see, the thing is ... she kissed me."

Ramon didn't say anything for a moment. He appeared stunned, his jaw slightly slack, his eyes wide. When he recovered, he seemed to think he'd heard incorrectly.

"Sofia? The extremely hot kayak chick?"

"That would be correct. Um ... yes."

"Dude. You are my hero. Seriously."

Patrick was simultaneously uncomfortable and gratified. Which seemed to be the case so much of the time.

"The question is, now that it's happened, what do I do next?"

"What do you mean, what do you do next? You ask her out on a second date. I'd have thought that would be obvious."

"You'd think so, wouldn't you?" Patrick squirmed a little in his seat. "But it just seems ... I don't want to annoy her."

Ramon was looking at him as though Patrick were either crazy or stupid, which, in this context, he might have been. "She asked you out the first time, right?"

"Yes. She ... yes."

"And she's the one who kissed you."

"Yes." He blushed a little at the memory.

"Then it's definitely your move. You have to ask her. If you don't, she'll be offended, and once a woman's offended, it's game over."

Patrick nodded. What Ramon was saying made sense. The only problem was that now, he actually had to pick up the phone and make the call. Which seemed impossibly frightening.

"Maybe I'll just wait a bit."

"The kayak thing was Saturday?" Ramon asked.

"Yes. Saturday."

"Then you can't wait. Nope. No can do. It's already been forty-eight hours. Two days without contact is okay, but if you go any longer—three days or, God forbid, four—she's going to get increasingly pissed, wondering why a guy like you thinks he's too good for a woman like her."

This was a surprise. "Really?"

"Really. You can ask Lucy if you don't believe me."

Lucy, Ramon's wife of five years, was a lovely, warm, vibrant woman. Given the fact that she'd surely married beneath her, Patrick had to wonder how much she might really know about the fine points of dating.

"Besides," Ramon went on. "If you had the guts to go kayaking again when it almost killed you the first time, calling a woman should be no sweat."

"You'd think so, wouldn't you?" Patrick said for the second time in the conversation.

～

He went through the rest of his workday distracted, thinking about Sofia. He taught two classes in the morning—the first, an introduction to Shakespeare's tragedies, and the second, a section of English 101—and held his office hours in the afternoon.

He'd hoped to find time during office hours to call Sofia, but a steady stream of students came in, asking questions or wanting to talk about the syllabus.

Patrick didn't believe that men were inherently better students than women; in fact, many—perhaps most—of his best students over the years had been female. So he could never understand the steady traffic of young women into his office asking questions about things he thought should be obvious.

Today, he'd met with a freshman who wanted to know the best place to buy the works of Shakespeare (anywhere books were sold, really, though Amazon was the easiest); a junior who wanted advice on whether her paper should be single-spaced or double-spaced; and a grad student curious about why she'd lost one point on her paper —*one point*. All were women. It baffled him.

The last one—the grad student—was just leaving when Ramon stopped by the office on his way home.

"I don't get it." Ramon plopped down into the visitor's chair once the student had gone.

"You don't get what?" Patrick was glad Ramon had dropped by, because it allowed him to procrastinate on his call to Sofia.

"You and the girls," Ramon said, as though that should have been clear. "I mean, you're okay-looking, I guess, but you're not exactly movie star material."

Patrick suddenly felt as though Ramon had started speaking a language he could neither understand nor identify. "I don't know what you're talking about."

"Ah, bullshit." Ramon waved a hand dismissively. " 'Oh, Professor Connelly, can you help me with my paper? Oh, Professor Connelly, what font should I use? Professor, I couldn't possibly write about the major themes in King Lear without a big, strong man like you to help me.' " Ramon was speaking in a high, singsong voice that, one assumed, was supposed to mimic the average female college student.

Suddenly, it occurred to Patrick what Ramon was saying, but the idea was so absurd that he couldn't imagine there was any validity to it.

"They're not flirting," he said. "Of course they're not. Why would they?"

"They are," Ramon said. "As to the question of why, there are mysteries that mere mortals will never solve."

Patrick, a bit stunned, sat at his desk and considered what Ramon was telling him. "They're flirting?"

"Good God, man, you're hopeless. Don't you think they could figure this stuff out on their own? That last one is an honors student."

"But ... why?" He was genuinely puzzled, considering the fact that he'd never imagined himself to have any skills with women.

"That's the question," Ramon agreed. "I think it's that helpless, boyish thing you've got going on. It's that *I've got a 140 IQ, but I need a good woman to make me whole* kind of thing."

"I don't have a 140 IQ," Patrick said. It was 145, but he saw no need to say that.

"Whatever. If I had that, it wouldn't have taken me five years to get Lucy to marry me."

Could it be that Patrick had actual magnetism that appealed to women? Was that why Sofia had asked him out and then, ultimately, kissed him? If so, that was a heartening prospect. It might mean that he had a chance with her after all, despite objective evidence to the contrary.

"Well," Patrick said, digesting it.

"Have you called Sofia yet?" Ramon asked. "If you haven't, you're an idiot."

He might, in fact, be an idiot when it came to women. If so, that was beyond his control. The least he could do was not be a coward.

SOFIA HAD NOT BEEN WAITING for Patrick to call. So what if she'd been keeping her phone nearby at all times with the ringer turned to top volume? She always did that. Well, she *didn't* always do that, but she should. There was no telling what kind of important calls she might miss.

It was her night to cook dinner, so she was in the kitchen boiling a pot of water for pasta and defrosting a container of Bianca's meat sauce when Patrick finally got around to calling.

For a moment, she considered letting it go to voice mail. She didn't want to appear too eager. But she felt a rush of excitement at the thought of talking to him. The excitement was alarming—she liked to play it cool this early on—but there it was. In any case, she was too mature to play games, so she picked up the call.

"Patrick."

"Sofia. Hi. Uh ... good. It's you. I was expecting to get your voice mail."

She couldn't help smiling at his adorable ineptness. "Nope. It's me. In the flesh." And, yes, she was teasing him a little with that last bit. So what? What was the harm?

"In the ..." He cleared his throat. "Right."

"How are you?" Maybe a little light chitchat would relax him enough that he could say whatever it was he'd called to say.

"I'm well, thank you. The reason I called"—the throat-clearing again—"I was wondering if you'd like to have dinner with me on Friday night. Or Saturday. It wouldn't have to be Friday or Saturday, now that I think of it, considering that Saturday and Sunday are work days for you. It could be any day that fits into your schedule. It doesn't have to be dinner, in fact. It could be lunch. Maybe coffee and a muffin ..."

What was it about his nervousness that charmed her so thoroughly? Maybe it was that he was so different than anyone she'd dated before. She felt warm and happy just hearing him struggle through the phone call.

"I'd love to have dinner with you. Or coffee and a muffin."

"You would?" He sounded surprised, which charmed her even more.

"I would."

"That's ... good. Great. That's great." He let out a puff of air. "Let's make it Friday night, then. Can I call you on Friday morning with the details?"

"Patrick?"

"Yes?"

She smiled and put a full, flirtatious spin on her tone. "You can call me whenever you like. You don't have to wait until Friday."

8

———

Patrick did wait until Friday to call, but not because he didn't want to talk to Sofia. The problem was one of logistics: If he called, she might ask where they would be going and what they would be doing on Friday night, and he didn't know yet. He wanted to plan the date well and wisely; he didn't want to blurt out something on the spur of the moment just to avoid the embarrassing admission that he didn't yet have any ideas.

But that raised another problem. The fact that she had told him he didn't have to wait until Friday suggested that she didn't *want* him to wait until Friday. Which meant that she wanted—even expected— a call sooner. He might show up for their date on Friday night already having made a terrible mistake by failing to meet her phone-contact expectations.

He couldn't worry about that, though. He had to stay focused on the main task.

For that, he couldn't rely on Ramon, but he certainly didn't want to leave it to his own possibly limited imagination. So he contacted the person in his life who had the best expertise on such things.

He called Ramon's wife, Lucy.

"I invited her to dinner. But now I'm wondering if that's too boring, too ... expected. In fact, it seems I couldn't have proposed a *less* creative option. I don't know what I'm doing. In fact, I'm going to call her and cancel." He wasn't really going to cancel, but it felt like a tempting idea.

"No, you're not," Lucy said. "And dinner's fine."

"It is?"

"Of course it is. It's a classic for a reason."

"Well ... all right. That's reassuring."

"Now, the problem is that *dinner* covers a lot of possible territory," Lucy said, her voice thoughtful. "You can go the formal route—Neptune or the Sandpiper, maybe—or more casual. Burgers, pizza, that sort of thing. Then there's the whole area in between those two ends of the spectrum. And that doesn't even cover the category of picnics, home-cooked meals, or takeout."

"Oh, God," Patrick moaned. "I really am going to cancel."

"No, you're not," Lucy said again. "Go with Neptune. The food's good, the atmosphere is nice, and they don't play loud music in the dining room, so it's good for getting to know someone."

"Neptune." He'd been there a couple of times since he'd come to Cambria, and he'd enjoyed it.

"Sure. That's where Ramon took me on our first date, and I married him."

According to Ramon, the route to marriage hadn't led immediately from Neptune to the altar. Rather, it had detoured through several failed proposals, a breakup, a reunion, years of cohabitation, and a course of treatment with a relationship counselor. Still, they'd gotten there eventually.

WHEN FRIDAY NIGHT CAME, Patrick picked up Sofia at her house, the way any gentleman would. He knocked on the door, his palms sweaty and his heart racing, and she opened it looking stunning, as usual.

She tried to usher him out to the car quickly, closing the door behind her, grabbing his hand, and pulling him down the porch steps and toward the curb. But her plan was foiled when a woman who looked like a slightly older, more staid version of Sofia opened the door and greeted him.

"Well, hello," the woman said. She was shorter than Sofia, maybe a little trimmer in build, with dark, shoulder-length hair that had been straightened. "What's the rush? Sofia, bring your guest in to meet everybody."

Patrick cleared his throat. "Um ... everybody?"

"We're in a hurry, Bianca," Sofia said. "We'll miss our reservation."

"Well, actually," Patrick said, "our reservation's not until six-thirty, and it's barely six, so ..."

"Perfect," Bianca said.

SOFIA WASN'T sure how she'd ended up introducing Patrick to her sisters on what was only their second date. Having a guy meet the family was something one should do only after things got serious—if at all. Of course, her sisters had met most of her boyfriends in the past, and that was probably why she was hesitating now. They met, and then they judged, and then they offered unsolicited advice.

Still, Bianca had outplayed her, hauling ass to the porch before Sofia had a chance to get away.

Now, there was no choice but to go through with it—or she'd have to explain later, both to Patrick and to her sisters, why she hadn't wanted to.

"I'm Bianca. This is Martina, and that one over there is Benedetta." Bianca made the introductions while Sofia stood aside, considering ways to create a diversion so she and Patrick could escape.

"Ah ... Patrick Connelly." He shook hands with everyone, looking both nervous and intrigued. "You have a beautiful home."

He was looking around with interest, and Sofia knew the compliment had been more than an empty bit of courtesy.

"The kitchen ... is that redwood?" he asked.

Martina, pleased to be in her element, started giving him a tour.

"Yes! The countertop was custom made by a craftsman here in town. The floors are the original oak, and you see that window up there? The red one?" She pointed to a small red pane of glass set into the peak of the roofline. "That was from when the house was a den of prostitution."

"Before we got here," Benny pointed out.

"And ... is this a real log cabin?" Patrick asked.

"Two, actually," Martina went on. "Our parents had two small cabins joined into one to get the amount of square footage they wanted. This area here is one house, and if you go down that hall, you'll be in the other."

"It's wonderful," he said. He seemed to mean it.

"Can we go?" Sofia said irritably.

"Not so fast," Benny said.

"Yeah," Martina agreed. "You've got time." She grabbed Patrick by the arm and pulled him into a hallway so she could give him the complete tour of the house, including bedrooms, the vintage claw-foot tub in the largest bathroom, the loft—accessible only by ladder—off of the sitting room, and the library.

"You have a library." Patrick marveled at the array of books lining the walls in a large room off the kitchen.

"Our mom loved to read," Martina said, her voice dreamy. "This was one of the first rooms she set up when they renovated the place."

The room had rough-hewn oak floors, a high ceiling with exposed beams, some comfortable-looking leather club chairs, and, most importantly, the books. He took a volume off of a shelf and read the cover. *To Kill a Mockingbird.*

"Wait. Is this a first edition?" The cover was worn, but the book was still serviceable and intact.

"It is," she confirmed, clearly pleased that he'd spotted it. "It was given to my mother as a gift by one of her boyfriends before she met Dad. Do you like to read?"

He put the book back carefully. "Yes, I do. Ah ... I guess Sofia didn't tell you anything about me. I'm an English professor at Cal Poly."

"Really." The way Martina was looking at him, he might have said that he'd recently arrived from Venus. "Well, this is going to be interesting."

SOFIA COULDN'T WAIT to get Patrick out of the house, but by the time she did, it was too late. Her sisters had already had time to grill him. It wasn't that she didn't think he could handle it—more that she didn't like them poking into her business.

She loved them—of course she did. But why couldn't she have anything that was private, just her own?

He walked her to his car and opened the door for her. Typically, she didn't date the kind of man who opened doors for her. She probably should object on feminist grounds, but why? It was nice being with a man who had manners.

Once he was in the car beside her, his seatbelt buckled, he turned to her. "I wanted to tell you as soon as I saw you that you look lovely, but your sister came out, and I got sidetracked. You do, though. Look lovely."

She was wearing a little black dress with an A-line, knee-length skirt and a sweetheart neckline. She'd had to borrow the dress from Bianca; Sofia's wardrobe consisted almost entirely of items one might wear to the beach. When Patrick had said they were going to Neptune, she knew she would have to do better than that.

She'd fretted over her clothing choice more than she would have admitted; she wasn't used to dressing up, but she wanted to look good for Patrick. She wanted to please him, which was, in itself, a puzzling development.

He looked good, too—almost startlingly so. She'd thought of him as a too-thin, slightly nerdy-looking guy, but he looked almost ... *elegant* in a nice pair of slacks and a dark blue blazer over a gray dress shirt. When the word popped into her mind, she knew it was right. He'd have looked right at home in a 1940s Hollywood film next to some starlet.

"Your sisters seemed nice," he said as he drove toward the restaurant. "I take it you didn't want me to meet them."

She hadn't, but the reasons were complex enough that she didn't want to unpack them right now—not on a second date. Instead, she changed the subject.

"Do you have any brothers or sisters?" she asked.

The look he gave her told her that he knew exactly what she was doing, if not why. But, mercifully, he let her do it.

"Two. A brother and a sister."

So, he would understand sibling dynamics. That was something.

9

Clearly, she hadn't wanted him to meet her sisters. And clearly, she didn't want to talk about it. That was okay; it was far too early for either of them to force uncomfortable topics of conversation on the other. Still, it raised questions.

Did she think one side would disapprove of the other? If so, why?

He was already nervous enough about dating Sofia without the worry that her sisters might think he wasn't good enough.

Or, maybe that wasn't it at all. Maybe the sisters were horrible, and she hadn't wanted them to scare him away. Except, they hadn't seemed horrible. He'd liked them.

He was still pondering it when the hostess at Neptune seated them at a table near the front window.

Neptune was upscale, with polished wood floors, tasteful lighting, white tablecloths, an extensive wine list, and a seafood menu large and varied enough to earn the restaurant its name. Patrick had been here once for a colleague's retirement party and another time for a friend's birthday—but he'd never come here with a date.

Certainly, he'd never been here with anyone who made him feel the way Sofia did.

The way she looked—that dress had him distracted to the point that he wasn't sure he could remember how to order food, let alone eat it.

Somehow, he managed to get through the menu-reading and food-ordering part of the evening without incident. But the conversation—that was harder.

He'd already failed with his initial gambit—the one about her sisters. He didn't do much better when he asked her about her mother.

"Your mother's library is amazing," he said when they had their wine, a chardonnay for him and a cabernet sauvignon for her, and they were enjoying it with hot rolls from the bread basket. "That first edition of *To Kill a Mockingbird* ..." He shook his head in awe. "Did she have other rare editions?"

She looked down at her bread plate, avoiding his eyes. Then she changed the subject—again. "You must love to read, given what you do for a living."

"I do." He had a choice to make: push it or let it go. For the second time, he let it go. "The books I read when I was young—from as soon as I was old enough to hold a book—were what inspired me to teach. Books have always had a lot of meaning for me."

She told him about a book she particularly loved—a love story by an author whose name he knew.

He didn't try to talk about her family again.

By HALFWAY through the dinner entrée, he was sure the date was destined for disaster. He'd been so disheartened by his failed attempts at conversation that he was now venturing only into the least offensive topics: weather, attractive vacation spots, and current movies.

He was boring himself senseless; he could only imagine how Sofia must feel.

But just when he was starting to think the whole thing was hopeless, he was handed a gift in the form of the couple at the next table.

They were in their fifties, probably: him, balding with a bad comb-over, ruddy skin, and a paunch at his middle; her, recently blow-dried and manicured, with elaborate makeup and hair that looked like it would withstand gale-force winds.

The two of them had just arrived, and after a few moments of quiet conversation about some unknowable thing—their grown kids, maybe, or the mortgage—they started to argue about the menu.

It started simply enough, with her claiming she didn't like salmon. Patrick wasn't trying to eavesdrop, but their voices carried, and their table was only a few feet away.

"Since when do you not like salmon?" the guy asked.

"Since I was *five,* Albert, which is why I can't believe your inability to hold onto this particular piece of information."

Sofia shot Patrick an amused look, one eyebrow cocked.

"I didn't know you when you were five, Janice, so maybe that has something to do with it." The guy raised his menu and began to read it.

"If I hadn't *mentioned* it since I was five, then I suppose that argument would make sense," Janice countered. "But I've mentioned it *hundreds* of times."

"Hundreds," Albert repeated with a mocking tone.

"Yes, hundreds!" Janice began ticking off incidents on her fingers —though what she would do when she got past ten was a mystery. "I told you on our first date. And on our second date. I told you when we went to your mother's house that Christmas. I told you on my birthday. I told you on our *goddamned wedding day!*"

"We had salmon at the reception!" Albert protested.

"I know! I know! Which proves my point! You had one job. One! You and your mother were supposed to choose the reception menu. And you chose salmon even though you *knew I don't like salmon!*"

Patrick and Sofia did their best to pretend they weren't listening. Not that Albert or Janice would have noticed them if they'd set up bleachers and started selling popcorn.

The waitress, a woman in her twenties with blond hair pulled back in a neat chignon, approached and tried to head off an escalation by telling them that Neptune offered many fine non-salmon menu options.

"That. Is not. The point." Janice's eyes were fiery with righteous indignation. "Can you see we're having a private conversation?"

Albert was still looking at his menu as though he'd been through this same thing numerous times before—which he certainly had, Patrick reflected, perhaps once for each time his wife had mentioned her hatred of salmon.

Then, things took a turn.

"You know who likes salmon?" Albert asked, not looking up from his menu.

"Who?" Janice demanded.

"Carol." He put down his menu with a smack and gave Janice a dead-eyed stare. "Carol likes salmon."

Whoever Carol was, the mere mention of her name made Janice go white. "You son of a bitch," she hissed.

It seemed to Patrick that this situation needed a hero—someone to step in and be the blessed voice of calm. It might as well be him. The pleasant dinners of dozens depended on it.

"Excuse me," he said to Janice.

Janice turned on him. "Who the hell are you?"

"Just ... a man with no particular opinion on salmon. I wondered if I might be of help."

"Well, I don't know," Janice said. "Can you turn back time to before Albert fucked that salmon-loving whore?"

That was the moment when Sofia lost the composure she'd held onto so flawlessly through the entire episode. It started with a giggle. Then the giggle turned into a guffaw. Finally, the guffaw evolved into helpless laughter.

"I can't ... I don't ... I'm sorry." She was gasping for breath, her face flushed prettily, her body shaking with mirth. "Excuse me." She got up and headed across the restaurant and toward the hallway that led to the restrooms. She seemed to be having some difficulty between the high heels she was wearing and the convulsions of laughter.

Patrick stood up, Albert and Janice still looking at him. "I'd better

..." He pointed vaguely in the direction Sofia had gone. "I should see if she's ... in need of the Heimlich." He got up and sped past the other diners and into the hallway where Sofia had gone.

In the hallway, he found Sofia leaning against the wall outside the ladies' room, her hand clapped over her mouth, tears streaming from her eyes.

" 'Just a man with no particular opinion on salmon!' Oh, my God. I can't." She dissolved into helpless laughter again.

Laughter was contagious by nature, and before long, Patrick found himself gripped by the kind of desperate, stomach-clenching mirth that has its sufferer gasping for oxygen.

They both leaned against the wall for support. The hallway was narrow, and he had to squeeze closer to Sofia to allow a waitress to pass through.

When he realized how they were positioned—his hands on the wall on either side of Sofia, so close to her that he could smell her hair—he gradually stopped laughing. Then, so did she.

Everything fell away: the bickering couple, the restaurant, the tension they'd both felt at the beginning of the date. Now, there was just this exquisite nearness, this yearning.

He leaned forward and kissed her, and he didn't feel nervous or awkward anymore. He felt that he was exactly where, and who, he was supposed to be.

～

SOFIA WAS LOST in the kiss when, through the fog of her desire, she heard the waitress talking to them.

"You two want to get a room? Because we need this hallway."

So many things about Patrick were endearing, and one of them was that he had a tendency to blush—which he was doing now.

"Ah ... sorry," he told the waitress.

Sofia wasn't sorry, though. She wasn't sorry at all.

～

Albert and Janice were gone when Patrick and Sofia got back to their table. Whether they'd been asked to leave or had cut the night short on their own was unclear.

Either way, Patrick and Sofia were able to continue their date without the distraction of a fight at the next table—and without the awkward tension that had marked the beginning of their evening together.

They talked easily and comfortably through the rest of their meal —though Patrick was careful not to approach the topics of her sisters or her parents. That didn't matter, because they had so much more to say.

Patrick told her about Ramon and Lucy and their toddler son, Joe.

Sofia told him about the things she loved to do: hiking, camping, running.

By the time the check came, Patrick should have felt completely at ease with her. And he would have, if not for the suffocating sexual tension he was feeling.

He wasn't the kind of man who would try to get into a woman's bed on the second date. Even if he thought he could accomplish such a feat, he wouldn't have wanted to, because he'd always found sex so much more satisfying when he truly knew someone.

And yet, there was the kiss and the way it had made him feel.

He drove her home reminding himself that he absolutely, certainly, without a doubt was going to walk her to her door without trying anything. What kind of man would he be otherwise?

As it happened, when they got to her house, she was the one who tried something.

Not that he minded.

He needed glasses when driving after dark, and he was wearing them when she grabbed him by the shirt and hauled him to her as they stood outside the front door of the log cabin, the porch light shining down on them in the warm evening air.

She reached out, took the glasses off of him, and set them down on a small table that sat between two Adirondack chairs. Then she kissed him long and hard, still with a fistful of his shirt in her hand.

The blood was rushing to his nether regions; maybe that was why he felt so lightheaded. The taste of her mouth was more intoxicating than the wine he'd had at dinner.

He leaned into the kiss, into her, his lips exploring hers, his tongue tasting hers. Just when he was about to abandon his ideals about sex and getting to know someone and what, exactly, constituted respectful behavior, she let go of the shirt and stepped back, a languid smile on her face.

"Call me," she said. Just that. And then she disappeared into the house and closed the door.

He waited a moment for his rational mind to start working again, then went down the steps and toward his car.

Patrick was all the way to the car before he realized that his glasses were still on the porch. He went back up, grabbed them, then started to leave again.

He meant to go to his car and go home, he really did. But the window next to the front door was open, and he could hear Sofia and her sisters talking. Still, he wouldn't have listened. Except for the fact that they were talking about him.

At first he just heard his own name along with some unintelligible words. Then, someone—probably Bianca, if he remembered her voice correctly—came closer to the window, and he could hear her clearly.

" ... nothing like the others," she said. "He's got a brain, for one thing."

"And he's cute," another voice said. Martina? "But he's not ... you know ... drop-dead gorgeous."

Patrick wasn't offended by that; after all, it matched his own assessment of his relative attractiveness.

Sofia made some noises about how they all should mind their own business, but the others kept on.

"Oh, come on, Sofia, don't deny that you always date super hot men," said a third voice that had to be Benny. "They've all been either weightlifters, or models, or ... or there was that guy who acted in a soap opera. What was his name?"

"Blake!" Martina said triumphantly. "Oh, I remember him. He used to wax his eyebrows."

They all laughed at the memory of the eyebrow-waxing, then he could hear Sofia again.

"There is nothing wrong with Patrick just because he's not as ... well ... as conventionally attractive as the other guys."

"Believe me, I know," Benny said. "I think you might finally have a good one. Give this one a chance before you crush him into dust, would you?"

"Please," Martina agreed.

10

———

In the days following the date at Neptune, Patrick couldn't stop thinking about the things he'd overheard.

If he'd been more secure about his place in Sofia's affections, he might have focused on the fact that her sisters had praised his intelligence and had even suggested that he was superior to the men she'd dated before.

But he wasn't entirely secure, so he focused instead on the fact that they'd said he was less attractive than the others.

Weightlifters? Models? A soap opera actor?

How in the world was he supposed to compete?

"Be honest. Am I hot?" he asked Ramon at school the following Monday. The two of them had met at a coffee kiosk on campus before Ramon's first class.

"Dude. I like you a lot, but not that way," Ramon said.

"Very funny." Patrick accepted his latte from the barista, opened the lid, and added sugar from a packet. "I'm serious. If you were a woman, would you find me attractive?"

"I'm not a woman," Ramon pointed out.

"But if you were. Use your imagination."

"My imagination isn't vivid enough for that," Ramon said. "You want to ask Lucy?"

The idea of asking Ramon's wife if he, Patrick, was hot made him flush with humiliation. On the other hand, a woman's perspective might prove enlightening. And yet, there was the humiliation again.

"No," he said. "Absolutely not. But ... maybe."

So Ramon called Lucy and put her on the phone with Patrick.

"*Hot* isn't the right word," she said after considering the question. "*Hot* implies a certain kind of generic good looks with the body and the attitude and all of that. You're something different. You're ... compelling."

"Compelling," he repeated, trying the description on in his head.

After he hung up and returned Ramon's cell phone, Ramon gave him a side-eyed look. "Why is my wife calling you compelling?"

"Well ... you'd have more to worry about if she'd called me hot, wouldn't you?"

Ramon shoved the phone into his pocket. "No, I wouldn't, and you know it."

COMPELLING WAS NICE, but it didn't put him in a league with Sofia's previous boyfriends. Patrick thought about what he could do to improve his odds. He couldn't change his genetic makeup, and he couldn't change his basic personality.

There was one thing he could change, though, so he went to a gym near the college after his classes finished the next day and asked about a membership.

"You ever worked out before?" Chad, a guy in a bright red Fantastic Fitness T-shirt, sat across from Patrick at a fake wood-grain desk in a glass-walled area next to the free weights. Chad was so bulked up it seemed likely that the sleeves of his shirt might split should he unexpectedly flex. The room smelled like sweat and synthetic carpet.

"Ah ... no."

Chad made a note on a clipboard. "You do any cardio?"

"Well, I take long walks sometimes between classes, so ..."

"That's a *no*." Chad made another note. "Let's just get your weight and measurements."

There was a scale, a measuring tape, and a pair of calipers, and Chad made notes and grunted to himself as he contemplated the data he was writing down.

"It's not looking good for the home team," Chad said, his eyebrows raised, as he looked at his clipboard.

PATRICK LET himself be talked into the personal training package, which on the one hand seemed like an extortionate scam, but on the other hand might prevent him from seriously injuring himself.

He got started the next day, at an obscenely early hour when he normally would have been sipping his first cup of coffee or reading the news online.

"Let's warm you up with ten minutes on the treadmill, then we'll run you through a nice beginner routine," a guy who wasn't Chad, but who was pretty much interchangeable with Chad, told him as the machines whirred and clanged around him. A bank of TVs mounted on the walls showed a variety of morning programming, ranging from CNN to a cooking show.

The warmup went well enough—no matter how out of shape he might be, he could manage ten minutes at a brisk walk on the tread- mill—and he had settled into a false sense of security by the time not-Chad came to get him.

He'd expected to be taken to the machines with their neat stacks of weights on cables and their padded seats and handles that made everything seem so doable and straightforward. Instead, not-Chad steered him to the free weights.

"Aren't we going over there?" Patrick asked, gesturing plaintively to the machines.

"Nah." Not-Chad waved off the idea. "Those are for the members who pass on the personal training—we send them over there so they won't hurt themselves."

"But won't I hurt myself?" Patrick wondered.

"Not with me showing you what to do. Let's start with the bench press."

HALF AN HOUR LATER, Patrick left the gym freshly showered, dressed in the clothes he'd worn to work, and feeling weak as a kitten recovering from a bad bout of the flu. His limbs were rubbery and shaky, and he had the odd sensation that they might give up at any moment, refusing to hold him upright and leaving him to collapse onto the surface of the parking lot.

It was possible he'd overdone it.

Not-Chad had reminded him not to strain himself, saying he should take it easy for the first week or so until his body began to adapt. But there were two problems with that: one, he didn't want not-Chad to think he couldn't handle a basic beginner's workout, and two, he didn't have a lot of time. If he took months to get into shape, Sofia would either have seen him naked by then—proving that he wasn't up to her usual standards—or she'd have decided she didn't *want* to see him naked because he wasn't up to her usual standards.

No, he had to speed up the usual timeline for this kind of thing. So he'd lifted a little more than not-Chad had suggested and he'd done it a few more times than what he'd been told to do.

And this wasn't so bad, really. Yes, he was tired. But he also had the satisfaction of knowing he'd embarked on the manly occupation of sculpting his body into something superior to what it was today.

He and Sofia had a date for the following night, and Patrick would see her with a little more confidence.

That was the plan, anyway.

Of course, Sofia Googled Patrick. In this day and age, only an idiot would fail to Google the person they were getting involved with.

And Sofia was not an idiot.

Mostly, she wanted to make sure he wasn't some sort of lunatic who seemed perfectly normal at first but who eventually ended up sending you a live wolverine in the mail.

What she found was pretty much what she'd hoped for: all of the normal things, with no references to wolverines, crackpot conspiracy theories, or restraining orders.

But the more she read, the more uneasy she felt—for a different reason.

It turned out, Patrick wasn't just some English teacher toiling away at a thankless job teaching eighteen-year-olds to diagram sentences. If anyone even did that anymore.

He was actually kind of a big deal.

He'd graduated with honors from Princeton, he'd been a Rhodes Scholar—she'd had to look that up to even know what it was—and he was, according to Wikipedia, the world's foremost authority on some Scottish poet she'd never heard of. He'd published a book about the poet, which had been reviewed in *The New Yorker*.

Sofia didn't usually feel insecure when it came to men. That was one area in which she tended to hold the upper hand. In every relationship, there was one person who was more desirable—more of a catch, at least on paper—than the other one. The less worthy of the two was generally the pursuer, while the more worthy one was generally the pursued.

Sofia was always, always the pursued.

Now, she was beginning to wonder if she might be losing her spot at the top of the dating food chain. Yes, she looked the way she looked, and that was always an advantage. But Patrick wasn't just smart. He was *brilliant*. How could she compete with that? How could she possibly hold his interest in a conversation about ... oh, let's say ... iambic pentameter?

Sofia wasn't even sure what iambic pentameter meant, though she did know it had to do with poetry.

How could she hope to be attractive to Patrick when she couldn't even define iambic pentameter?

She liked to read, but she read thrillers, for God's sake. Romance novels. *Game of Thrones*. She didn't read poetry! She didn't read *literature*! She'd gotten through high school English mostly with the aid of CliffsNotes.

She was starting to become slightly hysterical by the time Bianca came home from work to find her at the kitchen table with her laptop, her hands fisted in her hair.

"You look like you just read that a giant asteroid is going to wipe out the Earth," Bianca remarked as she put her purse on the table and grabbed a water bottle out of the refrigerator. "It's not, is it?"

Sofia stared at the screen, where the *New Yorker* review of Patrick's book was displayed.

"Hello?" Bianca waved a hand between Sofia's face and the screen.

"I'm doomed," Sofia said. "Doomed."

"Oh, God, *is* there an asteroid?"

"What? No." Sofia snapped the laptop closed and laid her head on it. "But, now that you mention it? That would solve my problems."

Bianca pulled out a chair and sat next to Sofia. "All right, spill it. What's going on?"

Sofia just moaned.

Bianca slid the laptop out from under Sofia's head, opened it, and looked at the article displayed on the screen.

"Why are you upset about this guy Calum Mc something or other?" Bianca asked.

"I'm not."

"Then what ..." Bianca scanned the article, and her eyes widened. "Patrick wrote this book. Your Patrick."

"Apparently. And he's not *my* Patrick. He's never going to be *my* Patrick. He's a freaking genius, it turns out. And I'm just ... me!"

Sofia hadn't realized how interested in Patrick she was until this. Until she'd learned that she wasn't good enough for him. And she certainly hadn't planned on talking about it with any of her sisters.

But who else was she supposed to talk to? Where else was she supposed to turn?

"You're joking, right?" Bianca said. "Of the four of us, you're the one most likely to cause a traffic accident bending over to pick up a dollar from the sidewalk. You've got nothing to worry about."

"That's fine, until he wants to talk about ... about iambic pentameter!" Sofia threw her hands into the air for emphasis.

"Sof, you're hysterical."

"He should be dating you, not me," Sofia said. "You're a doctor! You know things. You've read books that aren't sold in the checkout line at Walmart."

"That's true," Bianca allowed. "But he doesn't want me. He wants you."

"He won't, once he knows I'm not smart enough for him."

Benny had come in the front door in the middle of the conversation, and she swung her messenger bag—full of books, papers, and God knew what—on the kitchen island. She was wearing a Superman T-shirt, a pair of ripped jeans rolled up to midcalf, and a pair of Converse sneakers.

"What are we talking about?" she asked.

"About how Sofia isn't smart enough for the new guy she's seeing."

Benny's eyebrows drew closer to one another, causing her forehead to wrinkle. "You're smart."

"I'm smart in the sense that I can balance my checkbook and manage my life and ... and have conversations at parties. But Patrick ..."

"Patrick what?"

"Patrick was a Rhodes Scholar and he wrote a book that was reviewed in *The New Yorker*," Bianca said, filling her in. She pointed toward Sofia with one thumb. "She's freaking out."

Benny still looked puzzled. "Since when do you freak out about men? Men freak out about you, not the other way around."

"This one's different," Bianca said pointedly.

"It's just ... he makes me feel things," Sofia wailed.

"Oh, boy," Benny said.

"I'll bet he's only dated really smart women in the past," Sofia said. "Other professors, or writers, or ... or poets." She said the word *poets* as though she were saying *lepers* or *crack addicts*.

"Oh, I doubt that's true," Bianca said, her hand on Sofia's shoulder.

"You want me to find out?" Benny sat down at the kitchen table, a bottle of Coke in her hand. She twisted off the top and took a long swig.

"You can do that?" Sofia perked up.

Benny shrugged. "I can ask around at the college, see if anyone knows."

This was what sisters were for. They comforted you when you were freaking out over a man—then they stalked him so you wouldn't have to.

11

As a marine biologist, Benny frequently did research at the college, but she wasn't on the faculty. Still, she knew a number of people in the science department, and they knew people in the math department, who knew people in the English department.

By the next day—the day of Sofia's date with Patrick—she was ready to offer her report.

"You weren't wrong about him mostly dating eggheads." Benny came into the kitchen around noon, plunked her messenger bag on the table, then plopped down into a chair next to where Sofia was sitting with a cup of tea.

"Uh oh," Sofia said.

"I talked to Will Bachman in the science department, and he didn't know anything, but he's friends with a guy over in math named Ramon Alba, who pals around with Patrick." Benny looked pleased with herself, maybe even a little smug. "Ramon says Patrick dated another English professor before this and a novelist before that."

"Oh. A novelist. Well, that's not so impressive," Sofia tried.

"She was shortlisted for the Pulitzer," Benny said.

"Oh ... God." Sofia was starting to feel sick. It was worse than she'd imagined. Sure, he was attracted to her now. But what happened when he realized she didn't have the intellectual heft of his previous girlfriends? What would she do then?

"Look, Sof. You don't have any reason to feel insecure about other women. You're much hotter than either one of them."

"You've seen them?"

"Google," Benny said. "And anyway, maybe he's tired of dating women who make him feel like he's on *Jeopardy* every time they go out to dinner. Minus the cash prizes, obviously."

"I want to see them," Sofia said. She got up, went into her room, and came back with her laptop. She opened it and turned it toward Benny. "Show me."

While Benny tapped the keys, Sofia imagined what she might see. Mousy women, she hoped—the kind with thick glasses and limp, colorless hair. The kind who never had a date during high school because they were too busy dissecting the themes in *Of Mice and Men*.

It didn't work out quite that way. The English professor looked attractive if somewhat plain. But the author—long, glossy, chestnut-colored hair. Big, blue eyes. And a smile that looked both intelligent and a little bit mischievous.

Sofia almost wanted to date the woman herself.

"Look at her," Sofia said miserably.

"That's her author photo," Benny pointed out. "You know those are always professionally done, with a stylist and Photoshop. She probably doesn't even look like that. And even if she does, you're still hotter."

Maybe. Sofia knew, objectively, that she was an attractive woman. But looks weren't everything. What if he wanted to be challenged intellectually? What if he wanted someone who was his equal professionally?

"You must really be into him if you're this worried about it," Benny remarked.

"No," Sofia said, more out of reflex than honesty. "No, no. I'm just … I want to know what I'm up against."

"I've met the guy—he's not exactly a ladies' man," Benny said. "He ought to worry about what *he's* up against."

PATRICK WAS WORRIED about that very thing, and that was why he woke up that morning feeling like he'd been hit by a runaway cargo van.

When he'd tried to get out of bed, his muscles had protested so much that he'd wondered if this was how someone felt after a bar fight. He'd never been in a bar fight, but it seemed plausible that the aftereffects might be similar to this. But only if various implements such as baseball bats and wooden chairs had been used as weapons.

He'd taken a couple of ibuprofen and a hot shower, and that had helped somewhat. But now, in the middle of his teaching day, all such measures of relief had worn off, and he cursed himself for his failure to follow not-Chad's warnings about starting slowly.

Live and learn.

"Dr. Connelly? Are you okay?" A young woman in the front row had been looking at him with concern as he'd lectured about Shakespeare's *Titus Andronicus*, and now, as he paused and winced in pain, she finally spoke up.

"I'm fine, thank you," he said. "I was just"—he struggled to come up with an explanation that would make him seem less pathetic than he was—"playing tennis earlier, and I pulled a muscle."

It seemed to him that anyone—even a perfectly fit person—might hurt himself playing tennis, while only a complete novice would be stupid enough to disable himself lifting weights. He didn't like to lie, but one did have to save face.

"Now, back to the themes of the play. Is revenge the same thing as justice?" He looked to the class for responses. "Anyone?"

THE LIE FELL APART when the young woman from the front row came to up to him after class to ask about his interest in tennis.

"I love tennis," she told him, looking blond and perky, the ponytail on the back of her head bobbing hopefully. "We should play sometime."

Sitting behind his desk at the front of the class, he'd opened his mouth to make some excuse—some line about lack of time or the inappropriateness of him spending his free time with a student—when he simply deflated. "I didn't hurt myself playing tennis," he admitted.

"You didn't?"

He gave her a wry grin. "No. I joined a gym. I must have ... pushed it a little too hard."

"Ooh." She winced. "You should get a personal trainer."

"I've got one. He warned me." He should have ended it there. But for some reason—maybe it was how fresh and young she looked, how open, how innocent and guileless—he told her the truth. "It was stupid. I was trying to impress a woman."

"Oh." Her face fell, and he realized for the first time that her offer to be his tennis partner had been more than that. Had Ramon been right? Were his students flirting with him? How had he failed to notice?

"Anyway, thank you for your concern." He put on his professor voice again. "I appreciate it, but I'll be fine."

She shoved her books into her backpack, zipped it up, and started to go. At the last moment, she turned back to him.

"For what it's worth, you don't have to try so hard," she said.

"Pardon me?"

She shrugged. "You just don't, that's all. If she doesn't get it, then that's her problem."

He blinked a couple of times, as though he'd just emerged into bright sun. "If she doesn't ... get what?"

She smiled in a way that made him think of high school cheerleaders and Ivory soap. "You really don't know, do you?"

And before she could explain to him what it was he didn't know, she shouldered her backpack and left him alone with his insecurity and his sore muscles.

LATER THAT AFTERNOON, well before she was set to meet Patrick, Sofia went to her mother's library and breathed in the scent of the books—a smell that always reminded her of Carmela.

Sofia's mother would have loved Patrick, she was sure of it. For just a moment, Sofia opened the box filled with her grief over her parents and let a little bit of the pain seep out. She wanted her mother to meet him, but that would never happen. She wanted to ask her mother's advice about love—about this giddy feeling that she'd met someone important—but she couldn't do that.

Sofia felt the sorrow of it like a soul-deep ache, and then she put the pain away again.

The first edition of *To Kill a Mockingbird* was sitting on the shelf in front of her. Sofia took it down and wondered whether she should read it. The book was valuable, and she didn't want anything to happen to it, so she carefully replaced it on the shelf.

She did think she should try reading one of the classics, though, to get some insight into Patrick's interests. She selected another book: *Ulysses* by James Joyce. She sat in one of her mother's comfortable leather club chairs and began to read.

AN HOUR LATER, it was only by sheer will that she didn't hurl the book across the room. What in the world was happening here? Was this book even in English?

Martina came into the room at just about the time Sofia thought her brain might start leaking out her ears.

"What are you reading?" Martina was holding a book of her own —one she'd apparently finished—and she put it back on a shelf.

"Who the hell knows?" Sofia snapped. "I don't know what this is! I don't know why anyone would subject themselves to ... this!" She held up the book as Exhibit A.

"*Ulysses*? Oh, Sofia, no." She said it as though she'd found Sofia shooting heroin and was shocked that it had come to this.

"I want to be interesting! I want to be able to talk about the things he enjoys. But I don't know if it's worth it." She plunked the book down on the table next to the chair, defeated.

Martina sat down beside her in the club chair's twin. "Look. Just be yourself. He already likes you. He likes *you.* He doesn't expect you to suddenly become someone else."

"I guess." Her shoulders fell, and she didn't meet Martina's eyes.

"I've never seen you this worried about a guy before," Martina said. "You're usually so ... casual."

Sofia usually approached dating as though it were merely fun, something to pass the time. But her instincts told her this one mattered. She wasn't sure why; she didn't know him well enough yet to base the feeling on anything rational, anything logical. Instead, she was basing it on her gut.

Her gut told her something important was happening in her life, and that it had everything to do with Patrick.

But he was an accomplished author, a professor, an academic who'd been showered with honors and accolades. What was she?

She was a kayak tour guide.

"I should have gone to college," she told her sister. "I should have gone to ... I don't know ... law school."

"Do you *want* to go to law school?" Martina asked.

"No! Why would I want to go to law school?!"

Martina composed her face into an image of serenity and patted Sofia on the knee. "Sof, I love you, but you're losing your mind."

12

———————

They'd decided to go to a movie at the multiplex in San Luis Obispo. They hadn't settled on what to see yet, so they discussed their options on the drive down.

Sofia wanted to see the latest Marvel Cinematic Universe flick, but she was afraid if she said so, he'd be even more certain that she was lowbrow and not smart enough for him.

Instead, she suggested the most highbrow, intellectually challenging movie she could think of—a film by a French director about a group of middle-aged friends coming to terms with their mortality. Or something. She'd heard that it was full of symbolism and meaning, so it seemed perfect.

"Oh. Really? Okay," Patrick said when she offered her suggestion. He hesitated a little when he said it. Sofia imagined that he'd hesitated because he was surprised that someone like her would want to see a movie like that. Which she didn't, if she were being honest. But him *thinking* she didn't offended her, so she stayed firm.

"Sure. The critics say it's brilliant and incisive. But if you want to see something else ..."

"No, no. That's fine."

They found a spot in a parking structure across the street from the theater, bought their tickets, and got settled into their seats with popcorn and a soda for him, and a bottle of water for her. She'd wanted popcorn and a soda, too, but it didn't go with the image she was trying to project, so she'd refused his offer and had settled for the water.

One of the best things about this particular theater was that it offered plush reclining seats that put the filmgoer in a nearly horizontal position. It was like watching TV in a Barcalounger at home, except that the screen was huge and the sound was as loud as a jumbo jet during takeoff.

Usually, Sofia was delighted by the seats, but now, with the characters on the screen having endless metaphor-filled conversations in beige rooms while listening to dour music and looking depressed, she found that she could hardly keep her eyes open. That, combined with the comfort of the seats, had her fully out—probably snoring and drooling—before the movie was half over.

PATRICK BECAME aware that Sofia was sleeping sometime before the main character's suicide attempt but after the dinner party scene in which everyone talked about the books they were reading but were really talking about death.

Death seemed pretty inviting at the moment, if it meant he wouldn't have to sit through the rest of this movie.

He was puzzled by Sofia's suggestion that they see it, but he'd wanted to make her happy. Now here he was, with a bad movie in front of him and a sleeping date beside him. He'd have welcomed finding Sofia sleeping beside him under other circumstances, but as it was, he simply felt disappointment that their date seemed to be a bust.

These seats really were comfortable, though.

His muscles were sore and tired, and the film was dull and impen-

etrable, and Sofia was making soft sleeping noises. Before he knew it, he was asleep, too.

SOFIA WOKE to the sound of a male, teenage voice speaking to her.

"Ma'am?"

There was some sort of light in her eyes, and she was groggy and disoriented as she slowly opened them.

The reality of the situation dawned on her slowly: the movie theater. The boring film. The comfortable seats. Patrick.

Oh, my God.

She bolted upright in her seat, her face heated with embarrassment. She and Patrick both put their reclining seats into their upright positions, gathered their things—her purse, his empty popcorn and soda containers—and left the theater, which was now empty except for the employee who'd awakened them.

"I ... ah ... must have dozed off." He was blushing.

"I guess so." She made no mention of the fact that she had, too. If he'd been too out of it to notice, then she certainly wasn't going to point it out to him.

"I'm sorry. Sofia, that was—"

"Let's just let it go, okay?" She walked a little faster, wanting to get out of here and away from this whole ill-fated situation.

He hurried to keep up, tossing his trash into a bin and lengthening his stride to keep up with her.

"Sofia? Are you *angry* with me?"

"Of course not. Don't be stupid." But she *was* angry, and everything about her body language said so as she went out the front door and into the plaza beyond.

He shoved his hands into his pockets and followed her. "Do you want to get something to eat?" It was about eight p.m. and they hadn't had dinner, so it was a reasonable question. Still, Sofia reacted as though he'd suggested bungee jumping.

"Why? Why would we do that, Patrick? What's the point?" She whirled around to face him.

"The point? Uh … hunger, I suppose."

"Well … you do what you want. I'm going to the car." She headed across the street to the parking garage, Patrick hurrying after her.

He had every right to react to her anger with anger of his own. She knew that. If someone had treated her like this, she'd have made him sorry for it. And yet he said nothing as they went to the car. He simply followed her, unlocked the car, and held the door open for her as she got in.

He was calm as they exited the parking garage and headed north toward Cambria. And that—the calm—made her realize she was acting like a fool.

"It's just … that movie! I mean, if you want to talk about sex, talk about sex! Don't pretend you're talking about ripe peaches! For God's sake!" It wasn't an explanation for her behavior—not really—but it was a start.

"I thought you wanted to see that movie," Patrick said.

"I only said I wanted to see it because I thought *you* wanted to see it."

He shot her a glance as he drove. "I wanted to see the Marvel movie."

Somehow, that was the last straw. "You … I … You *what*? Well, that's just freaking *perfect*."

"If we're going to fight, I need to pull over." He drove into a convenience store parking lot, found a spot, and turned off the car. "Sofia, could you please tell me what's going on?"

She considered her options: Pretend it all was somehow his fault? Claim that some outside factor, like a stomach bug, was causing her behavior? Tell the truth?

She remembered something her mother used to say: *Whatever's wrong, Sofia, lying about it will just make it worse.*

"I wanted to see the Marvel movie. But I didn't want to say that, because you're so brilliant, and I didn't want you to think I'm not as smart as you are. So I said I wanted to see the other movie, because it's the kind of thing your other girlfriends probably liked. But it was so boring! And I fell asleep. And falling asleep is the worst thing you could possibly do on a date—unless it's after great sex—so now I've ruined everything. And I felt awful about ruining everything, so I took it out on you and acted like a raging bitch to deflect. All right? That's what's going on."

THAT WAS a lot for Patrick to digest, especially since his brain had gotten stuck on the words *great sex*. The phrase had set a mental picture in motion, and he had to push that aside before he could proceed.

When he could answer coherently, he began ticking off points one by one.

"First, I do think you're smart. Second, your choice of movie wouldn't have changed my mind about that. Third, things don't have to be ruined. And fourth, what did you mean about my other girlfriends? What other girlfriends?"

She opened her mouth to speak, closed it, then sat back in her seat and avoided looking at him. "I had my sister ask about you at the college. She said you only dated super intellectual women. I guess that made me feel a little insecure."

He guessed it did, too, given how the evening was going.

"I don't date super intellectual women." But, was that true? He was surprised to realize that it was. "Or, actually, I guess I have done that in the past, now that I think about it."

"And I'll bet they'd have loved that boring-ass movie," Sofia retorted.

"They probably would have," he admitted. "And I'd have sat through it just to make them happy. Which was what I was doing tonight, with you."

Then, in a gesture bold enough to rival his initial kayaking attempt in its reckless grandeur, he reached out, pulled her to him, and kissed her thoroughly and passionately, his hands tangled in her hair. After a time that seemed long but not nearly long enough, he said, "I can't imagine why you'd feel insecure, Sofia. You're the most beautiful, vibrant, fascinating woman I've ever met."

Then he let go of her and sat back in his seat to gather himself.

"Oh," she said.

DURING THE DRIVE HOME, Sofia didn't speak. She was too busy replaying what Patrick had said to her. And—more vividly—how he had kissed her.

She wasn't used to feeling a lack of confidence with men, and it had thrown her off her game. Then the kiss had left her so thoroughly off balance that she'd begun to wonder what other assumptions she'd made that were utterly, foolishly false.

She'd seen Patrick as inept socially, a little out of his depth with her, perhaps somewhat inexperienced with dating and women. But the kiss had been so masterful, so commanding ...

One of them was out of their league—but she was no longer sure which one it was.

She didn't set out to sleep with him in order to regain the upper hand. That would have been too calculating, too manipulative ... hell, too *sleazy*. And she wasn't any of those things. All she knew was that she wanted him and that she needed to do something to feel better about her place in his life.

She wasn't naïve, and she wasn't innocent. When she wanted sex, she had it. She liked going after what she wanted.

Why shouldn't this be the same?

When they got to her house, he walked her to the door. She put her arms around him, pulled him to her, brought her mouth to within an inch of his, and said, "Patrick, come inside. Come with me to my room."

Patrick didn't just hear what she'd said. He felt it, along his scalp, down his spine, and lower, where all of his blood was beginning to surge.

How many times since the day he'd seen her at Jitters had he imagined this? How many times had he willed this very thing to happen?

She kissed him, her tongue slipping into his mouth, warm and caressing.

She wanted this. She wanted *him*. So why did it feel so ... wrong?

Knowing that he would regret this—and soon—he pushed her away gently and took a deep, shaky breath to steady himself.

"Sofia ..."

"My sisters aren't home." She pushed her body against his. "It'll just be us. Come on." She took his hand and pulled him toward the door.

If he were any other guy, he'd follow her. If he were any other man, he'd accept her offer, have an amazing experience, and never think twice about it.

But he wasn't any other man. He was the man his mother had raised him to be. And he couldn't do this—not now, not like this.

"Sofia, thank you, that's a lovely offer. But I ... I can't."

And, oh, God, the way she was looking at him. With a combination of lust, confusion, and hurt.

"What do you mean?"

"I mean ... it just doesn't feel like this is right for me. Or for you. Not yet."

A spark of something lit in her eyes as they stood in the glow of the porch light. Anger? Offense? Whatever it was, it made her even sexier than before. God help him.

"You're turning me down." She said it as though she were struggling to comprehend it. As sexy as she was, it seemed unlikely that anything like this had ever happened to her before.

"I'm sorry," he said.

She let go of his hand as though it were made of plutonium.

"Sofia ..."

"Goodnight, Patrick." She pulled her keys out of her purse and unlocked the front door.

"You're upset. I didn't mean—" But she didn't hear whatever it was that he didn't mean, because she'd already closed the door.

"Nice job, Connelly," he muttered, feeling utterly baffled by the mysterious ways of women.

13

S ofia was in the kitchen angrily working her way through a bag of Oreos when the others came home. It was just past midnight, and Martina and Benny were a little bit drunk. Bianca, the designated driver, reached into the cupboard for a partially full bottle of wine now that she was finally free to enjoy an adult beverage of her own. She pulled the cork and poured herself half a glass of Chianti, which was typical Bianca. A whole glass would have been far too indulgent for her.

"How was your date?" she asked Sofia. "Judging from the fact that you're here, and not still with him, it can't have been very good."

"It was fine." Sofia shoved another cookie into her mouth.

"You should have come with us," Benny said. "Martina flirted with that guy from the bank—what was his name?"

"Jim Putney," Bianca supplied.

"But I wasn't flirting," Martina said.

"Oh, my ass." Benny dismissed Martina's denial with a wave of her hand. "If you're going to practically invite a guy to do you on the pool table, at least own it."

"I don't know what you're talking about." Martina's eyes widened.

"Shut up," Benny said.

"Both of you shut up," Sofia said. "Shove a cookie in your mouth if you think that'll help you stop talking." She pushed the bag of cookies toward them.

"What crawled up your butt?" Benny wanted to know.

"She was just about to tell us how her date with Patrick went horribly wrong," Bianca said.

"No, I wasn't."

"But it did. Didn't it? Oh, no." Martina, always the nurturer, reached out and rubbed Sofia's arm. The silver bangles on her wrist jingled as she rubbed.

"Don't be nice to me," Sofia snapped. "If you're nice to me, I'm going to feel even worse, and I'd rather not. I'd rather just ... load up on sugar and artificial ingredients." She grabbed the cookies back, since she hadn't gotten any takers.

"Look. Whatever he did to upset you, it makes him an asshole." Benny pointed one finger at Sofia. "It's not worth bingeing on cookies over an asshole."

"Except that he didn't do anything! It's what I did! If there's an asshole in this scenario, it's me!" Sofia gestured with her hands, which were dusted with dark cookie crumbs.

"Uh oh. What did you do?" Bianca sat down at the table across from Sofia, focusing on her.

"I fell asleep at the movies. And then I offered him sex."

The other three were silent for a moment.

"Well ... okay," Bianca said. "The first part was a little unfortunate. But the second part probably made up for the first part."

Martina nodded her agreement.

"It should have," Sofia said miserably. "But it didn't. Because he turned me down. And then I was just ... just some woman who fell asleep on a date and then begged for sex, which he didn't even want because he was desperate to get the hell out of here!"

"Ouch," Benny said.

"The next time he and his friends are getting drunk and talking about the worst dates they've ever had, he's going to tell them about this one. And they're all going to laugh."

"They won't laugh." Martina laid her hand over Sofia's on the table.

"Well ... remember the time you told us about Jared Wilkerson?" Benny asked Martina.

"That *was* pretty funny," Bianca said, smirking.

"See? See?" Sofia dropped her face into her hands.

"Why did he turn you down?" Martina asked, squeezing Sofia's hand.

"He said it didn't 'feel right.' " Sofia put air quotes around the words *feel right.*

"Aww," Bianca said, going a little dreamy-eyed. "He's a romantic."

"Where do you get that?" Benny asked.

Bianca explained, "He wants to wait until he's in the right place emotionally. Which is really sweet. How many guys do that?"

"That's a good point," Benny conceded. "Most guys would think it feels right if the room's not on fire."

"No." Sofia shook her head. "No. He's not just waiting. He's not just holding out for the perfect time, or place, or for us to get to know each other better, or ... or marriage, or whatever damned thing. He said no because it was the date from hell, and he never wants to see me again."

"I doubt that," Martina said.

"And even if it's true," Benny put in, "who cares? Screw him. You just started seeing him, it can't be that big of a deal yet."

Except that it was. Somehow, it was. Despite it being early, and despite the fact that they hardly knew each other, despite all of that ... she'd gotten her hopes up. Her hopes had been irrationally up. And she'd ruined it.

"It was a desperation pass," she concluded. "Me offering him sex? It was desperation, because I knew the date had been awful, and I was just trying to fix it. I was using sex like duct tape."

"I'd have combined sex and duct tape in an entirely different way," Benny mused.

Martina ignored Benny's quip and focused on Sofia. "If that's true, then he was right—it would have been a mistake to sleep together.

He knew that. He knew you were offering for the wrong reasons. And he could have taken advantage of it, but he didn't."

Bianca nodded. "Not only is he smart and kind of cute, he's also insightful. And caring. He didn't want you doing something you'd regret."

All of that just made Sofia even more miserable, because he really was all of those things, and she likely would never see him again.

PATRICK DROVE HOME WONDERING how he could get things back on track, and when he could see Sofia again.

It was clear he'd hurt her feelings when he'd turned down her offer—an offer so generous, so astoundingly miraculous, that he still couldn't believe he'd refused it. He wanted her to make that offer again, under better circumstances, at a time when he could accept enthusiastically.

And he wanted that to happen as soon as possible.

But she'd been angry when he'd left her, and that wasn't good. The whole date had fallen apart the moment they'd reclined the overly comfortable seats and the characters on the screen had started talking about Jean-Paul Sartre.

They needed a do-over. And they needed to do it soon, before the memory of the bad date calcified in both of their minds in such a way that no amount of well-intentioned effort could hope to break it loose.

The big thing that had gone wrong, he thought, was that she'd pretended to like something she didn't in an attempt to be someone she wasn't. Maybe the key was to put her back in her own comfort zone—even if it meant taking himself out of his.

It was an intriguing idea.

He would refine the idea and come up with a plan. But tonight, he was too busy trying to get the idea of what he'd turned down out of his head.

At home in his cottage, he settled into bed, looked up at the dark ceiling, and tried to think of things other than sex—like algebra, the best way to get stains out of grout, and his mother's recipe for meatloaf.

When none of that worked, he thought of Jean-Paul Sartre. That had put him to sleep earlier this evening; there was no reason to think it wouldn't work now.

14

———

On Monday morning, Patrick got up early, showered, shaved, and dressed, then drove to the college for his eight a.m. graduate seminar on postmodern literature. Confronting postmodernism was hard enough on an average day, but it was even harder when he was distracted by thoughts of Sofia.

What was she doing right now? Was she still sleeping? Going for a run on a trail through the woods? Maybe enjoying an early morning of kayaking, alone out on the water, at peace with her thoughts?

He'd been struggling with the fact that he hadn't slept with her. Images kept flittering through his mind—images of what would have happened if he'd said yes.

Only an idiot would stand at the very gates of paradise and say to himself, *Well, no, I don't believe I'll go in there today. Maybe some other time.* What kind of fool refused such an opportunity?

The kind of fool who wanted more than just sex.

If she slept with him and regretted it afterward, that would add baggage that neither one of them wanted. She'd feel bad for having done it, and he would feel bad for having made her feel bad. And none of that would lend itself to them having a long-term relationship, which he dearly hoped they might do.

No, if she felt anything negative after their first time sleeping together, he wanted it to be sorrow that it ever had to end.

He was playing the long game, and sometimes that was difficult and frustrating. It rarely lent itself to easy gratification.

He was thinking about all of that while one of his students, a defiantly unkempt twentysomething man-child with greasy hair and a battered motorcycle jacket, was discussing the themes of rampant consumerism in the works of Don DeLillo.

A young woman—a prodigy, just eighteen and already in grad school—was arguing with him, and Patrick was content to let them sort it out between themselves as he sorted out his love life.

Should he call Sofia today? Or did she need more time to get over her obvious irritation with him?

" ... ridiculous, asinine assumption. Right, Dr. Connelly?"

Somebody was talking to him, but he wasn't entirely certain who it was. He usually prided himself on giving his students his full attention, but Sofia had gotten into his head, and his professionalism was slipping.

"I ... That's ... Do you have more evidence to support your assertions?" The young woman—girl, really—launched into a well-thought-out argument for why the man sitting across the table from her was utterly full of crap, and Patrick got the impression that no one in the room had noticed that he hadn't heard a word they'd said until now.

AT LUNCHTIME, he met Ramon at Mustang Station in the University Union, and they wedged themselves in next to some students at a long wooden table with their pizzas and their soft drinks.

"How are things going with Sofia?" Ramon asked, after the preliminary chitchat was out of the way.

"We went out this weekend," Patrick said, somewhat evasively. If he'd hoped that the answer would be enough to satisfy Ramon's curiosity, he was mistaken.

"So? How was it? You guys do the deed yet?" He raised his eyebrows in question as he shoved a bite of pepperoni pizza into his mouth.

"We, ah ... no."

There must have been something in the way he'd said it, because Ramon chewed, wiped his mouth with a paper napkin, and focused on Patrick with sympathy. "Aw, shit. What happened?"

What, indeed? A lot had happened, but he wasn't sure he understood all of it. He laid it out for Ramon succinctly but thoroughly.

"We went to the movies and we both fell asleep. Sofia got mad and said she hadn't wanted to see that movie—even though she'd picked it. Then she complained that I only see intellectual women. We kissed, and then she ... ah ... made it clear she wouldn't mind more. But I left. And now she's angry with me—or, at least, she was the last time I saw her."

Was that everything? It didn't cover the subtleties, certainly, but it had hit on the relevant facts.

Ramon took a long slurp of his soft drink. "What movie was it?"

"Does that matter?"

"It matters. I can't give advice unless I know the movie."

Patrick hadn't asked for advice—he hadn't wanted to talk about this at all, in fact—but it was always possible Ramon had some insight. He told him which movie.

"Ah, jeez," Ramon said. "Of course it was a bad date. No good date ever started with a French art film."

"But—"

"Wait." Ramon pointed one finger at Patrick. "Somebody was asking around about you last week. Will Bachman over in the science department wanted to know about your ex-girlfriends. Said he was asking for a friend. Must have been Sofia, if she complained about who you date."

Patrick groaned softly. "What did you tell him?"

Ramon shrugged. "I told him about Stacy and Kim. I didn't think it was a secret."

"It's not." Stacy had been a full professor at Cal Poly until she'd left to take a job on the East Coast. And Kim had written a novel that had been featured by Oprah's Book Club. She was now in talks to sell the story to a Hollywood producer. He hadn't had particularly satisfying relationships with either one of them, but he could see how it looked—on paper, at least. "I wish you hadn't done that, though."

"Dude, I'm sorry. I thought he was asking for another one of those chirpy little undergrads who are always trying to get into your Dockers."

Patrick's brow furrowed. "I don't know what you're talking about."

"I know you don't." Ramon shook his head sadly. "It's a wonder you manage to feed and dress yourself every day."

Patrick didn't particularly want his pizza. He wasn't hungry, but he had a full load of afternoon classes and office hours, and he couldn't do it on an empty stomach.

"So, she picked an artsy film because she found out about your exes and wants to seem as smart as they are. But the movie was crap, and you both fell asleep, and she tried to drag the date out of the Dumpster with a little naked romp, a little mattress tag. But even that didn't work, so now she's pretty much had it."

"That's ... amazingly accurate," Patrick concluded.

"So, what are you going to do now?"

That was, indeed, the question.

"I thought ... running."

Ramon looked at him blankly. "Running where? You mean, dumping Sofia? Dude, I know it was a bad date, but ..."

"Running as recreation," Patrick clarified. "I thought I would ask her to go running with me."

Ramon nodded. "Right. Do something active and outdoorsy. That's her bag. Give her the home field advantage, get things back on the right track."

"That's the general idea," Patrick agreed.

"Do you even run?"

"Of course. I wouldn't suggest it if I didn't. I'm not eager to be humiliated." It wasn't strictly true that Patrick ran. Not regularly, anyway. But he had jogged a little in the past, and he'd been increasing his speed on the treadmill since he'd started working out at the gym. Certainly, he could manage a couple of miles respectably enough.

"Okay. So, when are you going?"

"I haven't asked her yet."

Ramon picked up his slice and paused with it halfway to his mouth. "Have you talked to her at all since the bad date?"

"Ah ... no."

Ramon shook his head in pity. "Every minute you wait, she's getting more and more angry about the whole French film debacle."

"She is?"

"I'm married, man. Trust me. The clock is ticking. Tick-tock."

PATRICK WOULDN'T NORMALLY ASSUME that Ramon was right about anything, but the man did have more experience with relationships. That had to count for something.

Figuring that a phone call might be fraught with peril—too many variables might come into play—he texted her after lunch, before his next class.

When can I see you again? Some morning this week, maybe? I thought we might go running.

There. Going running together before work was casual, it was non-threatening. And it wouldn't lead to the question of sex, because they both would have somewhere they needed to be.

He normally wouldn't have added *won't lead to sex* as an item in the dating-scenario plus column, but one had to adapt to the circumstances.

When she didn't answer right away, he figured she hadn't seen his text. And when she still hadn't answered an hour later, he wondered if he'd blown his chance with her.

That, he thought, would be tragic.

15

———————

Sofia didn't see the text until more than two hours after Patrick sent it. She'd been out on a kayaking tour when it had come in, and she didn't notice it until after she'd gotten showered and dressed.

Running? That was unexpected.

She wasn't sure how to answer. She wanted to see him—she'd thought of little else since their ill-fated Saturday night—but was there any point? They were too hopelessly mismatched for this thing between them to go anywhere.

Did Patrick call you yet? Martina texted while Sofia was considering her options.

He texted. He wants to go running.

Why running? Martina asked.

God knows.

She had an idea about his reasoning, though. She'd told him that she'd felt out of her element on their date, and he wanted to put her back into a situation where she'd feel comfortable. It was sweet.

I don't know what I'm going to say, she told Martina.

Say yes!!! The response came almost immediately. *He's sweet, Sof. If you don't go out with him again, I will.*

And that decided it. The force of sibling rivalry was strong enough to overcome any doubts Sofia had.

The hell you will, Sofia answered.

THEY SCHEDULED their run for a Wednesday morning before work. Patrick didn't have his first class until ten, and Sofia didn't have a tour group until late morning. They met at upper Fiscalini Ranch, and Sofia unfolded a map that she'd taken from a rack at the trailhead.

Patrick's first hint that he'd made a tactical error came when she showed him the map and proposed a route.

"We can head up this trail to the Forest Loop, curve around here to go down to the bluffs, follow the bluff trail down to here, and then circle back to the starting point." She looked at him expectantly.

He blinked a few times, looked at the map, then looked out at the trail before them. The route she was suggesting had to be at least four miles, maybe five. And a substantial portion of that was steeply uphill.

"Oh. Ah ... hmm." Yes, he'd been sure that he could handle a run. But he'd imagined a couple of miles at the most, on relatively flat ground.

"If that doesn't work for you, we can take a different route," she said.

He should have confessed then that the route was too hard, too uphill, too long. He should have admitted that he was daunted by the prospect of it. But the blow to his manly pride would have been too much.

"Have you run this route before?" he asked.

"Oh, sure. When I'm training for a triathlon, I do this on my low-intensity days."

This piece of information offered two bits of alarming news. One, that she competed in triathlons. And two, that she considered this route to be "light intensity."

Chances were good that he would end this outing injured, humiliated, or both. He began wondering how he might get out of it. Could he fake some kind of emergency that would require him to leave early? Pretend that he had a bad knee or a sore ankle that demanded a shorter route at a slow pace?

He could try that, or he could just man up and do his best not to embarrass himself.

"So, what do you think?" She was stretching a hamstring as she spoke.

"After you." He gestured gallantly to the trail ahead.

One benefit of the outing was the view. The rolling hills, the golden grass, the wildflowers, the sweeping vistas of the forest and the ocean, the vast, blue horizon. And then there was the view straight ahead of him: Sofia in a cropped workout top and spandex running pants, every curve and plane of her body in clear relief.

If he'd thought she was magnificent before, she was even more so now, her muscles working flawlessly, a light sheen of sweat glistening on her skin, her shiny, thick hair bouncing in its ponytail, a good two inches of smooth, tanned skin visible above the waistband of her pants.

He was enchanted.

At least, he was enchanted for the first part of the run, before all of his faculties became absorbed in survival.

Her pace was faster than he would have liked, but that was okay at first. He pushed himself a little, and he kept up. But as they headed uphill in the late September sun, his breathing became labored and his legs and lungs started to burn.

He could have called to her to slow down a little—she would have accommodated him—but, God help him, he wanted to impress her. So he imagined what he might do if rabid wolves were chasing him. He dug down deep into his reserves of strength and energy, and he kept pace with her as they rose toward the top of the hill.

By the time they were two miles into the run, he was gasping for breath, his legs felt like they were on fire, his vision was blurred with sweat, and he began to see his life flashing before his eyes.

Sofia, keeping her eyes on the trail in front of her, seemed oblivious until he stumbled. She looked back over her shoulder to see if he was okay, and surprise—then alarm—registered on her face.

"Patrick? Patrick! Oh, my God." She skidded to a stop and rushed back to where he stood in the middle of the trail.

AT FIRST SHE wondered if he was having a heart attack.

Patrick's face was bright red, he was gasping for breath, and his eyes were wide in either pain or panic. He dropped to his knees as she got to him.

"Patrick! Are you all right? What happened? Can you talk?"

He flopped onto his back and spread out like a starfish in the dirt, gasping.

"Oh, shit. Oh, shit. I'm going to call 911." Marveling that the man was going to require emergency services for the second time since she'd known him, she pulled her phone out of a pocket in her shirt and thumbed it on.

"No … no … no need …" Patrick gulped air. "I just … I need … a minute."

She knelt beside him and felt his pulse. His heart was racing.

"Can you sit up?"

He began to pull himself into a sitting position, and she helped him, supporting his back with her hand. She pulled a water bottle out of a pack she had strapped around her waist, and she offered it to him.

He drank deeply, gasped for air a few more times, then fell onto his back again, this time more in defeat than due to any kind of near-death crisis.

"Come on. There's a bench over there." She offered him her hand and helped him up, and they walked fifty yards to a driftwood bench that overlooked the ocean down the hill and far below them.

"You gave me a scare. Again," she said when they were settled and his breathing was slowing down.

He rubbed the back of his neck, then ran a hand through his

sweat-soaked hair. "I probably should have mentioned that I'm not a serious runner."

"You don't say." She might have smirked slightly. She wasn't proud of the smirk, but the situation seemed to call for it.

"You're a triathlete," he said.

"Well, yes." Suddenly, she was embarrassed that she'd failed to take that into account. What had she expected? Of course she was more fit than he was. Not everyone was prepared to run four to five miles at high speed up steep hills. Why had she assumed he was?

Probably because her previous boyfriends had been body-builders, long-distance runners, and cyclists—men who'd have thought today's run was a light warm-up, the way Sofia did.

She hadn't even thought about it—she'd simply expected more than Patrick could give.

"God, I'm so sorry," she said as they sat on the bench, looking out at the ocean. "I didn't think. When you said you wanted to go for a run ..."

"I meant a mile or two. At a slow jog." He smiled ruefully.

"You should have said something."

"Yes. And you should have said you wanted to see the Marvel film. We're even, I suppose." His color was improving, and his breathing was more or less back to normal.

She offered him the water bottle again. "I guess you're right."

Would they ever have a date that went smoothly, when someone didn't almost die or fall asleep unintentionally, or explode in a fit of insecurity?

She sighed and slumped down into her seat. "Patrick ... maybe this just isn't meant to be."

"I don't believe that." He was looking at her intently with those pale blue eyes.

"You don't?"

"No." He reached out and touched her shoulder where the T-back shirt left it bare. An electric tingle warmed her all the way down her spine.

"I invited you into my bed, and you refused. No one has ever refused before."

"Now, that I believe." He smiled, just a little, and the smile tugged at her.

"So, why did you say no?"

His hand slid off of her shoulder and down her arm, until he took her hand in his. "Because you weren't offering for the right reasons. You didn't want me. You wanted the upper hand."

"I ..." She'd opened her mouth intending to deny it, but she couldn't. It was true.

"I want you to want *me*, Sofia."

"I do." It came out as a whisper, a prayer.

"I'm not an athlete," he said.

"I'm not some intellectual, high-IQ MENSA member who—"

He cut her off with a kiss, and in a moment, she could no longer remember what she was or wasn't, or what he was or wasn't. She only knew she'd meant it when she said she wanted him. Her body was on fire with it.

His hands were on her face, holding her to him, and hers were in the fabric of his shirt, grabbing it, pulling at it.

She was utterly lost in him when they heard someone coming up the trail. They pulled apart self-consciously as a woman walked past with a corgi on a leash.

"This isn't over," Patrick murmured to her.

"God, I hope not."

16

It was confusing, that's what it was. They kept having disastrous dates, yet Sofia couldn't stay away from him.

He wasn't her usual type, that was true. But dating her usual type hadn't worked miracles for her love life, had it? Dating a man she could work out with was good; it was fine. The visuals were great, and the sex usually met her expectations. But when it came time to be quiet together or to actually talk, there was always something missing.

Usually, what was missing was any concern for her or her feelings.

But Patrick was different. He wasn't out to use her. If he had been, he'd have slept with her the night she'd offered, regardless of whether it was the right thing for either one of them.

But he hadn't done that. He'd wanted her to want it for the right reasons, and that was a revelation. That was refreshing as hell.

Normally, after two dates as bad as the ones they'd had, she'd have packed up her emotional bags and moved on. But somehow, she wanted to unpack and move in for a long stay.

Sofia took her tour group out at San Simeon Cove later that

morning. The weather was perfect for it: clear skies, warm temperatures, calm water in a color so blue it almost seemed painted on.

Her muscles were pleasantly warm as she paddled, keeping an eye on the group behind her.

Twice now, Patrick had risked both pain and injury to get close to her, to impress her. He was trying too hard—but then, so had she when she'd claimed to want to see a movie she had absolutely no interest in.

What if they both stopped trying so hard and just relaxed? What if they both tried being themselves? It was possible they'd discover they had nothing in common. But it was also possible that they would have a lot of fun. And it certainly would be safer for Patrick.

After she brought the group in, she got changed into workout clothes and went to the gym, where she put in a hard half hour on the free weights. She didn't feel quite right unless she'd had an intense workout. It was something in her DNA, something that had been true for her since she was a small child running on the beach with the wind in her hair, feeling a thrilling surge of energy and the immutable strength of her own limbs.

When she was done and heading toward the showers, she ran into a guy she'd dated once—a muscle-bound jock who'd played football for the Mustangs and who now worked as a personal trainer. He was wearing shorts that showed the bulge of his quadriceps and a cropped T-shirt that offered a peek of six-pack abs.

What kind of guy wore a crop top, anyway? She marveled that the question had never bothered her before.

"Hey, Sof." He eyed her up and down while trying to pretend he wasn't. "How you been?"

"Logan. I'm good." Their time together had been brief and had ended amicably enough. The problem was that she'd gotten tired of talking exclusively about him—and he never had.

"Saw you running at the ranch yesterday with some guy," Logan said. The inflection he put on the words *some guy* indicated that what he really meant was *some stiff* or *some asshole.*

"Did you?" She smiled enigmatically.

"Looked like he was having some trouble. You training him, or what?"

"Or what," Sofia said, offering nothing more.

Logan grimaced. "What are you doing with that guy? Let me take you out, remind you what it's like with a real man." He flashed his artificially white teeth in what was supposed to be a winning smile.

"A real man?" Sofia said. "Why? Were you planning to introduce me to one of your friends?"

"Ouch!" Logan staggered theatrically, his hands over his wounded heart.

"Goodbye, Logan." Sofia continued on her way to the locker room.

"Think about it, babe!" he called after her. "You've got my number!"

She certainly did have his number. And that was the problem.

PATRICK MANAGED to get through his work day despite his sore muscles and his dearly held desire to take a nap.

He lectured, he moderated class discussions, he met with students during his office hours, and he graded papers. He tried not to wince when he got up from his chair.

He was torn in his feelings about his own actions since he'd met Sofia. On the one hand, a person could argue that he'd acted like a fool, pretending to be someone he wasn't and putting his own safety in jeopardy. On the other, how could he be faulted for giving his all for romance? What was life if not risk? And Sofia was more than worth a foolhardy gesture or two.

If he'd been more cautious, more prudent, then where would he be? Admiring her from afar, he supposed, instead of fondly remembering that sublime kiss.

Ah, the kiss.

He needed to kiss her again the way he needed food, shelter, air. It was hard to think about anything else. But he had a job to do, so he focused on the student who was sitting in the chair across from his desk during his afternoon office hours.

"... my financial aid," she was saying as she waved a stapled sheaf of papers in front of him.

"May I?" He reached out for the assignment she was holding, and she handed it to him. An analysis of the story structure in *The Sun Also Rises.* He'd given her eighty-eight percent—a B-plus.

"Eighty-eight is a very respectable grade," he said, handing it back to her.

"Yes, but Dr. Connelly, I need to get an A in your class or my overall GPA is going to fall below the requirement for my scholarship. I can't lose my scholarship."

He pulled up her grades for the semester—such as it was, this early in the term—and saw that she was averaging in the eighties. "There's plenty of time to pull up your grade," he reminded her. "We're only a month into the term."

"I know, but my mom's been in the hospital, so I haven't had time to study, and my dad died last year...."

"I'm sorry to hear ..."

"Could I maybe redo the paper? You made some notes on the introduction, what if I rewrote it?" She looked at him hopefully, her blond hair shining in the office's fluorescent lights.

"Miss Brooks, the assignment has been turned in and graded."

"I know, but ..." She launched into further detail of the sad circumstances of her life, up to and including her brother's drug problem, her grandmother's dementia, and her own struggles with anxiety and unemployment.

He got a couple of these a week, and he always told them the same thing: He couldn't change grades after the assignment was turned in and graded. If he did it for one student, he would have to do it for everyone, and then his professional life would be a chaos of sob stories, pleas, attempted bribes, and questionable ethics.

"I'm sorry, Miss Brooks, but there's nothing I can do. If you want me to help you arrange for some tutoring ..."

She got up from the chair and rushed out in a flurry of indignant emotion—the way they often did. He sighed, rubbed his eyes with his fingertips, and thought about Sofia.

Thinking about her was, more and more, the highlight of his day.

~

ONE OF THE problems with leading kayak tours was that business dried up when summer ended.

That meant Sofia had to look for a job.

Unlike her sisters, Sofia hadn't gone to college. She'd traveled a bit after high school, then had settled into a pattern of physically demanding tourism jobs in the summer and doing whatever work she could get the rest of the year.

The temperatures had stayed comfortable well into September, so she still had enough clients to keep her going. But that was going to change soon, so she figured it was time to start asking around.

The list of things she'd done in the past was long: barista, hotel maid, ranch hand, waitress, personal trainer, clothing boutique sales associate, and wine bar server, to name a few.

All of those jobs had been pleasant enough, but none of them paid much. Fortunately, she didn't have rent or a mortgage payment, so that helped. But she did have to pay for her share of the food and utilities, property taxes, and homeowner's insurance. And she was considering buying a car. Riding a motorcycle was fine during good weather, but the rainy season would be upon her before she knew it, and on wet days, she'd have to borrow a car when she wanted to go somewhere. Her sisters were nice about offering theirs, but it would be so much better if she had her own.

And even if money hadn't been a factor—even if she'd had no expenses at all—she liked to keep busy.

"Time for the annual job hunt," she announced to her sisters over breakfast a day or two after the running date that had gone wrong, and then right. She had a mug of coffee in front of her at the big kitchen table. Martina was eating one of her hippie breakfasts—

muesli with almond milk and flax seeds—and Benny had just emerged, yawning and tousled, from her room.

Bianca was puttering around the kitchen in her work clothes— black slacks, white button-down shirt, sensible shoes—making whole wheat toast in the toaster oven.

"You don't have to do that," she told Sofia.

"Well, I do if I want income. The tourists are starting to dry up." There would be another surge of tourism in October for the Scarecrow Festival, and again around the holidays, but very few of them would want to kayak. For some reason, the average family visiting from Des Moines didn't tend to put *Christmas* together with *kayaking*. A damned shame, Sofia thought, but it was the reality of her business.

"I didn't mean you don't have to work," Bianca said. "I meant you don't have to *look* for work. I'll hire you."

"You will?"

"Sure. You know Madison?" Bianca asked, referring to the receptionist at her pediatric office. "She's getting married and moving down to L.A. I was going to post some help wanted ads, but if you want the job, I won't have to."

Sofia had never worked in a medical office before, but there was no reason she couldn't. She'd answered phones and done paperwork in some of her other jobs, and that had gone well enough. "When is she leaving?"

"That's the thing." Bianca stood at the kitchen island with a hand propped on her hip. "She wanted to go last week, but I begged her to stay a little longer until I could find somebody. You could start right away."

"Don't do it." Benny was over at the coffee machine, poised to pour a cup from the pot.

"Why not?" Bianca asked, offended.

"Because you should never work for family." Benny shot Sofia a look. "Trust me on this one."

Sofia figured she should take the warning seriously, considering that Benny had worked for Bianca for a while during grad school.

Sofia seemed to remember a certain amount of angst. And fighting. Fighting wasn't good.

"Don't listen to her," Bianca said.

"Was she a monster?" Martina asked Benny. "Was she the boss from hell?"

"I was not the boss from hell!" Bianca insisted.

Benny looked thoughtful. She stirred cream and sugar into her coffee. "No, she wasn't the boss from hell."

"See?" Bianca said.

"But there was a certain big sister vibe on top of the usual boss vibe. A certain, *I know what's best for you, and now that you're working for me I can finally make you see the light* kind of thing."

"Uh oh," Sofia said. "Maybe I'll just ask around at the hotels on Moonstone Beach."

"No, you won't," Bianca said. "You're coming to work for me."

17

Sofia had a few more kayak tours before the end of the season, but not enough of them to keep her busy full-time. Summer was almost over.

When Sofia had been a child, the stretch between the end of summer break and the approach of the holidays had seemed like an endless wait. Time had seemed to stretch interminably, making her think the Thanksgiving turkey and the gifts under the tree would never come.

Then, as an adult, that had shifted. Time had seemed to speed up between September and January first, going so fast that the days seemed to vanish one after the other before she'd even had a chance to notice them.

That sense of fall dashing by in a blur used to be merely a curiosity. Now she dreaded it.

Sofia's parents had died in late November two years before, her mother right before Thanksgiving and her father soon after it. She no longer looked forward to the chilly weather, the festive lights, or pumpkin spice anything. If Sofia could have gone to sleep in September and awakened in January, she would have done it.

Since that wasn't an option, and she wouldn't have her kayaking clients to keep her busy for much longer, she decided to begin training at Bianca's office. The more work she had to do, the more she could keep her mind off of the time of year and all that it meant.

Besides, keeping busy would help her not to obsess about Patrick and the question of when they would see each other again, and how, and where that might lead.

She put on one of her professional outfits—she had a few for when she had to take the inevitable job that required them—went into the office, and let Madison begin showing her the routine.

If Madison could do this job, Sofia was sure she could, too. The girl—and Sofia could only think of her as a girl, rather than a woman—was a perky twentysomething with blond, bouncy hair and the manner of a high school homecoming queen.

"It's so awesome that you're coming to work here!" Madison told Sofia as they got settled behind the front desk. "My fiancé wanted me to move to L.A. to be with him weeks ago, but I told him I couldn't leave Bianca without anybody. And my fiancé was really understanding about it, but I know he was disappointed. When I told my fiancé that you were coming to take over for me, he was thrilled."

Clearly, Madison enjoyed saying the phrase *my fiancé*. Sofia wondered if she would enjoy the actual marriage as much.

Sofia knew Madison was usually efficient, because she'd heard Bianca praise her in the past. But now, the younger woman's excitement about her upcoming wedding seemed to have obliterated any number of her brain cells.

"So, when someone calls, how do I—"

"Did I show you my wedding dress?" Madison interrupted her. She clicked a few keys on the computer in front of her and brought up a picture of a princessy concoction of tulle and lace. "Isn't it amazing?"

"You'll look beautiful," Sofia said. With her creamy complexion, deep blue eyes, and perpetually shiny hair, Madison was the kind of girl who would look beautiful if she were stranded on a desert island with a nasty rash, no conditioner, and only a torn, dirty boat sail for clothing. Sofia wanted to hate her, but it was impossible. The girl's sunny disposition deprived Sofia of that simple pleasure.

"It's lovely, Madison," Bianca said warmly as she passed the front desk on her way to an exam room. "But if you could show Sofia the phone system, that would be a great help."

"Of course, Dr. R!" Madison chirped. As if on cue, the phone rang. Madison punched a button and picked it up. "Russo Pediatrics. How may I help you?" After a pause, Madison said, "Oh, Mrs. Cruz! Sure, we can get Rodrigo in this afternoon. When you come in, remind me to show you my wedding dress."

Bianca rolled her eyes and disappeared into a room where a six-month-old girl was waiting for her well-baby exam.

By lunchtime, Madison had settled down enough to teach Sofia some of what she needed to know. But now Sofia was the one having trouble concentrating, because Patrick had texted inviting her to his place for dinner.

When it came to dating a new person you hadn't slept with yet, everybody knew that *come to my house for dinner* was code for *let's just rip the Band-Aid off and screw like rabbits*. And Sofia wanted that—so much. But so far, their dates hadn't gone very well. What if their sex date continued the trend? What if he was awful in bed? Even worse, what if *she* was?

After the text came in, Sofia nearly sprinted to Bianca's office, skidding to a stop in the open doorway to make the announcement.

"Patrick wants to have sex."

"Of course he does. He's male," Bianca responded.

"Yeah, but he wants to have sex tonight."

"Of course he does. He's male."

"Would you stop that?" Sofia demanded. "What am I going to do?"

Bianca batted her eyes and cocked her head slightly to the side. "I thought Mom had this talk with you, but okay. Sometimes, when a man and a woman love each other very much—"

Sofia flipped her sister the bird discreetly, making sure no patients or their parents could see. "You're hilarious."

"Between you and Madison, this whole practice is going to grind to a halt," Bianca said. "Just have sex with him already so you can concentrate."

It was an idea.

OF COURSE, Patrick had wanted Sofia to accept his invitation. But once she did, his nerves began to play tricks on him, telling him it was an awful idea that would end in disappointment, humiliation, and possibly a devastating house fire.

The house fire thought came into play when he realized he'd invited her for dinner but he didn't know how to cook.

"I need to borrow your wife," he told Ramon as they passed each other in the halls of the administration building.

"That statement should probably worry me," Ramon said.

LUCY WAS NOT ONLY willing to help, she was enthusiastic. It baffled Patrick how intent some women were on seeing that the single men in their orbit found mates. There was probably an evolutionary reason for it—something having to do with the perpetuating of the species.

"Here's what you need to buy. Do you have a pen?" she said when he called her during his lunch break. He did have a pen, and he wrote down the items she dictated to him. "What time is she coming?"

"Ah ... around seven."

"I'll meet you at your place at five."

CERTAIN MATTERS HAD to be attended to when you were planning to have sex with someone for the first time, and Sofia threw herself into them as soon as she got off work.

First, there was the shaving. She generally kept her legs fairly smooth during the summer and early fall—she had to, because she frequently stripped down to her bikini in front of her clients and whoever else happened to be on the beach. But smooth enough to look at was one thing. Smooth enough to touch was another.

Then there was the tricky issue of her more intimate body hair. She usually waxed just enough for her chosen swimwear. But was that enough for this? If Patrick had preferences—turn-offs and turn-ons when it came to the proverbial trimming of the hedges—she didn't know what they were. What if she went for the mostly natural look and he preferred Brazilian? Of what if she chose Brazilian and he thought it made her look like a twelve-year-old girl?

As an Italian woman, she was not unfamiliar with issues of body hair—and even facial hair. And that was another issue, now that she thought about it. She hadn't had an eyebrow wax in a while. At least she didn't have a mustache, unlike her aunt Donatella.

"I have too much hair!" she announced to Martina when she got home at just after five.

Martina was sitting on the sofa with a sketchbook and her laptop, working on some designs for a client. "What are you talking about? Your hair is beautiful."

"Not the hair on my head," Sofia clarified.

"Ah." Martina didn't even pretend it wasn't an issue. She'd been blessed—or cursed—with the same genes as Sofia. "I can get you an appointment for waxing this weekend. Greta's down in Morro Bay, but she's great."

"I don't have time for Greta. Tonight's the night." She tossed her purse onto the sofa and freed her hair from the band that had been holding it in an office-appropriate bun.

Martina's eyebrows shot up. "It is?"

"God willing," Sofia said.

"I have a home waxing kit on the bottom shelf in the bathroom," Martina said. "Greta's better, but it'll do in a pinch."

WHEN LUCY GOT to Patrick's place, he was ready with the groceries she'd told him to buy. She'd come planning to cook the meal for him, but he insisted that he had to do it himself.

"It's no trouble," she told him. "It'll be fun."

"But wouldn't that be ... deceptive?" He settled on a word after thinking about the exact nature of his objections. "Part of the point of having her over is showing her that I'm willing to put in the work. That I don't mind going to some trouble for her. If you're the one doing the work and going to the trouble, it's cheating."

"Cheating," she repeated, her hands on her hips as she stood in his tiny kitchen.

"Well ... yes."

"Patrick, I swear, if she doesn't snap you up, I will." She pointed a finger at him. "Do *not* tell Ramon I said that."

He motioned locking his lips and throwing away the key.

"We'd better get to work," she said.

18

Lucy supervised Patrick as he prepared a meal of roast chicken with lemon and rosemary; fingerling potatoes; and a green salad with feta cheese and pine nuts. For dessert, he would serve slices of buttery pound cake—store-bought—with berries and fresh whipped cream.

The dessert idea was inspired, he thought; he would be able to pull it together in just minutes when the time came, yet it would look elegant and upscale.

"How do you think I got Ramon?" she asked when he complimented her on it.

Privately, he thought Lucy could have gotten Ramon simply by agreeing to take him, but he knew better than to say that.

By the time Sofia was scheduled to arrive, the chicken was roasting fragrantly in the oven and the table was set with nice plates, silverware, and cloth napkins he'd borrowed from Lucy.

Before she'd left twenty minutes earlier, Lucy had helped him to take care of everything except his nervousness. He supposed he would have to manage that part on his own.

He checked the chicken. Then he checked the salad. He looked at himself in the mirror to make sure his clothes were right. He straightened sofa pillows that didn't need straightening.

He was just contemplating the issue of music vs. no music—why hadn't he thought to ask Lucy?—when Sofia knocked on the door.

He took a moment before answering, because he didn't want to seem too eager. But who, exactly, was he fooling? He *was* eager.

He took a calming breath and settled his thoughts. If he could risk death kayaking for her, he could do this.

He was feeling pretty good about his sense of inner peace—until he opened the door and saw her.

ONCE SOFIA HAD GOTTEN the body hair issue sorted out as well as she could, she'd taken care with her clothes, her hair, and her makeup. She didn't usually worry much about those things—people could take her or leave her as she was—but this was different. This was special.

She knew her efforts had paid off as soon as he opened the door. Patrick was staring at her wordlessly, his jaw slack.

"Can I come in?" she prompted him.

"I ... Yes! Of course!" He stepped back to let her pass. Actually, he jumped back as though he'd been hit with a hot branding iron. "You look ... That dress ..."

The dress was something she'd worn only once before, for a guy who hadn't turned out to be worth it. Black, clingy, and short, with a low-cut neckline that exposed a generous expanse of cleavage, it carefully walked a tightrope between too slutty and just slutty enough.

Looking at his reaction, she wondered if she'd maybe fallen on the wrong side of the line.

"It smells good in here." The aromas wafting from the tiny kitchen were tempting enough to surprise her. Of course she knew that some men cooked. But with most of the guys she'd dated, "cooking" meant combining a scoop of protein powder with some fruit in a blender.

"Oh, that?" Patrick waved a hand casually. "That's nothing, really. Just a chicken. And some potatoes. And a salad. And ... dessert. Well, I haven't made the dessert yet, but it won't be hard. When I do, I mean. I had some help, but—"

She interrupted him with a kiss. It seemed like the kind thing to do, given his obvious discomfort. She held him close as she kissed him, and she could feel his body relax, bit by bit.

"Better?" she asked after a while.

"Ah ... yes. Much."

Not all of him was relaxed—part of him was noticeably not relaxed—but it was an improvement.

∼

SOFIA WAS NERVOUS, and it occurred to her that one way to deal with the nerves—both hers and his—would be to skip dinner and go straight to bed. But Patrick had worked so hard on the meal and everything that went with it, from the place settings to the garnish on the plates, that she knew she had to give it the attention it deserved.

She asked for seconds of everything, which was no hardship, as it really was delicious. Then she helped him clear the table. She would have helped him wash the dishes, too, but he shooed her away.

"I can't let you clean," he told her. "It would be ungentlemanly."

"Well ... maybe all of this could wait until later."

"Later?"

"Yeah. You know ... after."

He almost dropped the plate he was holding, and she giggled at his reaction. "Come on." She reached for his hand. "Show me your bedroom."

∼

PATRICK SIMPLY COULD NOT BELIEVE his luck. He was a good person generally, but what had he ever done to deserve a windfall of this magnitude?

As he led her to his room, he kept thinking that she would suddenly realize her error; of course *he* wasn't the man she'd intended to sleep with—she'd thought he was someone else. Someone better.

But that didn't happen, and it kept not happening as they stood at the foot of his bed and she slipped out of her shoes.

"Can you help me with this?" She turned her back to him so he could undo the zipper on her dress.

He swallowed hard and nodded. His hands shook a little as he slid the zipper downward, slowly exposing more and more of her perfect, silky skin.

She slipped the dress off of her shoulders and let it fall to the floor with a soft *whoosh*. Then she stepped out of it and turned to face him.

If there had ever been a more perfect woman, he couldn't imagine her. If there had ever been a more exquisite anticipation than this, he couldn't fathom it. She was wearing lacy black underthings, and he was immeasurably honored by the thought that she'd chosen them just for him.

He wanted to touch her, but he didn't want this moment—when everything was still pure and perfect—to end.

"Here. Let me." She began undoing the buttons of his shirt slowly, one by one. When she was done, she ran her hands inside the shirt and over his shoulders, sliding it off of him. Her touch was electric, and he groaned softly.

When she finished with the shirt, she reached for his belt, and he watched as she unbuckled it so slowly that every nerve ending in his body was trembling with need by the time she was done.

She was going to kill him, surely. And he had every intention of letting her.

"Touch me," she said.

The room was dim, with only the light from the kitchen filtering in through the open door. He cupped her cheek in his hand, then ran his palm down over her neck and shoulder, bringing it to rest on one perfect breast.

He ran his thumb over the erect nipple, through the lacy fabric, and felt her tremble at his touch. Emboldened, he moved the cup down, freeing her breast, and bent to take the sensitive peak into his mouth.

"Oh." She threw her head back and tangled her hands in his hair.

Every part of him wanted to grab, to push, to devour. But this woman deserved so much more than that. This woman deserved to be worshipped. So he moved slowly, reverently, tasting and touching her skin so that he would remember. He wanted to remember, in case this was the only time. In case this joy—this miracle—should ever be taken from him.

"Get undressed," she told him, her voice a rough whisper.

He did it while she watched. He knew his body didn't look like the men she was used to. He wasn't as strong, as sculpted; he wasn't the masculine ideal. But the way she was looking at him with such raw desire made him forget that he wasn't the man he wanted to be. He was the man *she* wanted him to be, and that was enough.

He put his arms around her, unfastened her bra, and let it fall to the floor. Then he hooked his thumbs in the waistband of her panties and drew them down so she could step out of them.

Nude, she was even more beautiful than he'd thought she would be. He hadn't imagined such a thing was possible.

"Lie down." She gently pushed at his chest.

"Just ... hold on a second." He went to his beside table and found a condom in the top drawer.

"Let me." She took it from him and tore open the wrapper.

Patrick lay on his back on the bed, hard and ready for her. She rolled the condom onto him, then climbed up and straddled him, poised above him on her knees. He slid a finger into her, and she let out a low, animal moan.

The sound she made drove through him like an electric current; that sound alone was almost enough to push him over the edge.

He touched the soft wetness of her, then put his hands on her hips and guided her down onto him. Eyes closed, she rode his body slowly at first, then faster.

Patrick reached up and buried his fingers in her hair. "Sofia. Look at me." He needed that connection, that knowledge that this moment was about the two of them and only them.

She opened her eyes and looked at him. He quickened his pace, drinking in the expression of pleasure on her face.

"Oh. God," she murmured.

He pulled her close to him and rolled her onto her back. She was holding onto him tightly now, her hands on his waist, fingernails digging into him. She was so close, he could see it, feel it. He reached between them and rubbed the pad of his thumb over her engorged nub without ever slowing his pace.

"Oh." She let go of him and grabbed the sheets, gripping fistfuls of fabric. "Oh. Oh. My God. Oh."

Then she stiffened and he could feel the orgasm tearing through her. His own hit at nearly the same time, leaving him gasping and shuddering.

It was only his deeply ingrained sense of courtesy and gentleman-liness that kept him from collapsing with his full weight on top of her.

When her breathing slowed, she let out a throaty laugh and said, "We finally got a date right."

All things considered, he thought it was worth a few near-death experiences to get here.

19

———————

If Sofia had known sex could be like this, she would have ditched the muscle men and the jocks and found herself a brainy college boy a long time ago. Then again, she doubted that brainy college boys in general would have this kind of effect on her. It was probably specific to one in particular.

She was still pondering whether there was a correlation between intelligence and sexual prowess when she sneaked into her house that night after her sisters were asleep.

At least, she'd thought they were asleep.

"Well, well, well," Benny said. "Out past curfew, were we?" She came out of her room wearing fuzzy Hello Kitty pajamas and bunny slippers, her hair askew.

"Are you planning to ground me, Mom?" Sofia asked.

"Should I? Have you been bad?" She wiggled her eyebrows.

Sofia's goofy, lovestruck grin said it all.

"Ooh." Benny sat down on the sofa and patted the seat next to her. "Do tell."

Sofia didn't sit. She had no plans to dish about everything that had happened between herself and Patrick. It was too big for that. Too important. "It was a really good date, that's all."

Benny cocked her head and regarded her sister. "Are you in love, Sofia?"

"Shut up," Sofia said.

SOFIA MIGHT HAVE SHUT down Benny's prying questions the night before, but that didn't stop all three of her sisters from grilling her about her date the next morning.

"Guess who came in at two a.m.!" Benny announced as they all puttered around the kitchen arranging breakfasts ranging from packaged donuts (Benny) to homemade granola (Martina).

"It wasn't me, so that narrows it down," Bianca quipped.

"It must have gone well, then," Martina observed. "Unless you spent most of that time walking aimlessly in the dark and sobbing."

"I did not," Sofia said.

"So the bad-date curse is broken?" Bianca wanted to know.

Sofia hadn't wanted to gloat about her evening, but right now, she couldn't help it. "We broke the curse. Twice." She could feel the idiot grin on her face, and she knew they would rib her for it, but she didn't care.

"Twice!" Benny said, impressed.

"So, does this mean you two are officially a couple?" Bianca stood in her work clothes, her hip propped against the kitchen island, a coffee mug in her hand.

"Oh ... I don't know about that." It was a question Sofia had considered more than a few times since last night, but she didn't want to admit that she'd given it a thought. She didn't want to seem like that woman who had good sex—okay, great sex—then fell immediately in love. She *was* that woman, but that didn't mean she had to advertise it.

"He's cute," Martina said. "Really cute. If the chemistry is there ... maybe this one will last."

"Maybe," Sofia said, as though she were considering it for the first time. "We don't have a lot in common, but ... maybe."

"Dating guys you have a lot in common with hasn't worked out all that well for you," Bianca remarked. "I'm just saying."

PATRICK WENT to work the next day feeling happy. Well, *happy* was an inadequate word for how he felt. He felt as though God or Nature or whatever higher power might exist had shone a golden light on him for reasons unknown. While he was sure there were others more deserving of such divine largesse—doctors who saved the lives of orphans, for example—he told himself not to question it. The tides of fortune would turn eventually, as they always did, and there was nothing to do but enjoy the bounty when it came.

Though, it wasn't entirely out of his control. If it were possible for him to deserve having Sofia in his life, he could strive for that. He could give her every reason to stay with him and no reason to leave.

He could start by letting her know he was thinking of her. Sending flowers seemed like a cliché. A box of candy? Poetry?

The last one held some appeal for him. He was an expert on the subject, after all. He considered sending her the work of one of his favorite poets, on the topic of sensuality. (He'd have opted for the topic of love, but he didn't want to scare her away.)

But, no. What use would she have for someone else's words, someone else's thoughts? The words, when she read them, had to be his. There could be no shortcut, not with Sofia.

He delivered an inspired lecture, led a class discussion, and met with a student whose grades were suffering due to a persistent health problem. Then, when he had a moment of privacy and quiet in his office, he pulled out a notebook and started to write.

SOFIA MIGHT HAVE EXPECTED to feel tired and groggy after staying up so late the night before. Surprisingly, she felt fresh and perky, if a little distracted. She put a patient with the wrong chart, and she accidentally hung up on someone who'd called to book an appointment. Other than that, though, she was holding up improbably well.

Last night's orgasms must have infused her with energy, she thought with a smirk. The concept had the makings of a blockbuster self-help book.

"You seem chirpy," said Madison, the local authority on annoying and unreasonable perk. "Did something happen?"

Sofia considered denying it, but she felt too damned good for deception. "I met someone."

"Ooh." Madison's eyes widened and she rubbed her hands together in glee. "Have you thought about wedding venues? Because I have a whole folder of ideas ..."

The word *wedding* hit Sofia like a slap. "Wedding? But ..."

"It's never too soon to plan. That's all I'm saying."

INEVITABLY—BECAUSE it was what women did—Sofia wondered if Patrick would call her that day and worried about how she would feel if he didn't. Fortunately, she didn't have to wait long.

Just after two p.m., while Madison and Sofia were reopening the office after its daily closure for lunch, she got a text.

I can't stop thinking about you.

It was simple, short—and everything she needed to hear.

"Is that him?" Madison asked. "Jeez, look at your face. You're already in love."

"I am not."

"Yes, you are. Now, about those wedding venues ..."

20

———

P atrick talked to his parents every week, at least. His mother had been unhappy about him moving all the way out here from Michigan, and he'd promised frequent phone calls—and visits, whenever he could manage them—to put her at ease.

He hadn't told either his mother or his father about Sofia yet, though. Still, some instinct on his mother's part—some sixth sense that came through the parent-child bond—had alerted her to a seismic shift in her middle child's life.

"What's going on? You sound different," she said when he called her a couple of days after the very good date.

"Different how?" The non-answer was disingenuous; he knew how he was different, he just wanted to know how *she* thought he was different. With any luck, it would be something unrelated, and he could avoid admitting to his mother that he did, in fact, have a love life.

"I'm not sure, honey. That's why I asked."

The edge in her voice said she knew he was being intentionally evasive. And that—the edge—activated his devoted-son guilt response. It was embarrassingly easy to make him come clean.

"Well ... ah ... there is something. I suppose. I ... I've started seeing someone." And could his delivery have been any more transparent? The stammering clearly said, *I've met The One, and I'm nervous about telling you.* Standing in his tiny kitchen as the early evening sun slanted through the windows, he closed his eyes, tipped his head back, and waited for the onslaught.

"Oh. That's lovely. Good for you."

Slowly, and with not a small amount of suspicion, he opened his eyes, peered at the phone in his hand, then put the device back to his ear. "That's it?"

"Should there be more?" Her voice was all innocence.

"It's just that I expected a certain amount of … curiosity."

"Well, I hate to be predictable, Patrick. Besides, you'll tell me about her when you're ready."

In the background, he could hear a football game on TV and his father's running commentary on the one side of the phone call he could hear from his easy chair: "What's lovely?" and "Predictable about what?" and "Tell you about who?"

His mother ignored his father and began chatting about other matters: Patrick's siblings, his aunt, the high price of deli meats at the Family Fare Supermarket.

Just listening to her voice comforted him, the same as it had when he was a child. It didn't matter what she was talking about. He was soothed by the mere fact of her and her steady presence in the world.

Once she'd exhausted all of her agenda items, she brought the conversation around to what she'd wanted to talk about since the phone call started: "So, are you coming home for Christmas?"

"Mom, it's barely October."

"Yes, but you have to book your flight early. Everything gets so busy around the holidays."

"Can I get back to you on that?"

"Of course, but, Patrick, Fiona and the kids are going to be there. And Sean is bringing his friend." By *friend,* she meant the man Patrick's brother had been seeing for the past few months. Aileen had no problem with her youngest son's homosexuality, but she still didn't seem to know what to call his boyfriend.

"I'll let you know soon, okay?"

"All right, but the flights—"

"Mom? Can I chat with Dad a little bit?" The deflection worked. He knew he was safe talking to his dad; Hugh Connelly had never, to Patrick's knowledge, had any particular opinion about anyone's plans for the holidays.

PATRICK WAS LOOKING FORWARD to Christmas at his parents' house, and he had every intention of going. He just didn't know whether he'd be going alone, and that made things problematic.

He was in murky territory, as he'd begun seeing Sofia at the least convenient time possible. They hadn't been together nearly long enough for him to invite her to come with him for the holidays. But by the time the actual holidays rolled around, they would, God willing, be a solid couple. If he asked her now, he'd seem like he was rushing things to an egregious degree. But if he *didn't* ask her now, he would A) end up going without her, possibly hurting her feelings and ruining his own chance to spend that time with her, or B) have to ask her at the last minute, when it might be too late to buy plane tickets.

What was the best course of action? Tell his mother he wasn't coming? Buy two plane tickets now, in the hope that Sofia would agree to come with him when he finally asked her two months from now?

Ramon wasn't much help when Patrick asked his advice.

"Dude, you can't ask her now. You've had, what, three or four dates? You're going to look like one of those crazy stalkers who make dolls out of a woman's fingernail clippings. You don't want to be that guy."

He certainly didn't want to be that guy, but none of the alternatives seemed viable, either.

"Buy the ticket and hang onto it," Lucy said when he asked Ramon to put her on the phone. "That way you cover your bases."

Sensible, yet it seemed to Patrick that he and Sofia were mature adults who could discuss this in a mature, adult manner. Despite both Ramon and Lucy imploring him not to do it, he brought up the issue with Sofia the next time he saw her.

"So ... it's hard to believe it's already October," he began as the two of them lay in his bed on a Saturday afternoon after a particularly athletic bout of lovemaking. They both were relaxed and drowsy and covered in a light sheen of sweat.

"Right?" she agreed. "It seems like summer just started, and now it's over."

He stroked her hair as she rested her head on his chest. "It's going to be Christmas before we know it," he said, approaching the subject as though it were a rabbit that might startle.

"I guess." There was something in her tone that had him on alert, but he couldn't identify it.

"My mother's already asking me about my plans." He kissed her lightly on the temple. Sofia didn't say anything, but he felt her stiffen.

Everything in her body language told him to abort. Clearly, he'd entered dangerous territory, a land filled with minefields and trip wires, booby traps and perhaps even poisonous snakes. He might have been foolishly in love, but he wasn't a fool. He let the topic drop, telling himself he could revisit it later.

"You know ... I'd better get going." Sofia got out of bed and walked, nude, into the little bathroom adjoining the bedroom.

Patrick enjoyed the view and looked forward to seeing more of it.

There would be time to think about holidays and family and what to do about them later.

SOFIA WAS SLEEPING with Patrick figuratively, but not yet literally. She hadn't spent the night with him yet, preferring to come back to her own bed after her time with him.

That came in damned handy when he started talking about Christmas, because it gave her a chance to escape.

The mention of Christmas freaked Sofia out for more than one reason. Her parents had died during the holiday season, so that made it impossible for her to think of the month of November and December with anything other than pain. But that wasn't all that was on her mind. She was also thinking about what Christmas with Patrick might mean for their relationship.

She was probably attaching more meaning to it than he'd intended. All he'd said was that his mother was pestering him about his plans. He hadn't said he wanted to present her to his parents and announce their impending nuptials.

Except that was where he'd been heading, clearly—not the part about the nuptials, but the rest of it was right on. He'd been gearing up to invite her to meet his family in Michigan, and that was a lot to process this early on.

She was thinking about all of that—while trying not to think about it—the next day over her morning coffee when Martina came into the kitchen in a flowy white nightshirt and said, "I'm thinking we should have a big Thanksgiving. We could all invite our friends and make some of Mom's recipes and—"

"Why the *hell* is everyone already talking about the damned holidays? It's *freaking October!*" Sofia snapped at her.

Martina stopped where she was and appraised her sister. "I'm sensing a problem with your energy."

Sofia flipped her a middle finger, then immediately felt bad about it.

Martina, unperturbed, sat down at the table across from Sofia. "You know, you don't have to celebrate Thanksgiving if you don't want to. I understand if you don't. But that doesn't mean I can't get excited about it."

"I know. I'm sorry." Sofia's shoulders slumped, and she looked into her coffee mug to avoid Martina's gaze.

"It's hard without Mom and Dad," Martina said softly.

Sofia didn't want to talk about that with Martina, or with anyone. What good did it do to poke at an open wound? How would that cause her anything but pain?

Sofia's mom and dad had died in late November two years before.

Slammed by shock and grief, Sofia and her sisters had not even acknowledged the holidays that first year. How could they? They'd had nothing worth celebrating.

Last year, the sisters had taken a trip to avoid the issue altogether. So, this would be the first relatively normal year without Carmela and Aldo. But that was just it. *Normal* wasn't a term that applied anymore. *Normal* had died with them, as far as Sofia was concerned.

"I have to get ready for work." Sofia got up and took her mug to the sink.

"You know what, Sof?" Martina said. "It might feel good to talk about it."

"I don't want to talk about it."

"What don't you want to talk about?" Benny had just emerged from her room.

"Mom and Dad," Martina said.

"Ah." She put a lot of weight into the *ah*—the acknowledgment not only of their shared grief, but also of Sofia's persistent refusal to deal with it.

"If you could just—" Martina began.

"I can't hear you!" Sofia put her hands over her ears like a petulant child and walked out of the room, closing her bedroom door behind her.

She felt pressure and heat behind her eyes, but she didn't cry. She hadn't cried since her parents' deaths—not once—and she was self-aware enough to know that was weird. But it was also easier, and she would take that. It was about time something got easier for her and her family.

Patrick wasn't sure what to make of it. Sofia had bolted the moment he'd mentioned Christmas—even though he'd never actually gotten around to asking her to spend it with him.

He was pretty sure it wasn't about him. Moments before she'd stiffened up and left his place, they'd been cuddled happily in his bed, talking and enjoying the glow created by great sex.

If she'd been ready to distance herself from him, he'd have felt it. He was sure of it. It was only when he'd mentioned his holiday plans that she'd tensed and then fled, as though she'd been alerted of some impending danger.

Assuming that he wasn't the problem, it was one of two things: either she sensed that he was moving too fast, or she hated the very thought of Christmas itself. He sensed it might be the last one. Lots of people dreaded the holidays, didn't they? Weren't the holidays hotbeds of family stress?

Of course, Sofia's mother and father were gone, so she wouldn't face the kind of parental judgment some people had to deal with.

Then it hit him: her mother and father were gone.

He didn't know how they'd died or when, but he did know one thing: it would be hard for her to spend the holidays—a time when families traditionally came together—without them.

Later, he would want her to talk about it. He would want to know more about what happened so he could know more about her. But that would come when she was ready. They weren't there yet, and that was okay.

As for his own holiday plans, he decided to tell his mother he was coming, buy two plane tickets to Grand Rapids, and then hope that, when the time came, he would need the second one.

He realized how foolishly optimistic it was to think this thing with Sofia would not only last, but would become serious enough that she would want to meet his family in less than three months.

But if he were a betting man, he would bet on love. Every time, he would bet on love.

21

S ofia's kayak tour business dried up by mid-October, as it did every year, so she began working full-time at Bianca's practice. Now that Sofia was used to the routine, she didn't need Madison anymore, and the younger woman had gleefully collected her final check and moved to Los Angeles.

Sofia was beginning to enjoy the work. The kids who came in for treatment were cute, their parents were mostly agreeable, and Bianca was easy enough to work with.

That is, until she started nudging Sofia on the topic of her lack of a career.

"I'm just saying, you could go to nursing school and become an LPN in a year. You'd make really good money. I mean, sure, if you want to be an RN, it takes longer, but—"

"I don't want to be a nurse."

They'd just closed the office for lunch, and Bianca was leaning against the counter next to Sofia's desk, her intimidating white coat on, her arms crossed in a stance that meant she was in big-sister mode.

"But why? It's a good career. And it's not like you've got other plans."

"I do have other plans," Sofia said. "I plan to lead kayak tours in the summers and work other jobs the rest of the year. Oh, wait, that's exactly what I'm doing. Looks like my plans are panning out nicely." She turned away from Bianca and started clicking at her keyboard in the hope that her sister would think she was too busy for conversation.

Unfortunately, it didn't work.

"Sofia, you can't do the kayak thing forever."

She looked up from the computer screen. "Why not?"

"Because! You're not going to be young forever!"

Sofia scowled at her sister. "I'm only twenty-eight."

"That's now!" Bianca threw her hands into the air. "What about in ten years? Or twenty? You're going to need something else to fall back on that's more substantial than ... than playing in the water!"

"That's what you think I do? Play in the water?" She could tell Bianca about the physical demands of her job. About the challenges of running her own business, keeping the books, making her clients happy. She could go into how seriously she took safety and how religiously she kept up with her water rescue and CPR skills. But what was the point? Bianca would believe what she wanted to believe. It didn't matter that Sofia was an honest-to-God businesswoman. She could never compete with her sisters—especially Bianca.

"I didn't mean that," Bianca said. "I just meant—"

"I know what you meant. But we can't all be doctors."

"Sof—"

"I'm going to lunch." Sofia grabbed her purse from the bottom drawer of the reception desk and walked out without listening to her sister's efforts to backtrack.

FOR PATRICK, mid-October meant midterm exams—first giving them, then grading them. Once that was done, there would be the inevitable flood of students wanting to meet with him to plead for better grades.

The entire prospect seemed exhausting, especially because these days, all he wanted was to spend time with Sofia. He'd been seeing her for a couple of months now, and they'd fallen into a happy routine of having lunch together, taking walks, eating dinner together at his place or hers, and having sex—lots of wonderfully satisfying sex.

Being with her was so lovely, so delicious, that it made the non-Sofia portions of his life seem dull and uninspiring by comparison. So he was happy—more than happy, really—when she called while he was writing an exam question.

"What are you doing right now?" he asked her.

"Oh … wasting my life, according to Bianca."

Patrick's brow furrowed. He never knew how to handle these sorts of comments. If he were to side with her against Bianca, there would be backlash when Sofia reflexively defended her sister. But if he sided with Bianca, Sofia would think he wasn't being supportive. Rock over here, hard place over there. And Patrick positioned squarely between them.

"Ah … why do you say that?" A question was usually safe.

"Because she wants me to go to nursing school so I can have 'a real career.' Not like kayaking or like running the front desk in her office, apparently."

"Oh. Do you want to go to nursing school?"

"No. But she can't get over the fact that I'm the only one of the four of us who didn't go to college."

Ah. College. A topic on which Patrick had some authority. He was happy to be on firmer ground.

"Do you *want* to go to college?" he asked.

She was quiet for a moment, then said tentatively, "Maybe. I'm not sure. But … maybe."

"You could try some classes at Cuesta College and see what you think," he suggested. The community college was near Cal Poly, which was a nice bonus—she could drop in to see him after her classes. "Of course, it's too late for this semester, but you could sign up for something in the spring. In the meantime, you could audit some of my courses. If you want to, that is."

"Audit?"

"Sure. You could just attend without formally signing up. Not all instructors allow it, but you've got some pull with a certain English professor, so ..."

"Hmm," Sofia said.

SOFIA DIDN'T THINK she wanted to go to college. If she'd wanted that, she'd have done it right after high school like everyone else. But she hadn't wanted to admit that outright, because she didn't want to seem like she was disrespecting what he did for a living. More than that, she didn't want him to think she couldn't handle college or that she was afraid to try.

So she'd said *maybe* when what she'd really meant was *hell no*.

But now that the idea was sinking in a little, she thought that sitting in on one of his classes might be nice. She could see him in action in his native environment. She was curious about what he did and how he did it. If she gave it a try, it might placate Bianca while satisfying her own need to learn more about Patrick's world.

He taught a class on Mondays, and Bianca's office was closed on Mondays, so that worked.

At the very least, it would give Sofia a glimpse of the road not taken, and that couldn't be a bad thing.

SHE COULDN'T VISIT his class the following Monday because he was giving a midterm and there would be nothing for her to do except watch a bunch of college kids huddle over their test papers. So they planned for her to attend the week after that. Exams would be over, and Patrick would be giving a lecture.

"What am I supposed to wear?" she fretted the morning of the class, sorting through the things in her closet. Benny was standing in the doorway watching her.

"It doesn't matter what you wear," Benny said. "It's a bunch of heavy-drinking teenagers on their own for the first time. It's a good day if they remember to wear pants."

"But most of them aren't sleeping with the teacher," Sofia said.

"Well ..."

"Stop." Sofia put up a hand. "If that's a thing, I don't want to know."

"It's not a thing with Patrick," Benny said. "I guarantee it."

"How do you know?" It was a question Sofia had never considered, but now that it was out there, she needed to hear the answer.

"Because he's too good. He's too ... Patrick. He'd take his responsibilities too seriously to ever sleep with a student."

Benny was right. She didn't know him well—Patrick had been spending some time around the Russo house, but not that much—and yet she was right. His basic decency was so fundamental that Benny hadn't been able to miss it.

"Well, not wearing pants isn't an option," Sofia said. "So get in here and help me pick something out."

SHE'D SPENT TOO much time fussing over what to wear and then searching for a parking place on campus. As a result, Patrick had already started his lecture when she arrived. She quietly slipped into a seat in the back of the lecture hall, trying to create as little disruption as possible.

Patrick was talking about the relative importance of theme vs. plot in contemporary literature and how the balance between the two had shifted over time when he saw her.

He didn't stop what he was doing. He didn't fumble or stammer the way she'd known him to do in the past. He didn't pause in any significant way that would be obvious to an impartial observer. But when his eyes fell on her, he smiled slightly; it was a small, private smile that touched every part of him in a subtle way—not just his lips, but his eyes and the way he held his body. He looked as though he'd just thought of something secret and wonderful, some quiet delight that he took just a moment to savor before moving on.

That was the moment. If there was one instant when her life became not only her own but his, too, it was this. The smile undid her.

As she sat there feeling her resistance melt, she marveled at how different he was here than he was elsewhere in the world. While he sometimes seemed uncertain out there, as though his confidence was faltering, here he was in command, at ease, and utterly natural.

The tone of his voice, the way he worked the room and the crowd full of students held a mastery she'd never seen in him before. She'd never thought of him as an alpha male, but here, in this place, there was no doubt who was in control.

It was ridiculously hot.

Gradually, she became aware that she wasn't the only one who thought so.

With growing unease, Sofia noticed that most of the students in the front four rows were women. Then she noticed how attentively those women were listening to Patrick's every word. Maybe they were just interested in theme vs. plot. Maybe they were just exceptionally eager students who wanted to master every nuance of English literature.

Bullshit. There might have been a few like that—one or two studious-looking types who had their heads bent over their notes—but the rest were hot for teacher.

Sofia resisted the urge to rush to the front of the room and stake her claim. Let all of these lithe young coeds find their own men at frat parties or wherever the hell college kids hooked up these days. Patrick was hers.

She hadn't thought of it in precisely those terms before, but now that she had, it felt true.

Patrick was hers.

Sofia saw no indication that he was flattered by or even aware of what his female admirers might be thinking about him. He worked the whole room, male and female, young and old, asking questions and listening carefully to the answers of middle-aged returning students as well as the newly minted adults around him.

When a student spoke, he listened completely, giving all of his attention to whatever they had to say. She herself had sensed that from him. Before she'd met Patrick, when had she ever felt that her words were so valued? When had she ever felt so *heard*?

It was a heady thing, getting full and caring attention from anyone, let alone from this man who, at the moment, seemed so commanding and so brilliant. She couldn't blame the students for falling for him.

How could she, when she'd fallen for him herself?

IF SOFIA HAD DOUBTED her instincts about the women in Patrick's class being infatuated with him, her suspicions were confirmed when the class session ended. He was immediately surrounded by students wanting to ask him questions—and almost every one of those students was female.

He dealt with them just as masterfully as he'd taught his class. Another professor needed the room in a few minutes, so he answered the quick questions, acknowledged the more complicated ones, and invited anyone he hadn't had time for to speak to him during his office hours that afternoon.

When his class had filtered out and the next one was straggling in, Patrick gave her a shy smile and she followed him out into the hallway.

"That was really something," she told him.

He ducked his head in an adorable show of humility. "Do you think so?"

"I do."

"I have some time now. Do you want to get some coffee?" he asked.

Normally, she'd have liked that. But after all of the things she'd seen and heard and felt over the past hour, all she really wanted to do was be alone with him.

"Could we go back to your office?" She grinned at him suggestively.

He got her meaning; she could tell by the way he was blushing. "I think ... ah ... yes. Follow me."

Patrick's office was small and simple, with a desk, a chair, a visitor's chair, and a compact sofa. A bookcase on one wall held a selection of novels, books of poetry, and textbooks, along with neat stacks of student papers waiting to be graded.

Sofia appraised the sofa and judged it too small. The desk was better.

"You don't have office hours right now, do you?" she asked.

"Ah ... no. That's later."

"Good." She reached out, grabbed his tie, and used it to pull him toward her.

"That's not to say that students won't drop by...."

"Hmm. That could be awkward," she purred, her mouth barely an inch from his.

"Just ..." He put up one finger in an indication that she should wait. He retrieved his tie from her, went to his desk, wrote something on a piece of paper, then taped it to the door of his office.

The paper said, BACK IN TEN MINUTES.

"Ten minutes?" She raised one eyebrow at him meaningfully.

"Hmm. I see your point." He took back the paper, crumpled it, and threw it away. Then he made a new sign: BACK IN TWENTY MINUTES.

Still not enough time, from her perspective, but it would have to do.

With the sign up, he closed and locked the door, closed the blinds on his window, and went to her.

"I'm pretty sure the dean would frown on this," he said in a voice rough with lust as she started undoing his tie, then working on the buttons of his shirt.

"The dean would be jealous as hell," Sofia said.

"Ah ... probably."

She propped her butt against his desk and parted her legs a little, and he slid a hand up her skirt, pushed her panties aside, and slid a finger into her. She squirmed against him, helping him to hit just the right spot. "There. There. Oh ..."

He knew he shouldn't be doing this. It was unprofessional and potentially scandalous. But that just made it more irresistible. He'd never behaved this way in his place of employment—had never even come close. And that quality of danger was so erotic that he thought he might evaporate into a million tiny pieces if he couldn't have this, have her.

"Please, Patrick." Her eyes were closed, her lips parted, and he could smell the heady scent of her arousal.

All semblance of self-control gone, he moved his body between her legs and unbuckled his belt. He unsnapped, unzipped, and then he was pushing himself past the panties she was still wearing and into the warm, hot depths of her.

He was still mostly dressed and so was she, because there was no time, no time. Someone might come to his office door at any moment, and if they got caught it would be shame and doom.

That prospect—the shame and the doom—heightened his senses and his arousal, taking this from a mere act of lovemaking to something animal, something elemental.

She grabbed at the sides of his desk to hold on, and a cup of pens and a stapler fell with a crash to the floor.

She started to cry out, so he covered his mouth with hers to silence her. He shoved one hand under her shirt to cover her breast, and wound the other in her hair, holding on as he moved inside her, moving both of them closer, closer.

He came so hard he saw stars. He'd always thought that was an expression—seeing stars—but there were honest-to-God flashes of light in front of his eyes as the spasms slammed through him.

He might even have blacked out for a moment, because when he caught his breath and became aware of his surroundings again, she was pinned under him and he didn't know if she'd reached the finish line or not.

Patrick lifted himself up a little so she could breathe. "Did you ...?"

"Twice," she said, gasping. "It was like a bomb going off. Two of them. Holy shit."

He kissed the side of her face and then her neck tenderly, feeling immeasurably grateful.

"Dr. Connelly?" a voice said, followed by a knock on the door. Outside, one person said to another, "That's weird. I thought I heard him in there."

22

As it turned out, Patrick was not the first one in Sofia's circle to issue an invitation for the holidays. But neither was Sofia. Bianca did it, when November was well underway and Sofia still hadn't asked Patrick to have Thanksgiving dinner at the Russo house.

Patrick had spent the night in Sofia's room—something he'd been doing more and more often—and Bianca caught him when he was heading out to go home and shower before work. Sofia was still sleeping.

"So, do we have an answer about Thanksgiving?" she asked, as though he should already know what she was talking about.

"About ... excuse me?" He paused on his way toward the door, his jacket in his hand.

"She hasn't asked you yet, has she? Good lord." Bianca scowled and shook her head in judgment.

"Ah ... I suppose she hasn't gotten around to it yet."

"Patrick," Bianca said, a hand on her hip, "would you like to have Thanksgiving dinner with us? Since my idiot sister won't ask you?"

"Oh." The question sounded simple, but it probably wasn't. "I'd love to, actually, but if Sofia hasn't asked me yet, she ... Well, I can only assume it was because she doesn't want that. For whatever reason."

Whatever reason encompassed so many possibilities, some of which probably didn't reflect badly on their relationship and some that might.

"*Pffft.*" Bianca made a dismissive sound halfway between a scoff and a snort. "It's not that she doesn't want you here. It's that *she* doesn't want to be here herself. But unless she decides to flee to Vegas or something ..."

It seemed to Patrick that he had an opening, so he decided to take it. He put down his jacket and walked into the kitchen where Bianca was standing.

"Bianca ... Since you brought it up, what exactly is Sofia's issue with the holidays? I've tried to ask her, but ..."

Bianca's eyes widened. "You mean she hasn't told you?"

"No."

"Oh, man." She gestured toward a chair at the kitchen table. "Have a seat."

He hesitated. "If this is something she doesn't want me to know, then I don't think ..."

Bianca sat across from him and folded her arms on the table. "You want to respect her privacy—I admire that. So, I won't tell you anything about Sofia. I'm going to tell you something about me."

"Oh. Okay." He sensed this was going to be significant, so he gave her his full attention. He had the idea that he might not want to hear what she was about to say—that it might change everything—but knowing was better than not knowing.

"My parents died almost exactly two years ago. Cancer got my mother a few days before Thanksgiving. And my father went just a couple of weeks later in a car accident that might or might not have been an accident. As you can imagine, we pretty much skipped the celebrations the past couple of years. So this year will be my first more or less regular holiday season without them. It's hard for me— and I'm not the only one who feels that way." She looked at him significantly.

The news gut-punched him. How could he not know this? How could it be that Sofia had never mentioned a word about the timing of her parents' deaths?

After a moment of stunned silence, he said, "I'm so sorry," his voice thick.

"Thank you. So am I."

"She's never told me the details. I knew they'd died, but ..." He rubbed his face with his hands, trying to absorb it.

"She deals with things by not dealing with them. By closing a door on them and deadbolting it shut. Which is a thing you're really going to need to understand if you're going to be with her."

It was a lot to absorb. He hurt for her—for all of them—but he was glad he knew about this, because it was key to knowing *her*. At the same time, he felt uncomfortable hearing it behind her back when she so clearly had wanted to keep it from him.

"I don't think you should say any more," he told Bianca. "Without her here, I mean. It feels wrong."

She considered that, then nodded. "Good for you."

Sofia's bedroom door opened and she came out dressed in a terrycloth robe, bleary-eyed, her hair askew. "Hey," she said to Bianca. "Are you trying to poach my guy?"

"I wouldn't dream of it." Bianca got up from the table and regarded Patrick. "Besides, something tells me he's unpoachable." She picked up her mug and went to refresh her coffee.

Patrick wasn't sure what to do with this new information. It was too big, too significant. Should he tell Sofia what he knew? Should he wait for her to tell him herself? And what about the Thanksgiving invitation? Should he accept, knowing that she didn't want to do any of it, with or without him?

He didn't want to seek advice from anyone who knew Sofia, because that would seem like a betrayal. He considered talking to his mother about it, but that was too fraught with peril—she cared too much about whom Patrick was dating and why, and where it might lead. If he confided in her and she decided that Sofia had too much emotional baggage, it could make things awkward when Sofia did, sooner or later, meet his family.

And that was how he thought of it—*when* she met them, not *if*. In his own mind, the relationship had taken on an air of inevitability, perhaps even of destiny. He didn't think Sofia was there yet, but he could wait. If he had to, he could wait.

In the meantime, he needed advice from someone who knew about women and who could look at things objectively. During his lunch break, he went into his office, closed the door, and called his sister.

Fiona, the oldest of the Connelly siblings, had been married for fifteen years to her high school sweetheart, a solid blue-collar man who worshipped her. They had three kids, ages twelve, ten, and eight—spaced with unlikely precision—and Fiona stayed home with them, making sack lunches and casserole dinners, attending PTA meetings and volunteering at the local food bank.

Patrick and Fiona didn't talk often—at least, not often enough—but he thought that, with her experience managing a long-term relationship, she'd likely have something useful to offer.

"I guess you didn't lose my number after all," she said when she picked up the phone.

His first impulse was to react defensively. After all, she hadn't called him in a while, either. As the oldest, she always seemed to think it was her privilege to be the one on the receiving end of phone calls and visits. But bringing that up would have distracted him from his mission. Instead, he got right to the point.

"Do you have a minute, Fiona? I need some advice."

"About what?"

"Well ... about ... You see, I've met someone...."

This was big, obviously. She became all business. "All right. Listen, I'm in line at the grocery store. Give me fifteen minutes and I'll call you back."

She made it in twelve.

"Okay, shoot," she said without preamble when she called him back. He could hear her in the background opening cabinets and the refrigerator, putting away her groceries.

"Well ... Sofia and I have been seeing each other almost three months...." He gave her the short version of that—how they'd met and how things were going between them—then told Fiona about the bombshell Bianca had dropped that morning. "I'm not supposed to know any of this, and I don't know what to do with the information. And there's the entire issue of the holidays...."

"Wow." Fiona had stopped rustling around in the background and was now giving him her full attention. "That's a lot. Are you sure you're up to dealing with all of this?"

"I'm coming to you instead of Mom precisely because I didn't want to be asked that question," he said.

She was silent for a moment, then conceded, "Yeah, I can see that. Well, look. Let's take this one issue at a time. First, you've got to talk to her about it. Let her know what her sister told you."

"Really? Are you sure?"

"Hell, no, I'm not sure. But it seems like your best bet. If you don't tell her, where does that leave you? You're still not talking about it. She's still not letting you in, and she's still not dealing with things."

He rubbed his eyes and slumped back into his chair. "That's true."

"If you tell her, sure, she's going to be pissed that you talked about her with her sister. But then she'll get past that, and you two can actually deal with all the shit she's got going on."

Fiona had been a problem-solver from the time they were kids, and she used that skill to great advantage with her own children. Now, her confident tone was making Patrick feel a little bit better about things.

"All right. But when we talk about it ... what do I say?"

"It doesn't matter what you *say*, Patrick. It only matters that you *listen*."

He bobbed his head in agreement, though she couldn't see him. "Yes. Of course. I can do that."

"As far as the holidays go, I think you've gotta be matter-of-fact about it: Thanksgiving's happening, and I'm going to be there, so let's eat some damned turkey."

He grinned, missing his sister. "It sounds simple when you say it that way."

"It is. If she skips it and hides in her room, she's going to feel like shit because she's wallowing in misery. And if she doesn't skip it, she's going to feel like shit because she *thinks* she should be wallowing. Either way, she's going to need you there."

"All right. You're right."

"But, Patrick?"

"Yes?"

"Don't tell Mom any of this."

He'd had the same instinct, but still, he had to ask: "Why not?"

"Because all she's going to see is, this girl has more baggage than the cargo hold of a 747. And you don't need to hear that shit, because it's too late, and you're already in love." Fiona said the last part as though it were a simple fact.

Patrick supposed it was.

"Thank you, Fiona. Give my love to Barry and the kids."

"You can tell them yourself. You're coming for Christmas, right?"

"Yes. But that's another thing. Sofia—"

"Patrick, trust me on this. Stick to one holiday crisis at a time."

23

———

Patrick was nervous about bringing any of it up with Sofia, but Fiona was right. There wasn't a good alternative. He raised the issue as casually as possible a couple of nights later while they sat across from each other in a booth at a pizza place in Morro Bay.

"Bianca invited me for Thanksgiving, and I said yes," he told her as he picked up a greasy slice of pepperoni pizza. "I know the holidays are going to be hard for you with everything that happened, but we'll all be there to help you get through it."

He took a bite of his pizza, trying to pretend the moment held less weight than it did.

Sofia didn't say anything at first. Instead, she sat motionless with her hands in her lap, staring at the table.

"You and Bianca must have had quite a talk," she said at last.

"I'm glad she told me. I'm sure you had your reasons for keeping it to yourself, but it's good that I know." The casual act wasn't working, so he put down the pizza and focused on her. "Sofia, I'm so sorry about your parents. You must be—"

"I don't want to talk about this." Her eyes were dry, her face hard. "And I wish Bianca had minded her own business."

He wiped his mouth with a paper napkin, then folded the

napkin carefully and put it on the table. "I understand that you didn't want me to know, but now I do, so if you ever *do* want to talk about it ..."

"Thank you. Really. But I don't."

He nodded. "Is it all right if I come for Thanksgiving, though?"

Sofia reached out and took his hand. "Of course it is. I should have asked you myself."

The conversation had been tense, but the touch of her hand was making him feel better. "I'll bring pie," he said, because it seemed impossible for anyone to stay upset while talking about pie. "What kind's your favorite?"

THE TALK they'd had at the pizza place had made Sofia both angry and ashamed. Angry, because Bianca had no right to tell Patrick everything she had, no right to invite him behind her back. And ashamed, because she should have invited him—and told him every-thing—herself.

She kept the anger in check for the rest of the evening because Patrick didn't deserve for it to be directed at him. But when Sofia got home that night, she confronted Bianca before she'd even closed the front door.

"What the hell were you doing telling my personal business to Patrick?" she demanded.

Bianca was on the sofa watching a movie with Martina and Benny. She was wearing a USC sweatshirt and yoga pants, with thick socks on her feet. Her hair was in a messy ponytail.

"Uh-oh," Martina said. She picked up the remote and paused the movie.

"Someone needed to invite him for Thanksgiving," Bianca said. "It's less than a week away, and you hadn't even asked him yet."

"Okay. Fine. But you didn't need to tell him ... everything."

"He wanted to know why you're so weird about holidays," Bianca said. "So I told him."

"He said that? He said *weird*?" Martina asked. "That doesn't sound like him."

"Of course not," Bianca said. "That part was implied. But you know he was thinking it."

"Bianca, damn it …" Sofia began.

"Why *didn't* you tell him about Mom and Dad?" Martina clicked on the lamp on the table beside her, bathing the room in soft light. "You've been seeing him for months."

"Avoidance," Benny said. "It's Sofia's way."

Frustrated, Sofia threw her purse and jacket onto an accent table next to the front door and closed the door against the cool night air. "I didn't tell him because … because things with him are happy! And I wanted them to stay happy. Is that so wrong?"

"Of course not." Martina patted the spot next to her on the sofa, and Sofia sat down beside her sister. "But it's not enough for a relationship to be happy. It's also got to be *real*."

Sofia knew Martina was right, but she wouldn't admit it because she didn't want to give her sisters the satisfaction. She slumped in her seat, defeated.

"So, are you going to let him come for dinner, or are you going to make the poor guy sit at home alone with a Swanson's frozen turkey dinner?" Benny asked. "Because, I've got to tell you, those frozen dinners suck."

"He can come," Sofia conceded. "He's bringing pie."

THE COLLEGE WAS CLOSED the week of Thanksgiving, so Patrick had plenty of time to obsess over recipes, plans, and preparations for his lemon meringue pie. He didn't bake, really—he made cookies on occasion—so it probably would have been a good idea to simply order the pie from one of the local bakeries.

But he wanted to impress Sofia and her sisters by doing it himself. Besides, how hard could it be?

He began to get a sense of how hard it might be on the day before

Thanksgiving, when he tried to make a pie crust from a recipe his mother had given him and he burned it to a crisp in the oven.

The problem was that he'd tried to do too many things at once; he'd become absorbed in some research he was doing for a book project, and he'd forgotten to set the oven timer. By the time he'd remembered that the crust existed in the first place, smoke was billowing out of the oven and the fire detectors in his little house were screaming.

He'd taken the crust out of the oven, doused it in the sink, then aired out the house for the next hour until it no longer smelled like he'd held a bonfire in the living room.

Clearly, he'd have to concentrate a little better next time.

He had enough flour to make another crust, but he was short on butter. He went to the Cookie Crock, bought more, then came back home to try again.

The hardest part was cutting the butter into the flour. His mother said she used a food processor for that, but Patrick didn't have one, so he had to settle for crisscrossing the blades from a pair of steak knives through the dough until he thought it looked right. The dough still had visible chunks of butter in it, but he thought it would have to do.

This time, it went better. He remembered to set the timer, and he was careful not to concentrate too hard on anything else while he was waiting.

No alarms went off on the second attempt, so that was a plus. The crust was nicely browned, but not *too* brown, and that was also good. But it didn't look exactly right; the bottom of the crust was puffy, arcing up into the area where the pie filling would be. And the outer crust looked weird. He'd tried to make a nice design with his fingers and the tines of a fork, the way he'd read about online. Instead, it looked like it had been partially eaten by weasels.

Doing it a third time didn't seem like a viable option, so he pressed ahead.

The directions for making the lemon filling seemed self-explanatory, but it didn't thicken up the way it was supposed to when he whisked the mixture over the stove. He went online to a baking message board to ask whether it might thicken up in the oven; the consensus was that it would not. He realized the problem: he'd forgotten to add the cornstarch. He tried adding it after the fact, but the result was a yellow, lemon-scented, gloopy mess.

He threw it out and started again.

On the next try, he got a filling that looked more or less like the YouTube videos said it should. He poured it into his messy but passable crust and got started on the meringue.

Ah, the meringue.

After the fact, it seemed to him that whoever had come up with the concept of meringue had to be a petty, vengeful person intent on inflicting suffering on his or her fellow man.

On his first try, the egg whites didn't rise into stiff peaks the way they were supposed to. The second time, the meringue did rise, but then it became grainy and lumpy. The third time, it did what it was supposed to do, but when he put it in the oven, the peaks burned and the rest of the meringue was dotted with condensation that looked unappetizing at best and like a series of oozing sores at worst.

He ended up throwing the whole thing out and was utterly dispirited by the time Sofia stopped by late in the afternoon.

She put down her things, kissed him, and said, "Smells like you've been baking. How did it go?"

He led her to his kitchen trash can and pressed the pedal with his foot to raise the lid. Inside were the broken yellow remnants of his pies, looking like the doomed casualties of some horrible pastry-related collision.

"Yikes." Sofia peered into the trash and then looked at Patrick with sympathy. "There's more than one in there. You've had a rough day."

"I followed the recipe," he told her. "Carefully. I don't know what went wrong."

The little galley kitchen was a shambles of mixing bowls, pans, ingredients, and various implements covered in yellow and white goo.

"Why don't you let me clean this up?" she said, her arms around him.

"No, no. It's my mess. I'll do it."

"But you made that mess trying to bake for me." She rose onto her tiptoes and kissed him. "Let me clean it up, then I'll find some way to show you my appreciation."

His eyebrows rose. "Really?"

"Really."

IT WAS true that Sofia was not going to have lemon meringue pie for her Thanksgiving dessert. But she had something far better: a man who was willing to go through hell trying to make one for her.

As she cleaned up the kitchen, plunging various cooking implements into a sink full of hot, soapy water, she realized that no other man had ever done anything this sweet for her. Yes, it was just a pie; it wasn't a kidney donation. Still, he'd worked hard, outside of his comfort zone, to do something he'd thought would please her.

She thought about the other men she'd dated.

Jason might have offered to bring a pie, but would have brought a six-pack of his favorite beer instead, claiming he'd "forgotten" about the pie. Steven wouldn't have offered anything in the first place. And Greg would have asked *her* to make the pie, saying, "You're so much better at it, babe. Why don't you do it?"

But Patrick? This man had thrown himself into the task with single-minded determination, trying and failing and trying again, all in an effort to provide something pleasurable for her.

It was a revelation.

When she'd finished cleaning up, she went into his miniature living room and found him sitting on the sofa, looking defeated. She sat on his lap and wrapped her arms around him.

"Well ... this is nice," he said.

"You think so?" she purred into his ear.

"I do."

"I'll bet I can make it even nicer," she whispered to him in her most sensuous voice.

"Oh. Ah ... all right."

She got up, offered him her hand, and led him into the bedroom.

Some things were even better than pie.

24

———

In lieu of pie, Patrick brought a bottle of wine to the Thanksgiving celebration at the Russo house. By the time he got there, the place smelled of turkey, sweet potatoes, and the pumpkin pie spice blend that was so ubiquitous this time of year.

"All right, here's the plan," Bianca was saying to Benny. "You get set up outside Target, and I'll take Barnes & Noble and World Market. Martina will line up at Express, then head on over to Bed Bath & Beyond. We'll meet up afterward at the Big Sky Café for breakfast."

"What about Sofia?" Martina sounded slightly whiny.

"We need Sofia at home to get the online deals as soon as they come up, Martina. Jeez. Don't you remember what happened two years ago?"

"Yes. All right," Martina conceded, looking unhappy about it.

"Ah ... What are you doing?" Patrick came into the kitchen and put the wine in the refrigerator.

"We're planning our Black Friday strategy," Bianca told him. "Those fifty-percent-off deals don't just buy themselves."

"I suppose they don't," he conceded.

Sofia, who'd been given the task of chopping celery for the dressing, was silently standing at the kitchen counter wielding a chef's knife as though she were planning some kind of bloody assault.

She didn't look up when he came in, and she didn't stop viciously hacking at the celery, which was piling up at a rate that far exceeded what was needed for the recipe.

"Sofia," he said gently, afraid that if he startled her she might lose a finger.

"What?"

"I just ... I wondered if you needed any help." He stood awkwardly beside her, his hands in his pockets.

"I don't."

He caught Benny's gaze; she rolled her eyes in sympathy with him.

"That's probably enough celery," he said. A veritable mountain of celery was accumulating on the cutting board, leading him to wonder exactly how many guests they might be expecting to require quite so much.

"Really. You think so? If you know so much about it, why don't you take over?" She smacked the knife down on the cutting board and stormed out of the room. She went into her bedroom and slammed the door behind her.

"I didn't mean ..."

"She's been like this all day," Bianca said. "It's not you."

He went to the door of her room and knocked softly. "Sofia? Can I come in?"

She didn't answer, so he tried again. "Sofia?"

He tried the door; it wasn't locked. He went in slowly, carefully, in case she was planning to throw something at his head. She was lying on her bed without any heavy objects in her hands, so he figured he was safe.

"Are you all right?" He closed the door behind him.

"This damned day." She stared at the ceiling, her eyes dry. "She had three days to live two years ago on Thanksgiving. Three days. She was in hospice. When I went to visit her, they had paper turkeys taped to the walls. As though there were anything to celebrate. As though there were any way to forget what was happening to her."

He lay down beside her and pulled her into his arms. "You can cry if you want to. It's okay." He tucked her into the curve of his arm and stroked her hair.

"I can't, actually."

He looked at her. "What do you mean?"

"I can't cry. Not about this. I haven't been able to, even once."

Could that be true? "Not once?"

"No. There's something wrong with me."

He didn't think that was true, but he also didn't think it was healthy that she'd never released her feelings. "You'll cry when you're ready."

It seemed to him that when she did—when she was ready to fully experience everything she'd been through—she would need him to be here for it. And he had no intention of letting her down.

PATRICK'S PIE would have been superfluous. Once everyone who was invited had arrived, many of them bearing desserts, it came out to ten people and five pies—half a pie for everyone in attendance. The varieties included pumpkin (of course), sweet potato, pecan, mince, and apple crumb. Patrick was pleased to see there was no lemon meringue, because that would have meant someone had shown him up, and his ego had been damaged enough as it was.

When they were all seated, the parties around the table were the four sisters; Patrick; two nurses from Bianca's practice; a couple of teachers from the science department whom Benny had invited because they'd had nowhere else to go; and a contractor Martina regularly worked with in her interior design business.

It was a pleasant mix of backgrounds and interests, and Patrick enjoyed the conversation. Even if he hadn't, the food would have been enough to occupy him. Bianca was an excellent cook, and she'd prepared twice as much turkey, dressing, potatoes, rolls, salad, and cranberry sauce as the group could possibly eat, even if everyone were to indulge in third helpings.

A couple of people—including Bianca and one of her nurses, a motherly middle-aged woman of generous proportions—commented that Patrick was too thin, and they urged more food on him. Who was he to argue, when everyone had gone to so much work?

Sofia didn't say much during the meal, and she picked at her food. But she didn't snap at anyone, so they all took that as the best they could expect under the circumstances.

After dinner, the two other men present, along with Benny, left the table to settle into the well-worn leather sofa and watch football on TV. In the spirit of the thing, they'd traded in their wineglasses for beer bottles, and they were all yelling things at the players on the screen as though they thought it might make a difference in the outcome of the game.

In all of the Thanksgiving dinners Patrick had eaten at home over the years, he'd never seen his father help his mother clean up. Patrick loved his father, but that was one habit he didn't want to inherit. He got up from the table, took a serving dish of leftover potatoes out of Bianca's hands, and said, "Let me do this."

Her eyes widened. "Really?"

"Yes, really. Go sit down. You've worked hard enough."

"If you're just doing this to try to win me over," Bianca said, "it's working."

He hadn't been doing it for that reason, but the idea of having her approval pleased him anyway.

WHEN THE GUESTS had gone home and the last dish had been put away, Sofia and Patrick went to his house so they could spend the night together in privacy. She was glad one holiday, at least, was behind her, and though she'd had a lot of difficult feelings, it hadn't gone that badly.

"Your sister's quite a cook," Patrick said when they were in the car on their way to his place. She knew he was attempting to make conversation that wouldn't blow up in his face.

"She is." Sofia hadn't said much all day, but this was hardly something she could disagree about. "Our mother was an excellent cook. She taught Bianca everything she knew."

Sofia understood that, by mentioning her mother, she was opening a door. And maybe she was ready for that. Maybe she was ready to talk, just a little, on the most superficial level. It was something.

"Today must have been hard," he said. That was all. He didn't claim to know how she felt; he didn't try to guess what kind of hard she must be feeling. And he didn't insist that she tell him. Somehow, that made it easier for her to let out just a fraction of the truth.

"It wasn't as bad as I thought it would be," she told him in the seclusion of the car, with only the lights from the dashboard to illuminate them. "It was hard. But somehow I thought ... I didn't think it would be survivable. I got through it, so ..."

There was so much more to say. For instance, there was the question of how her sisters had managed to behave as though nothing was wrong. How they'd laughed and talked and ate as though it were any other Thanksgiving, as though their parents were still there to celebrate with them.

She didn't understand that and didn't know if she ever would. It created a feeling of resentment like a bright, burning lump in the center of her chest.

But she wasn't ready to tell him everything, so she kept that part to herself, a malignant secret.

Still, what she'd told him was true. It hadn't been the emotional cataclysm she'd expected.

"You did. You got through it." He reached for her hand and held it, warm and safe in his, as they drove to his place.

"That's one down. Now I've got to get through Christmas."

He shot her a glance as they pulled into his driveway. "Right. About that ..."

"... And the next thing I knew, I'd agreed to fly to Grand Rapids to meet his parents." Sofia let her head thunk down onto the table at Jitters, where she'd met Martina for coffee. Well, *she* was having coffee. Martina was having one of her frou-frou organic herbal teas— probably made from grass clippings and hemp and God knew what else.

"Oh, Sofia. That's wonderful!"

The coffeehouse, which sat at one of the busiest stretches of Main Street, was moderately busy, with about half of the café tables full of tourists, locals, and people tapping away on their laptops. The smell of espresso filled the air, along with the sound of the coffee grinder and the milk steamer. The place had a funky vibe, with polished hardwood floors, ancient wainscoting, and mismatched tables and chairs that had seen better days.

"What's wonderful about it?" Sofia moaned. "I'm meeting the parents? It's only been four months!"

Martina reached out, her arm covered with jingling bangle bracelets, and put her hand on top of Sofia's. "What's wonderful is that he's a really great guy and he loves you."

Sofia raised her head off the table, just a little, to look at her sister. "He's never said that."

"If he didn't say it, it's because he doesn't think you're ready to hear it. He invited you to have Christmas with his parents. He loves you."

Of course, Sofia already knew it. Everything about Patrick's demeanor—the way he talked to her, the way he looked at her—said it was love. Still, hearing that it was obvious even to onlookers made Sofia feel warm and fuzzy inside, and she didn't know how to deal with feeling warm and fuzzy at the same time that she was feeling sad and scared and unsettled.

"Maybe I don't love him back." Sofia was just being petulant, and Martina knew it.

"Yes, you do."

"Oh, God. Yes. I do. But ... it's a lot! I don't know if I'm ready to be in love."

Martina scoffed. "Since when does being ready have anything to do with it? You expect love to follow your timeline? Sof, it doesn't work that way. I wish it did. I'd have found someone years ago."

Sofia lifted her head off the table and regarded her sister. Was Martina lonely? Sofia had never considered that. With her artsy lifestyle and everything that came with it—the meditation, the yoga, the whole at-one-with-the-world vibe she gave off—Martina had always seemed content.

"I didn't know it bothered you, being single," Sofia said.

"Oh ... it doesn't." Martina waved off the thought, her bracelets jingling. "It's just ... it would be nice, that's all. And here you are, with this sweet, brilliant guy who adores you. You have what everybody wants. I'm a pacifist, Sofia, but if you let him go, I swear to God I'll kick your ass."

Well. That was another reason to go through with it, Sofia supposed.

25

As pleased as Patrick was that Sofia had agreed to come home with him for Christmas, he wasn't confident that it would actually happen. He sensed that she was ready to change her mind at any moment—that she might suddenly come up with an obligation or a crisis that would make it impossible. Waiting for the trip felt like carrying a baby bird in his hands—he was mindful that with one wrong move, he might drop it or crush it in his clumsy hands.

And Sofia was only part of the issue—he also had to prepare his mother to behave herself during the visit.

He called her shortly after Sofia agreed to make the trip. The idea that his mother might disapprove of Sofia was only one danger. Another was that she might approve of her so wholeheartedly that she would start designing wedding invitations at the dinner table.

"Oh, honey," Aileen greeted him when he called her after work one day in late November. "I'm so glad you called. How have you been?"

They dispensed with the chitchat about his work, her volunteering, how he'd been eating, and the various activities of relatives he hadn't seen in decades and wouldn't remember if he did.

"So, Mom ..." He wanted to hit just the right casual note,

suggesting that what he was about to say was no big deal, but was not, at the same time, *not* a big deal. "About Christmas ..."

"Oh, no." Aileen's voice filled with dread. "Please don't tell me that you're not coming, Patrick, because I've already told everyone—"

"No, no. I'm coming. It's just ... I wondered if I could bring a friend."

"Well, of *course* you can bring a friend, Patrick. The more the merrier." Her relief was palpable. "Is this someone from the college, or ...?"

"It's ... well, Mom, it's a woman I've been seeing."

At first, there was only stunned silence. Then: "Oh, Patrick. Oh, honey. How wonderful. Oh!"

He cut her off, hoping to stop her assumptions before they got too deeply embedded. "Mom? It's not a big deal. Don't—"

"It's about time you met someone!" she interrupted. "Someone nice, I mean. I never trusted that Kim.... And it's been so long! Why, the last time you brought someone was, what, four years ago?"

"Two. But—"

"Tell me about her! Is it serious? It's time you settled down, honey. I've always said—"

"Mom."

This was exactly what he'd wanted to avoid. Talk of "settling down" and the like would surely spook Sofia, because it was early in their relationship, and also because she'd been so reluctant for them to spend the holidays together in the first place. Meeting the parents was a momentous occasion—he knew that—but he had to do whatever he could to lower the stress and the expectations.

"Well ... what is it, honey?" Aileen sounded irritated that her gleeful planning had been disturbed.

"Can you just ... take it easy, please? Sofia and I haven't been seeing each other that long, and—"

"Sofia! What a lovely name. Is she Italian? Oh, when your father and I went to Italy for our honeymoon, it was simply divine. The people ..."

Patrick closed his eyes and counted slowly to ten. He took a deep breath and started again.

"Mom, please don't scare her." It was more blunt than he'd intended, but sometimes it paid to be direct.

"Scare her? What do you mean?"

"I mean, no talk about weddings. No talk about 'settling down.' No talk about ... well ... anything. We've been seeing each other for four months, and we're not there yet. I don't want her to feel pressured."

Privately, he could admit that he was very nearly *there*, in that place where he was thinking about some permanent future for himself and Sofia. But he couldn't expect Sofia to be thinking that way—not when she was dealing with the crushing grief of the anniversary of her parents' loss. Later, they would consider where their relationship might go. For now, he just had to get her through the next month.

"Well, I'm not talking about *pressuring* her, son." She sounded wounded, and Patrick immediately felt guilty.

"I know you won't *mean* to pressure her, but ..."

" 'No talk about anything.' " She repeated his words back to him, a tinge of bitterness in her tone. "Do I need permission before I say hello? Is it all right if I ask her to pass the potatoes?"

"Very funny, Mom. You know what I mean."

"I'll be on my best behavior," she told him, their small rift already repaired. "And, Patrick, I'm thrilled. Honey, you deserve someone. I'm just thrilled."

SOFIA WAS LESS THRILLED. She was putting on a brave face in front of Patrick, but when he wasn't around, her dread took over.

"If you're going to be this pissy about it, you shouldn't even go," Benny said at dinner a couple of nights after Thanksgiving as they were all seated around the table feasting on leftovers. Sofia's tone when she spoke about Patrick's invitation suggested that she'd agreed to a series of painful electric shocks instead of a holiday celebration.

"I'm not pissy," Sofia snapped at her.

"Benny's right," Bianca said. "You're pissy. If you don't want to go, don't go. Backing out is better than going and then making it clear that you'd rather be in a Soviet work camp."

Sofia's shoulders slumped, and she put down her knife and fork. "You're right. I don't want to be like that. And I don't want to back out. I want to go and be charming and fun and lovely."

"All right," Martina said encouragingly. "That sounds nice."

"But—" Sofia began.

"But it'll be too hard when you're thinking about Mom and Dad," Martina finished for her, tears glimmering in her eyes.

"This isn't about ... about Mom and Dad." Sofia could barely force out the words. Maybe because she didn't like to talk about them, or maybe because she was lying.

"Then what?" Bianca asked.

"It's a lot of stress, that's all." Sofia threw her hands up in frustration. "It's ... it's Meeting the Parents!" She said it with implied capital letters. "What if they don't like me? What if I don't like them? What if everybody likes everybody and Patrick and I hurtle way too fast toward moving in together and getting married and having kids, and ... and buying a house! I'm not ready for a mortgage!"

It had started as a lie—the part about it having nothing to do with her parents—but had careened dangerously into the truth. What if all those things happened? She loved Patrick—she knew she did—but the thought of where things might go was terrifying.

"Wow," Benny said, impressed. "You're already thinking about marriage?"

"No!" Sofia exclaimed. "That's the point! I'm not thinking about marriage!"

"And yet you said the words *married*, *kids*, and *mortgage*. All without ever thinking of those things," Bianca replied.

Sofia sputtered, caught. "Well ... I'm thinking of those things abstractly! As general concepts!"

"Uh huh," Martina said.

"Oh ... go screw yourselves." Sofia turned her focus back to her meal.

They all ate in silence for a moment, then Benny said, "Well, at least you're not pissy."

PATRICK AND SOFIA didn't talk much about the trip in the following weeks. They were spending more and more time together, sharing a bed—either at his place or hers—more often than not.

Sofia alternated among being tense, sad, and perfectly fine, but she didn't talk about her parents or about what might await her in Michigan.

The fact that she wasn't talking about it worried Patrick. He pictured her emotions as a dormant volcano that was going to erupt with little warning, showering lava on scores of unsuspecting villagers.

Any sane man would be miles away when it happened, but that wasn't an option for him. If Sofia was in pain—if she needed him—he couldn't imagine being anywhere but by her side.

He'd tried to talk about it with her a few times, but to no avail. Any time he mentioned Christmas, or the trip, or, God forbid, her parents, she found something she urgently needed to attend to, excusing herself and walking out of the room.

So he'd stopped trying to draw her out, deciding that she would talk to him when she was ready. In the meantime, the trip was getting closer and closer, and Patrick wondered if this was all a mistake.

He could hardy withdraw the invitation now, though—not without making some kind of statement he didn't intend. Instead, he worked and went about his routine, and waited.

And tried to figure out what to give Sofia for Christmas.

"Jewelry's always a winner," Ramon said when Patrick consulted him on the matter. "You can't go wrong."

"But ... jewelry sends a statement, doesn't it?" The situation was already so fraught that he had to consider any message he might send carefully.

"That's the point," Ramon said. "It sends the statement that you're serious about her. That you were willing to drop some cash."

He *was* serious, and he *was* willing to drop some cash. Still ...

"What if it sends *too much* of a statement?" he asked.

"You're not buying her an engagement ring, for freak's sake. Just something pretty. Women like pretty things."

Patrick and Ramon were hiking at Fiscalini Ranch, the site of his near death with Sofia. This time, they were taking it slowly, walking at a leisurely pace and enjoying the scenery as they hiked.

"I guess you're right," Patrick said.

"Of course I'm right."

"Maybe I should ask Lucy...."

"You don't need to ask Lucy, you wuss," Ramon said. "Just buy her a damned bracelet or something. Expensive, but not *too* expensive. Something that says you love her but you're not rushing her."

Patrick considered it. "That's a lot to communicate with a bracelet."

"Look, suit yourself," Ramon said. "But the night I gave Lucy that first piece of jewelry? Best sex of my life."

It was hard to imagine sex better than what Patrick and Sofia had already had, but if such a thing were possible, it seemed foolish not to try.

Patrick went to a jewelry store on Main Street in Cambria on a day when he didn't have a class until late morning and he knew Sofia was at work. He peered into the lighted glass cases at the necklaces, the bracelets ... and the rings.

He couldn't buy Sofia a ring, obviously. Neither of them was ready for that. But he hoped the day would come when he would look at diamond solitaires and accept congratulations on his impending engagement.

He was already imagining the proposal—something involving the poetry he was working on for her.

"Are you looking for an engagement ring?" the saleswoman asked gleefully, coming over to where Patrick was standing.

He could feel himself beginning to blush. "Ah ... no. Not yet, anyway."

"Not yet means soon!" the woman sang. "You're that professor who's seeing Sofia Russo, aren't you? My goodness, she's a lucky girl!"

Patrick didn't know the saleswoman, but he was sure he'd seen her around. And even if he hadn't, that was how things were in a small town: everyone knew who everyone else was and what they were up to.

It occurred to him that he should have done his shopping in Morro Bay.

"Ms. ..." he began.

"Eleanor Green," she supplied. "But please, call me Ellie."

Ellie was in her midfifties, with professionally styled blond hair, carefully applied makeup, and clothing in the loose, flowing style that upscale, artistic women of a certain age seemed to favor.

"Ellie," he said, "if you could maybe not mention this to Sofia ..."

"Oh, of course not!" Ellie put a hand to her chest as though the very idea might stop her heart. "I would never tell a woman that her special someone was planning to propose. Why, I wouldn't last long in the jewelry business pulling stunts like that!"

Patrick closed his eyes and rubbed his forehead, beginning to feel a headache coming on. "No. That's not ... I'm not planning to propose to Sofia."

"Oh." Ellie deflated slightly.

"Someday. Maybe. But she's not ready yet, and I don't want ..." He was rambling. He forced himself to stop and begin again. "I'm looking for a Christmas gift for Sofia. That's all. Not an engagement ring."

The news that the relationship was alive and well, and that Ellie might, in fact, make a sale, revived the woman, and she perked up considerably. "Of course! That's wonderful. What, exactly, did you have in mind?"

Patrick explained his need to find something that said he was serious about Sofia but not so serious that they should start shopping for china patterns. He wanted to charm her, not spook her. The gift had to hit just the right note.

"I know exactly what you mean," she reassured him.

They settled on a necklace: a circular gold pendant on a delicate chain. Simple but elegant. The color would look lovely against her tanned skin, Patrick thought, and the design was very Sofia—classic but not at all showy.

"It's lovely," Ellie said as Patrick handed over his credit card.

"Do you think so?"

"I do." She hunted around for a gift box under the counter, and frowned. "I don't seem to have any pendant boxes. Do you mind if I use a different size?"

He didn't mind at all, and in a few minutes he'd finished the transaction and had emerged onto Main Street feeling pleased with himself. He'd managed to invite Sofia, he'd purchased an appropriate gift, and he'd broken the news to his mother.

Now all he had to do was live through December twenty-fifth.

26

With just one day to go before she and Patrick were scheduled to fly to Grand Rapids, Sofia was beginning to feel the pressure. Or, more accurately, she'd been feeling the pressure for a month. The difference was, now she was beginning to think it might cause her limbs to fly off.

"Shit! I don't even have a gift! Shit!" She was rushing around her room plucking things out of her closet and dresser to pack while Bianca looked on from the doorway.

"You still haven't bought Patrick a gift?" Bianca looked appalled.

"Of course I did. I bought five. And the reason I bought five is that none of them are right! I can't give him a sweater or ... or a coffee mug! What am I going to do?"

"Show me what you got." Bianca, always the calm one, took charge of the situation.

Sofia brought out the items—the sweater and coffee mug, and also a wallet, a pair of gloves, and a keychain.

"I bought a keychain. What the hell was I thinking?" Sofia moaned.

"This isn't so bad." Bianca picked up one item, then another. "The sweater is nice."

So was the keychain, for that matter—Sofia had ordered it from Tiffany's—but it was still just a keychain, and it didn't come close to communicating anything about what she felt for Patrick.

"Yeah, it's a nice sweater—if I'm buying a gift for somebody's favorite uncle."

"Hmm," Bianca said.

"I don't have time for more shopping. I've got to do my laundry, and pack …"

"I have an idea," Bianca said.

"Great. What is it?" Sofia stood amid the chaos of her room, her clothes and other various items strewn everywhere, and waited hopefully.

"I need to talk to Benny and Martina," Bianca said.

"You … wait. What? Why?"

"Just let me talk to Benny and Martina."

When Sofia saw what Bianca had in mind, she was speechless.

"They said it's okay. I knew they would. They really like Patrick." Bianca held their mother's first-edition *To Kill a Mockingbird*.

"I can't give him that." Sofia didn't take the book Bianca was offering her.

"Of course you can."

"But … it was Mom's. And it's valuable. And … why would they say I could give him that?"

But even as she asked the question, she knew why. Her sisters thought it was okay to give him the book because they thought it was likely to remain in the family. They'd already pegged him as The One, and something about that irked and upset Sofia—even if she had more or less concluded the same thing.

"No." She pushed the book toward Bianca. "This belongs to you, Benny, and Martina as much as it belongs to me. I can't take it away from you."

"Do you love him?" Bianca asked.

Sofia wanted to say yes, but she couldn't make the word come out. She nodded silently instead.

"Then you *can* give it to him, and you should. He's an English professor; he'll appreciate it as much as any of us could. And it makes a statement, Sofia. He's making a statement by taking you to meet his parents, and you need to make one, too, if you're serious about him."

Sofia still wouldn't take the book, so Bianca went to Sofia's open suitcase and tucked it inside. "Just take it with you and think about it."

After Bianca left the room, Sofia stood next to the suitcase and stared down at the book. She didn't want to give Patrick something of her mother's. She wanted her mother to be here to meet him, to get to know him. She wanted her mother to be a part of this important moment in her life.

Because the moment *was* important, no matter how she might want to pretend it wasn't.

She went back to packing, thinking that this was all wrong. She couldn't enjoy the major milestones of her life without her parents to share them with her.

PATRICK AND SOFIA flew into Grand Rapids, but his parents and siblings lived in Muskegon, a city of 38,000 about a forty-five-minute drive away.

They got a rental car at the airport and took Interstate 96 northwest, out of the urban center and toward Lake Michigan. There'd been a recent snowfall, but today the skies were clear and the roads had been plowed. The temperature hovered around thirty-five, and they were grateful that the car had reliable heating.

He'd told her the basics about his family, of course, but the drive gave him a chance to add details: here was the office furniture factory where his father had worked for more than thirty years; here was the hospital where his mother was a nurse in the intensive care unit; here was the high school he and his siblings had attended; and here was the grocery store where he'd had his first job when he was sixteen.

At about six p.m., they arrived at his parents' home, a two-story midcentury house with pale green wood siding and white trim. A small, scraggly tree reached up through the snow in the front yard, and the concrete walkway that led to the front porch had been freshly shoveled.

The sun set early this time of year so the skies were already dark, but the streetlights and the porch light glowed. The windows on either side of the front door shone with a welcoming golden light.

It was a house, that was all. A house made for a family just like hers. It was well-tended and unimposing, a house that spoke of middle-American values and Sunday dinners.

So why was she so damned scared of it?

"You okay?" Patrick turned off the engine and looked at Sofia with concern. He took her hand and held it in his.

"Me? Sure. Of course."

"Because you look a little green," he said.

"Oh, it's just ... I get a little carsick."

"You've never mentioned that before."

"Why are you grilling me about it?" she snapped at him. "I ought to know if I get carsick, shouldn't I?"

"You should, yes." He squeezed her hand. "Sofia, it's going to be fine. They're going to love you."

"Listen, I was thinking ... Maybe we should get a hotel room. Maybe—"

She was interrupted when a woman in her midfifties came out the front door, exclaimed, "Patrick!" and began hurrying down the front steps toward them.

Patrick got out of the car and met her halfway. "Hi, Mom." They embraced, and Sofia felt almost overwhelmed with emotion.

"Come and meet Sofia," Patrick said.

Sofia supposed it was too late now for her hotel plan.

~

THEY'D ARRIVED in time for dinner, and Sofia ate pot roast, mashed potatoes, fresh rolls, and peas as Patrick's mother questioned her about every aspect of her life while trying to seem as though she wasn't questioning her.

"So, a kayak instructor!" Aileen said when they were about halfway through their meal. "How fun! I've always wanted to learn to kayak. Haven't I, Hugh?" she asked her husband. "Remember the time we went to Hawaii, when Patrick was ten? I told you then that I wanted to learn to kayak."

"You told me," Hugh agreed pleasantly enough, though he barely looked up from his plate.

"It's not too late to learn," Sofia said. "I could teach you. When the weather's warmer, I mean, or maybe when you come to Cambria."

"Oh, I don't know." Aileen laughed. "I'd probably end up in the emergency room."

"I certainly hope not," Sofia said. "One Connelly almost dying in a kayak accident is enough."

Sofia noticed the look of alarm on Patrick's face, but it was too late. She'd already said it.

"What do you mean, one Connelly almost dying in a kayak accident?" Aileen looked horror-stricken. "Patrick? What is she talking about?"

~

"WELL, THAT WAS A ROCKY START," Sofia observed later, when she and Patrick were lying side by side in the upstairs guest bed. The mattress had probably been bought when Patrick was a toddler, judging by the way Sofia could feel springs digging into her back.

"She could clearly see that I wasn't dead," Patrick commented. "And yet ..."

Aileen had insisted on hearing every detail of the story, then had grilled her son on why he'd gone kayaking when he couldn't swim; why he hadn't told her that he'd been in the hospital; and whether he was having any lingering effects from the head trauma. Her experience as an intensive care nurse meant she was more knowledgeable than most people on traumatic brain injuries, so her interrogation was both extensive and annoyingly specific.

Patrick had eventually stopped answering her questions, reasoning that it was the only way to get her to stop asking them. That had irritated Aileen to the point that she'd stopped talking entirely, leaving Sofia to try to make small talk with Hugh, who limited his remarks to the route Sofia and Patrick had taken from the airport.

"Did you come up through Coopersville?" he'd wanted to know. "Because Aileen's cousin Louise came by way of Kent City last spring, and that was just stupid."

Sofia had worried that Aileen might hold her responsible for her son's near death experience, but the opposite turned out to be true. When Sofia was in the kitchen after dinner, offering to help clean up, Aileen grabbed her and pulled her into a fierce hug.

"Why, honey, you saved his life," she'd said, her voice thick with emotion. "I don't know how I can ever pay you back for a thing like that."

"You certainly earned a lot of points," Patrick said now as they recapped the day, looking at the popcorn ceilings in the guest bedroom. "I, on the other hand, was lucky not to be disowned."

"She loves you." Sofia rolled onto her stomach to be able to see Patrick better. "I get that, because I do, too."

Sofia had told Patrick she loved him before, so it didn't have the gravity of the first time. But every time she said it, she still felt the same nervous quiver in her gut, the same sensation of the magnitude of it. She loved him, and that made her vulnerable in a way she hadn't been since her parents' deaths.

She still wasn't sure how she felt about that.

"I love you, too, Sofia." He put a hand on the side of her face and caressed her cheek with his thumb. "Thank you for coming with me."

"I don't—"

But he didn't wait to hear what she didn't do, didn't want, didn't feel. He kissed her and pulled her into his arms, and after that, they were both too busy to talk.

27

The next couple of days were a blur of activity. Sofia met Fiona and her family, then Sean and his boyfriend, Ethan, an accountant at the Meijer headquarters in Grand Rapids.

The family occupied themselves with a great deal of fussing over gifts, decorations, and food—and over Sofia.

She fielded question after question: "Tell me how you two met," and "When are you moving in together?" and "Has Patrick told you he wants kids?"

The first one was easy enough, now that Aileen had gotten past her horror over Patrick's accident, but the others seemed to Sofia to be breathtakingly presumptuous.

Did everyone assume they were going to live together, get married, and have children? Was that even what she wanted?

The atmosphere in the house was chaotic but warm and loving, and everyone seemed to want to pull Sofia into the center of it. There seemed to be some sort of conspiracy to make her feel like part of the family.

Aileen drew her into the kitchen to help cook and to talk. Fiona told her stories about Patrick's childhood and teen years. Sean kept offering her food. Fiona's kids begged her to play video games and then board games with them.

The effect was both intoxicating and disorienting. Every glimpse she had of this full, complete, and thriving family reminded her that her own family had been shattered. Every gesture of acceptance from Patrick's family made her want to be a part of it—but that left her feeling guilt-stricken, as though she were betraying her own parents.

She wasn't ready for this—for any of it. And yet she felt as though she were being swept along on an irresistible tide of longing. Everything she wanted was here, and she was being beckoned to reach out and take it. But how could she, when her own parents were irreplaceable? How could she take hold of her own happiness, when her mother and father had been robbed of theirs?

And—most troubling of all—how could she move toward a permanent relationship with Patrick when her parents would never be there to see her engagement? Her wedding? The birth of her children?

It had been a mistake to come. And Sofia didn't know how she'd been foolish enough to make it.

PATRICK HAD THOUGHT things were going well, but now he wasn't so sure. His family were all being nice to Sofia—not a given, after the way they'd treated Kim—but with each passing hour that they stayed here, he could see her withdrawing bit by bit.

"Sofia? Are you all right?" They were taking a walk along the Lakeshore Trail on the morning of Christmas Eve, the icy waters of Muskegon Lake stretching out to their left.

"I'm fine." She wrapped her arms around herself, tucking her hands into her armpits. The weather was in the high thirties—not too bad, from Patrick's perspective—but she looked like she was freezing despite her down jacket, hat, and gloves.

"Are you cold?" he asked.

"I said I'm fine."

They walked a while longer in silence, their boots crunching on the snowy trail.

"Is it my family? Has someone done something?" he tried again.

"No, Patrick." She stopped walking and faced him. "They're wonderful. All of them."

"Then what's going on?" He put his hands on her biceps and peered into her face.

"Nothing's going on." She avoided his gaze. "You know what? I am cold. Can we just go back?"

Sofia tried to hold it together the best she could. She'd thought that once she was there, in Patrick's childhood home, she would be able to handle all of the emotional connections that represented. She'd been wrong. Being here had stirred up such a potent soup of longing, grief, and resentment that she could barely face such simple tasks as showering and feeding herself, let alone being pleasant and gracious to the Connellys.

Still, she told herself that it was almost over. One more day, that was all. Today was Christmas Day, and they would do the gift exchange, eat the holiday dinner, and be back at the airport tomorrow morning. Then she could get home, go back to her normal routine, and pretend that what was happening between her and Patrick—this irresistible force drawing them toward eventual marriage—wasn't really happening.

But getting through one more day was harder than she'd thought it would be.

It started with the pancakes.

When Sofia got up that morning, the kitchen already smelled of warm pancakes and maple syrup. Aileen was standing at the stove in a holiday apron, Christmas carols playing softly on the stereo.

"Good morning, honey!" she called to Sofia. "Merry Christmas! Do you want some pancakes?"

It wasn't that she looked like Sofia's mother, because she didn't.

Carmela's hair was a glossy black, while Aileen's was auburn shot with gray; Carmela had been a sturdy woman, short and stocky, while Aileen was tall and willowy. Yet, something about the circumstances —the Christmas morning greeting, the use of the word *honey*, and especially the pancakes—gave Sofia a flashback to her childhood that was so intense and vivid that she nearly swooned.

Aileen must have seen it on her face, because she suddenly looked alarmed. "Sofia! What's wrong? Are you all right? Come on, sit down." She hurried over to the kitchen table to pull out a chair for Sofia.

"Just ... a little dizzy for a minute," Sofia said, lying to cover the truth.

She realized within seconds that the lie had been a mistake.

"Oh ... Sofia, are you *pregnant*?" Aileen stage-whispered the last word. "Does Patrick know? Oh, I know it's not ideal, with the two of you not married yet, but how wonderful! What a marvelous Christmas surprise. Oh—"

"No!" Sofia exclaimed. "No, no! I'm not pregnant! No! There's no Christmas surprise. I'm not ... There's no way I could be pregnant."

But even as she said it, she knew that wasn't true. That time in his office, they'd been too rushed, too caught up in the moment, to use a condom. Afterward, she'd chastised herself for being careless and had gone on the pill. But still ... She didn't have a calendar in front of her, but wasn't it possible that she was late?

She'd lied about the dizziness, yes. But she'd been especially irritable lately....

"Sofia?" Aileen was looking at her intently. "You look a little pale. Let me get you a glass of water."

Sofia drank the water gratefully when Aileen brought it. Then she told herself to calm down. She definitely wasn't pregnant. Probably. But that didn't change the fact that being here, in this kitchen with the carols and the smells and the rosebud wallpaper made her think of her mother, and that was almost more than she could bear.

"What's going on?" Sean, a tall, handsome man in his late twenties with dark hair and a slim build, came into the room and looked at Sofia, and then at his mother. "Is everything okay?"

"Sofia feels *dizzy*," Aileen said, loading the word with meaning. "And we were just wondering if maybe there's a *reason* she might be having *morning sickness....*"

"Oh," Sean said. Then: "Oh!"

"No, I'm just—"

"Does Patrick know?" Sean asked.

"There's nothing for him to know!" Sofia could feel the situation slipping out of her control—not that it had been firmly in her control in the first place.

"Here. Have some pancakes." Aileen set a plate in front of Sofia. "Having something in your stomach will make you feel better. At least, it always worked for me."

"Sofia? Are you sick?" Patrick came into the room, looking adorably tousled in pajama pants and a Cal Poly San Luis Obispo T-shirt. He ran a hand through his hair, which made it stick up at odd angles.

"No," she said.

"Just dizzy," Sean supplied, leaning against the counter with a glass of orange juice in his hand. "And maybe a little nauseous. In the morning." He winked at Patrick.

"I never said I was nauseous!" Sofia insisted. But she was, a little bit, now that she thought about it. Oh, God.

"Wait, did something happen?" Patrick squinted, confused. "Is there something going on?"

"I just ... Thank you, but ... I need to take a shower." Sofia got up, leaving her pancakes untouched, and left the room.

As she left, she heard Aileen say, "Dizzy and no appetite first thing in the morning. That's a dead giveaway. Oh, Patrick, it's so wonderful."

～

BY THE TIME Sofia got into the shower and away from the Connellys, she really was feeling sick. How had she let this happen? How had she let Patrick's family believe she was pregnant?

Which she wasn't, she was sure. Almost sure.

But what if she were? It was all just moving so fast, and she wanted to talk it over with her mother. She wanted that good, solid reassurance from her father. But they weren't here, and they never would be again.

She should feel better than this after two years, shouldn't she? Why didn't she? Why was it that Bianca and Benny and Martina could function normally and get on with their lives, while Sofia couldn't?

It's because I never cried. That's what Bianca would say. Because I never talk about it, never got it all out. But what good would that do? It wouldn't bring her mother and father back.

She got under the hot water and tried to feel better. When Patrick knocked softly on the door and called to her, asking if she was all right, she told him that she was. She wasn't, but it was the only thing she could say that would make him give her the space she needed.

She thought about getting dressed and escaping through the little window above the toilet, but she was unlikely to fit. Besides, it was snowing.

Just one more day, that was all she had to get through. One more day.

SHE MIGHT HAVE MADE IT, too, if it hadn't been for Patrick's gift.

They'd finished breakfast and were gathered at the tree for the gift exchange. The Connelly kids presented their mother and father with their gifts, followed by much *oohing* and *aahing* and thank-yous and hugs. Sean gave Ethan a new iPhone, and Ethan gave Sean a cashmere scarf. Fiona's kids ripped open a stack of gifts, leaving snowdrifts of torn wrapping paper on the carpet.

Then Patrick brought out his gift for Sofia.

It was the size of the box that undid her: a two-inch cube, suitable for pretty much only one thing—a ring.

This couldn't be happening.

Sofia wasn't the only one who'd assumed what was in the box. As soon as Patrick brought out the tiny package, his mother said, "Oh, Patrick!" Other members of the Connelly family followed up with "Oh ho!" and "Oh, my God! Patrick!"

Patrick himself looked confused about all of the excitement, but he pressed on gamely. He held out the box to Sofia and said, "I hope you'll like it."

Sofia stared at the box and then at the people around her. This family. This perfect, complete family.

And she knew she couldn't do it.

"Patrick ... I'm sorry."

She got up, rushed up the stairs, and went to pack.

HE COULD HAVE YELLED. He could have argued with her. He could have told her she was being ridiculous, or demanded an explanation.

But Patrick didn't want to do any of those things. All he wanted was to help her through whatever it was she was feeling.

He knocked gently on the door to the room they'd been sharing before opening it a crack and peering inside.

"Sofia? Are you okay?"

"I have to go. I'm sorry." She was stuffing clothes and toiletries into her suitcase without bothering to fold anything. "Will you apologize to your family for me? They're going to hate me now, I'm sure, but ..." She left the thought hanging.

"Nobody's going to hate you." He came more fully into the room. "Sofia ..." He put a hand on her arm, and she didn't shake it off. He guessed that was something.

"I have to go home," she said.

"Just ... wait a minute." When she stopped what she was doing and looked at him, he pulled her into his arms and held her, stroking her hair. She clung to him for a moment, then she let go and went back to packing.

"Do you want me to come with you?" he said.

"No. Please. No." She shook her head. "Do they have Uber out here? Or do I need to get a cab? I can—"

"I'll drive you to the airport."

"I can manage myself. I need ... I just want to be by myself."

"Okay, then take the rental car." He found the keys on his bedside table and handed them to her. "I have plenty of people who can drive me to the airport."

"Thank you." She took the keys from him. The way her eyes shimmered, he thought for a moment that she might cry. He'd never seen her do that, but it seemed like she might. Instead, her expression hardened and she went back to packing.

"You might not be able to get a plane ticket on Christmas Day," he said. "Let me check online and see before you go."

"I'm going now." She zipped up her suitcase and lifted it.

"Let me take that for you." Patrick reached for the suitcase.

"No. Please. No. Just let me do it." She pushed past him and headed for the door.

He was hurt and bewildered, but he let her go. If it had been anyone but Sofia, he would have thought this was the end—that the relationship was over. But it *was* Sofia, so that thought never occurred to him. The two of them, what they had, seemed so inevitable that he wasn't worried about their future. He was only worried about her.

"Sofia. If you have to go, then go. But take a minute first. I don't want you out there on the icy roads upset. You're not used to driving in this kind of weather, and if you're preoccupied ..."

That seemed to get through to her. "You're right. But I'll be okay. The roads have been plowed, and the rental car has good tires. I'll drive slowly, and if I have any trouble, I'll pull over. I promise."

She sounded rational, and now that Patrick considered it, she didn't seem especially emotional. She was just determined to leave here as soon as possible.

"Call me when you get to the airport." He wanted to kiss her goodbye, but he could see that she didn't want that. Instead, he opened the bedroom door and held it for her so she could maneuver her suitcase through the doorway.

"I will. Patrick ... I'm sorry."

She went downstairs and out the front door before he could say anything else.

HE'D HELD it together remarkably well when Sofia was still in the house. Now that she'd left, he realized how little restraint he had remaining for his family.

"Patrick! What happened? Where did Sofia go?" Aileen demanded when he came downstairs.

It was hard enough dealing with everything that had happened without also having to explain it to his mother. "I'm going out." He took his coat off the hook by the door.

"But, honey, it's Christmas morning! And we're still opening our gifts, and—"

"Mom, I just can't right now." He'd never used that tone with her before, and she looked stricken. He could deal with the guilt of that later. Right now, he needed space. He needed to clear his head.

He went outside and began walking.

28

During the drive to the airport, Sofia had worried that Patrick might be right—it might be impossible to get a flight on Christmas Day. But that turned out not to be the case. The airport was noticeably less busy than usual, probably because every sane person who celebrated the holiday was at home enjoying their day.

Because Sofia did not, at the moment, qualify as a sane person, she was here. And she was able to book a flight with no trouble—though she did have to pay a whopping fee to change her reservation.

Still, her departure time was more than two hours away. That meant she had plenty of time to sit around and think about what she'd done and why she'd done it.

Maybe later she would look into her own heart and see the real reasons for her actions. But not right now, as she sat in a molded plastic chair under fluorescent lighting and waited for her flight to be called. Now, she blamed Patrick.

What the hell was he thinking, trying to give her a ring? Because that was almost certainly what was in that tiny box. What else could it be? What else would have had his family gasping in pleased surprise?

He knew she was having trouble getting through the holidays. He knew that meeting his family was hard for her. And yet he'd raised the stakes even further, raised the tension until it was inevitable that something would break.

That something had turned out to be Sofia.

How clueless was he about what was going on in her head that he would pull such a stunt at the worst possible time?

"God, men are idiots," she murmured.

Except, Patrick didn't actually seem like an idiot, and he didn't seem clueless about her emotions. If he had been, he'd have blown up at her when she'd left so abruptly, hurting both his feelings and his mother's.

And hadn't a part of her *wanted* him to blow up? Because that would have made things so much easier. Then she could have made this all about him. She could have broken up with him on the spot and made it about his reaction to what she'd done.

But he hadn't, so now there was no way to avoid the truth of the matter: he'd been gracious and caring, and she'd been the one who was irrational and needlessly cruel.

And he'd wanted to marry her.

The inevitability of that idea was what had frightened her so thoroughly. Part of her—a substantial part—thought that *of course* they were going to be married eventually. And something about that—something inextricably linked to her grief over her parents—had made her feel like a rabbit with its foot caught in a metal trap. In her panic and her fear, she'd gnawed off her own foot to get away.

She wanted a life with him, so much. But it was a gift she just couldn't accept.

She pulled out her phone, texted him that she'd arrived safely at the airport, then turned off the phone. If he responded, she didn't want to read what he had to say. It would be too hard to resist him if she did.

BY THE TIME Patrick got back to the house more than an hour later, his family had dispersed, leaving the partially opened gifts exactly as they'd been when he'd left. He imagined they'd all been talking about him, but that was okay. He'd have done the same thing in their place.

He walked up the stairs feeling tired, as though his limbs weighed twice as much as they should have. He felt like he'd aged several years in the past hour.

Merry Christmas to him.

He went into the guest room, lay down on the bed, and closed his eyes. When he heard a knock on the door, he was certain it had to be his mother. Instead, Fiona poked her head into the room.

"Can I come in?" In true Fiona style, she didn't wait for the answer. She'd never been the type to wait for permission for anything.

The mattress sagged beside him as Fiona sat down on the bed.

"I guess she just wasn't ready to get engaged," she said softly.

Patrick's eyes flew open. "Engaged? What are you talking about?"

"What am I talking about? What are *you* talking about?" She gaped at him. "You mean there wasn't a ring in that box?"

He sat up. "A ring? What? No! Why would I give her a ring when we've only been seeing each other for four months?"

"Oh, boy." She explained to him what he'd been missing up to this point: that Sofia had run like hell because she'd thought Patrick was about to propose. "You brought her to meet the family—which is a lot to deal with on its own—and then you were about to spring a ring on her. Jesus."

"I was not about to spring a ring on her," he insisted.

"Well, that's what she thought you were about to do. It's what all of the rest of us thought, too."

"But—"

"On top of all of that, she's pregnant."

"*What?!*" Patrick leaped off of the bed. "She is? She told you that?"

"No, she didn't tell me that." Fiona waved away the question. "But she was feeling dizzy this morning and she had no appetite. Dizzy and sick in the morning, Patrick? You're a smart guy. You do the math."

"Oh, God." Suddenly, Patrick was the one feeling dizzy and sick.

Sofia's flight came in late on the afternoon on December twenty-fifth. She didn't have a car at the airport in San Jose—they'd taken Patrick's—so she had to rent one for the three-hour drive to Cambria.

By the time she walked in her front door pulling her suitcase behind her, she was exhausted physically and emotionally, so she was in no mood to field a barrage of questions.

It seemed unlikely she would be able to avoid it, though. She came in to find her sisters in their pajamas on the sofa, eating popcorn and watching *It's a Wonderful Life.* As one, they stared at her in shock while James Stewart insisted that he would never marry the young and dewy Donna Reed.

"What are you doing here?" Benny demanded.

"Uh oh," Martina said.

Bianca snatched up the remote from the coffee table and turned off the TV. "Where's Patrick? Did somebody die?"

"Nobody died." Sofia dragged her suitcase across the threshold and closed the door behind her.

"You're not due home for two more days. Why are you here if nobody died?" Martina asked.

Sofia wanted to tell them what she'd done and why. She wanted to tell them not to worry about her; that she'd made a decision and followed through on it, and she was willing to accept the consequences.

But she was too drained, too used up. Instead, she simply went into her room and closed the door.

If she'd thought that was going to put them off, she was wrong. Within moments, the three of them were standing outside the door, calling to her.

Martina: "Sofia? Are you okay?"

Benny: "Get the hell out here, or at least open the door. This is stupid."

And Bianca, to the other two: "Maybe we should leave her alone. She'll tell us when she's ready."

Bianca, always the sensible, adult one. They must have listened to her, because Sofia could hear the three of them retreating, muttering theories about a sudden breakup, Patrick's family scaring her away, or fruitcake-induced food poisoning.

Of course she was going to tell them eventually, but right now, she was so tired. She climbed under her covers, still fully dressed, and waited for sleep.

Sofia didn't know what time it was when her sisters came into the room, but bright sunlight was shining through her window, so it had to be late morning.

"Sofia. Get up." Bianca, of course.

"Leave me alone." She pulled the covers up over her head.

"Bullshit," Benny said. "You've moped long enough. Get the hell out of bed."

"I'm not moping." The fact that Sofia had the covers pulled over her head probably undercut her credibility on the subject.

"Sofia, please? We're worried about you," Martina said.

At the same time, Bianca pulled the covers away, revealing Sofia in her jeans and sweatshirt, her hair tangled around her face, her makeup from the day before smeared.

"Well, that's not good," Benny remarked.

"Come on." Martina took Sofia's hand and gently pulled her to a sitting position. "Let's get you a shower, then you can tell us what happened."

There didn't seem to be much point in fighting it; they would get it out of her sooner or later. Sofia took a hot shower, as she'd been ordered to do, and got dressed in clean sweatpants and a T-shirt. Then, her hair wet, she went into the living room and sat down on the sofa. Martina brought her a cup of coffee with cream and sugar, the way Sofia liked it.

"Okay, what happened? What did he do?" Benny wanted to know.

"He didn't do anything," Sofia said.

"I told you," Bianca said to Benny. "This wasn't Patrick's fault—he's too sweet. It's got to be his mother."

"It's not his mother," Sofia said.

"Maybe it really was the fruitcake," Martina speculated.

"Would you all stop it?" Sofia wrapped one hand around the warmth of her coffee mug and rubbed her face with the other. "Nobody did anything. Or, no, that's not true. Patrick did something. Or, he was *going* to do something."

"All right, I give up," Benny said dryly. "What was he going to do? Sleep with a hooker? Kick a puppy? Vote Republican?"

"He ... he was going to ask me to marry him."

There wasn't much that could make her sisters go silent, but that did it. They all stared at her. After a moment, Martina said, "Whoa."

"He asked you to marry him?" Bianca said, recovering herself.

"No. He was going to. At least, I think he was going to. He handed me my gift, and it was a tiny, square box, and his family all started saying things like, 'Oh, my God, Patrick!' and 'Oh, Patrick!' And I just ... couldn't!"

"So, naturally you had an adult, rational conversation with him about your needs and goals and expectations," Bianca said.

"I'm guessing no," Benny said when Sofia didn't answer. "I'm guessing she ran out of there like it was the zombie apocalypse."

"Pretty much," Sofia admitted.

"Oh, no," Martina moaned.

"So, wait." Bianca perched on the edge of her sofa cushion. "You don't even know if he intended to propose? I mean, the gift could have been a pair of earrings, or a brooch, or ... or one of those Pandora charms."

"It wasn't a Pandora charm," Benny guessed. "That man is in love, capital L, capital O, capital V, capital E. If she thinks it was a ring, it was a ring."

"See?" Sofia said plaintively.

"Well ... she still should have had an adult conversation about her needs and expectations," Bianca pointed out.

"I know I should have!" Sofia wailed. "I know! But there was just so much going on, with everyone acting like I was part of the family ..."

"The monsters," Benny quipped.

" ... and they probably told Patrick that I'm pregnant," Sofia concluded.

"Oh, shit. You're pregnant?" Bianca said.

"No! But they think I am, because I lied about being dizzy."

They were all silent for a long beat. Then Benny said, "I wish this conversation had CliffsNotes so I could read the summary and figure out what the hell's going on."

Sofia slowed down and told it all from the beginning: the way his family had assumed she and Patrick were already all but engaged; the way she'd lied about being dizzy to cover for being upset; the way Patrick had sprung the tiny box on her in front of everyone, which hadn't given her a chance to talk to him about his intentions. And then, how she'd fled the house as though she were escaping the scene of a crime.

"So where does this leave you and Patrick?" Martina's voice was gentle.

"I don't know," Sofia moaned. "He's probably finished with me now."

"He's not finished," Benny said. "Capital L, capital O, capital V, capital E."

"Well ... maybe *I'm* finished." She wasn't, but she'd said it out loud just to see how it would feel. It felt like the cruelest kind of lie—the kind intended to hurt, to destroy. It felt like blasphemy to have uttered the words.

"You're not finished, either," Benny said, and Sofia didn't correct her.

PATRICK DIDN'T WANT to leave his family on Christmas Day. His mother would be devastated. Besides, he thought Sofia needed a day or so to cool down from whatever it was that had upset her.

But he did leave on December twenty-sixth, a day earlier than he'd planned. Giving Sofia space was one thing, but if she really was pregnant, he needed to talk to her about it. He needed to let her know that he was in—one hundred percent. He needed her to know that he wanted it all: her, the baby, a life they could build together.

"I'm sorry, Mom," he told Aileen as he gathered his things after breakfast.

"Oh, honey, that's all right. I'm just sorry things didn't go better." She was in the kitchen making a sandwich from leftover turkey for Patrick to take with him.

"I have to talk to her," he said. "I waited a day to give her some space, but ... I don't think it can wait any longer."

"Well." She wrapped the sandwich in a plastic bag and handed it to him. "I just hope things go the way you want them to."

She had conspicuously avoided saying she hoped he and Sofia would work things out. He didn't blame her, given everything that had happened, but still, it concerned him.

"Mom? I know Sofia didn't make the best impression. But she has a lot on her mind. She has ... issues with this time of year."

"I just hope she's all right. And if she really is pregnant, Patrick ..." She left the thought unfinished.

If she really was pregnant, then what? He couldn't make her marry him. He couldn't make her stop being scared and start giving herself to their relationship wholeheartedly. He couldn't even make her have the baby.

That thought, popping into his mind unbidden, scared him. One thing at a time, he reminded himself. First, he just had to talk to her.

Aileen pulled him into a hug, and he clung to her harder than he meant to. "I trust you to make the right decision for yourself, whatever that is," she told him.

Whatever that is.

It seemed that neither one of them knew.

29

Sofia had started to convince herself that she was pregnant. So when her period came and she discovered that she wasn't, emotions hit her from all directions.

Relief, certainly. But also disappointment and a certain amount of despair. Because part of her wanted the life that Patrick and a hypothetical baby represented, but another part of her couldn't accept it. None of this was happening the way it should. It wasn't supposed to happen without her parents.

"I'm not pregnant," she said in Bianca's car while the two of them were on their way to the office a couple of days after Christmas.

"You already said you weren't pregnant," Bianca reminded her.

"I know, but … that was kind of a lie. I thought I might be. But I'm not."

Bianca drove quietly for a few minutes, until she could no longer keep silent. "How do you feel about that?"

"You sound like a psychiatrist, and that's not your specialty," Sofia pointed out.

"Shut up. Just tell me how you are."

If this were another day, and if Sofia were in a different kind of mood, she'd have teased her sister—told her that it was impossible to both shut up and explain her feelings. But today, she couldn't manage lightheartedness.

"I feel ... like I've ruined everything." She slumped in the passenger seat. "Like I've thrown away any chance I had at happiness." A thought occurred to her, and she smacked her face with her hand. "And, oh, God. Mom's book. I left it under the tree at Patrick's mother's house. I left before he had a chance to open it."

"So you were going to give it to him," Bianca said.

"I ... Yes."

Bianca grinned, just a little, and Sofia was outraged that her sister was smirking at her pain. "What the hell are you smiling about?"

"You."

"Why? Because you enjoy seeing me miserable?"

"No, you jerk. I'm smiling because Patrick's the one, and you know it. You wouldn't have given him the book—or *planned* to give him the book—if he wasn't. You know you wouldn't have."

"Oh." Sofia couldn't deny it. "But now I've lost the book...."

"You didn't lose the book. It's safe at his mother's house."

"But ..."

"And you didn't ruin everything, Sofia. If he really was about to propose, he's not going to be put off by your one little attack of cold feet. He's better than that."

"Oh," Sofia said again.

"The question is whether you can get past whatever it is that's holding you back so you can enjoy what's going to happen between the two of you."

Yes, that was the question, Sofia mused. "It's just ... too soon."

"Well, four months is soon," Bianca agreed. "Then tell him that. He'll wait."

"That's not what I meant. I mean, yes, four months is too soon, but ..."

"But what? What did you really mean?" Bianca had just parked the car. She turned off the engine and gave Sofia her full attention.

"I meant it's too soon after"—she could barely say it—"after Mom and Dad."

Bianca's eyes shimmered with tears. "Oh, Sof. It's not too soon. They would want this for you. They would want you to be happy."

Sofia didn't answer. She just sat there, looking out at the parking lot.

"What's going on in there?" Bianca asked, poking Sofia's forehead gently with her finger. "Don't shut down on me. What are you thinking?"

"I'm thinking ... we'd better get to work." Sofia didn't look at her sister.

"Sof ..."

"You've got patients." She got out of the car and headed toward the office.

PATRICK'S SISTER drove him to the airport. It was a moderately long drive, and he should have known she couldn't make it the whole way without offering advice. That wouldn't have bothered him if only she hadn't been telling him exactly what he didn't want to hear.

"I'm just saying, she's got issues," Fiona told him as they headed southeast toward Grand Rapids.

"So do I," he countered. "I have issues."

She shot him a doubtful look. "Name one."

Now that he was on the spot, he couldn't seem to think of one. But he didn't want to hand her the point, so he searched for something that made him look as troubled as Sofia had seemed to be.

"I ... well ... I don't fit in with our family. At all." Now that he thought of it, that wasn't a random thing he'd come up with to appease her. It was true.

"Oh, that's crap, Patrick. Don't be stupid."

"And when I try to express how I feel about it, I'm dismissed." He looked at her significantly.

She opened her mouth to say something, seemed to realize that she was about to prove his point, then closed it again.

"Everyone in the family loves you," she said.

"I know that."

"Then what …"

"Everyone loves me, yes. But I'm different." Patrick's life had always been like a game of "one of these things doesn't belong," but instead of the game pieces being four circles and a square, it was four salt-of-the-earth, blue-collar middle-Americans and one intellectual with an Ivy League degree.

His life was like an episode of *Frasier,* but without the nearly identical brother to make him feel less like a freak.

"So you're different," Fiona said. "There's nothing wrong with that."

"Tell that to Dad," Patrick said.

"Wait. Dad? What has Dad ever done wrong?" Fiona sounded offended.

"Nothing. Nothing at all." Hugh had never criticized Patrick, never berated him, had never expressed any disapproval of his son's choices. But he'd stopped trying to talk to Patrick at about the same time Patrick had been accepted to Princeton. Oh, they still talked, but never about things that mattered. It was small talk now. How's the weather? How was traffic? Did you remember to get your car serviced?

"Look." Fiona was using her big-sister voice, the one that told him she'd taken quite enough of his crap, thank you very much, and the sooner he fell in line, the better. "Has it ever occurred to you that Dad feels like you passed him by? Like you just sort of moved on without him?"

"What else was I supposed to do besides move on, Fiona? I couldn't just stand still."

"Because that's what Dad is doing? Is that what you mean?" The edge in Fiona's voice was sharp and dangerous.

"No. That's not what I meant." Of course, it was exactly what he'd meant, but he said the words to placate her. He didn't want to fight with Fiona.

She drove for a while, and he could feel the tension radiating from her.

"I guess you do have issues," she said.

30

———

By the time he got home, he told himself it was too late to talk to Sofia. She was probably tired, maybe even in bed already. The thought of her in bed without him made him ache with longing. He didn't want her to be in bed without him ever again.

He wanted to rush to her house, bang on the door, and insist that she see him. But he was exhausted from a long day of traveling and from being unable to sleep the night before. He wasn't sure he could be rational and coherent if he saw her right now, and he knew that he needed to be at his best when he spoke to her.

His phone pinged with a text message.

Did you get home all right, honey? His mother.

Home safe and sound, he answered.

Good luck when you talk to Sofia. XOXO

He smiled, heartened that his mother wanted things to work out between them, even if Fiona didn't.

One more message came:

I found your gift from Sofia under the tree. I didn't know what to do with it, so I put it in your suitcase.

That was interesting. He'd forgotten all about the gifts when things had imploded on Christmas morning. He went to his suitcase, unzipped it, and rooted around amid the folded shirts and socks.

He found the package, wrapped in red paper with Santas cavorting on it, underneath a sweater. He held the gift in his hands and considered it. Should he open it? It had been intended for him, after all. She'd never opened his gift, though, so maybe he should hold off.

Maybe they could both open their packages after they resolved this thing between them.

If they resolved this thing between them.

The thought that it was an *if* rather than a *when* made him feel vaguely sick. Of course he had to fix things with Sofia. There was no other option. At least, none that he would let himself consider.

WHEN PATRICK FINALLY CALLED SOFIA, she didn't pick up the phone. She saw the notification that she'd received a voice mail, but she didn't listen to it.

She wasn't angry with him, because he hadn't done anything wrong. She simply didn't know what to say to him. She knew she should apologize for leaving the way she had, but what then? What would happen if he tried again to give her the ring? If she accepted it, she'd be betraying her parents by moving on as though they'd never existed. If she refused to accept it, she'd run the risk of him ending things with her.

She knew she had to talk to him about this—about everything—but she didn't know how. For him to understand why she'd done what she had, he would have to understand her feelings about her parents. Sofia didn't understand those fully herself.

"Are you going to answer that?" Martina asked over dinner when Sofia's phone rang for the third time that hour.

"No." Sofia continued eating as though her phone wasn't ringing—as though she hadn't heard anything at all.

"You're being stupid," Benny said, as diplomatically as ever.

Sofia didn't respond.

Later, Patrick abandoned his efforts to call and tried texting instead.

Can we talk?

Sofia didn't answer. She turned off her phone, because every time he tried to contact her, it was hard to breathe. She really needed to just breathe.

CALLING WASN'T WORKING. Texting hadn't worked, either. Patrick considered his options and decided to go over there. He figured he would be much harder to ignore in person.

It was around eight p.m., so there was a high likelihood of someone being home. He needed to clear some things up, and he needed to do it today.

A light shone through the front window as he parked his car, and he could see someone moving around in there. He didn't see Sofia's motorcycle at first, but then he noticed it parked a few houses down on the curb.

So, she was there. Good.

His stomach felt unsteady, and he was sweating. He doubted he would be this nervous even if he had been trying to propose to her.

He turned off the car, walked up the porch steps, and knocked firmly before he could talk himself out of it.

The door opened, and Martina was standing there wearing some long, flowing top over leggings. Her hair was in two high knots on either side of her head.

"Oh," she said.

"Is Sofia here?" His voice sounded steady, he thought, so that was good.

She didn't answer, but she stepped back and held the door open wider so he could come in.

He'd caught the women in the middle of cleaning up after dinner. Bianca was at the sink rinsing dishes, Benny was putting plastic wrap over a ceramic dish, and Sofia was holding two plates smeared with red sauce in her hands.

"Ah ... Sofia. Hi. I was wondering ... Could we talk?"

The look on her face was everything at once: surprised, hurt, vulnerable, dismayed. And it was possible that, underneath it all, he might have seen a little bit of love.

"Patrick." It was all she said—just his name. It sounded like a plea.

"I'm sorry to disturb everyone, but ..."

Bianca was the one who took charge. "Hey, Benny, Martina? Could you help me in the other room with the ... you know. The thing I need help with?" The three of them scrambled off into Bianca's room, sneaking looks over their shoulders at Sofia.

When they were alone, Patrick approached her carefully, as though she were a small woodland creature who might easily be startled into fleeing. "I tried to call you."

"I know." She was still holding the plates in her hands.

"And I tried to text."

"I saw that." She didn't offer any explanation for why she hadn't answered him.

He had several options for how he could start the conversation: *Why did you leave? Are you okay? What can I do to fix this?* Instead of any of those things, he said, "It wasn't a ring."

She blinked a few times, then seemed to realize for the first time that she was still holding the plates. She put them down and wiped her hands on a dish towel.

"It wasn't?"

"No."

"But, the box ..."

"They didn't have the right size box, so they gave me a different one. I never thought about that, about what you would think."

"Oh." She was still standing in the kitchen, with Patrick more than ten feet away. He didn't make an attempt to close the distance, and neither did she.

"Are you ... Are you pregnant?" There. He'd finally gotten out the question that he most wanted the answer to. He was shaking a little just asking it.

"No. I thought I might be, but no. I'm not."

A rush of conflicting feelings flowed through him, and he could barely identify all of them. Relief? Disappointment? Elation? Sorrow?

"Ah. That's ... Look, Sofia, can we just get past this? Can we just ... pretend it didn't happen and start over?"

"I want to, but ..." She was struggling with what to say—he could see it in her eyes, in the way she held her body. He thought for a moment that she was going to shut down on him again. Instead, she said, "I want to be someone who can think they're getting a ring and be happy about it. I want that, Patrick. And part of me *was* happy, but another part ..." She shook her head in frustration. "I have all these feelings, and I don't even understand them. They're all tangled up, and it hurts." She pressed a fist to her breastbone. "Being happy hurts."

It was more than she'd ever said to him about her emotions. She was trying—he could see that. And yet, none of what she'd said sounded promising for him. And none of it made sense.

"So where does that leave us?"

"I don't know." She picked up the dish towel again and wrung it between her fists.

"Sofia—"

"You're not the one who caused this, Patrick, and you're not the one who should have to fix it." She took a few steps toward him, but didn't completely close the distance. "I just ... I need you to give me time."

"All right. I can back off. I can let you figure it out without pressuring you about it. Let's just go back to my place and get a good night's sleep, and—"

"No." She shook her head. "I need you to give me time *alone*, Patrick."

"Oh." He felt as though he'd been slapped. He left her standing there and turned to walk out the door.

HE WALKED out to the car feeling sick and miserable. What did she mean that being happy hurt? What was he supposed to do with that? He was confident that she loved him, and he knew he loved her. So why couldn't they just be together? Why couldn't they just enjoy what they had?

The front door opened, and Bianca came out and hurried over to him. "Can we talk a minute?"

"Ah ... of course. Yes."

The night was cold, so they both got into his car, and he started the engine and turned on the heater.

"Patrick, this isn't about you." Bianca clearly meant it to be comforting, but it wasn't.

"It is about me, though," he said. "Isn't it? Otherwise, I wouldn't feel so terrible right now."

"Point taken."

"I know it's about your parents," he said. "But I don't know how to get her past this."

"You can't get her past it," Bianca said. "She has to get past it herself. If you push her, she's just going to run farther away."

He rubbed his face with his hands, suddenly feeling older than he had just a couple of days earlier. "I can't just do nothing."

"I think you have to," she said. "For now, anyway."

He'd managed to hold back his frustration until now, but he couldn't anymore, and it came rushing out. "I wasn't even going to propose! I mean, that's what spooked her, right? But it wasn't a ring! It was a necklace! For God's sake, I should have just gotten her a ... a sweater, or a purse, or a gift card or something, and none of this would have happened."

And that reminded him of the other thing he needed to do. He reached into the backseat of the car and pulled out the wrapped gift that Sofia had intended to give him.

"Here." He handed it to Bianca. "Give this back to Sofia. I'm not sure she even wants me to have it anymore."

Bianca took the package and turned it over in her hands. "She never gave it to you?"

"She left before she had the chance."

She handed it back to him. "Open it."

"But …"

"Just open it."

He carefully untied the ribbon and tore off the wrapping paper. He recognized the book immediately. It was Sofia's mother's first-edition *To Kill a Mockingbird*. It was valuable in its own right, even before he considered the sentimental value to the family.

He opened the front cover and read an inscription that had been written to Carmela from the suitor who'd given it to her.

"I can't keep this." He pushed the book back into Bianca's hands.

"Yes, you can."

"But it's important to your family. It's—"

"That's why I want you to keep it. This is how Sofia feels about you. This is how important you are to her. She was going to give you this. You know she would never give this to someone she didn't think would be a permanent part of her life. And the rest of us would never have agreed to it if we hadn't thought you were the one."

He looked at the book and then at Bianca. "But she didn't give it to me. Did she?"

"Keep the book," Bianca said. "If things don't work out between you and Sofia, you can give it back. Think of it as a bet. I'm putting my money on you." She reached over and kissed him on the cheek, then got out of the car. "Hang in there, Patrick."

He watched her go back up the walk and disappear into the house.

31

———

The New Year came and went, and Patrick had to go back to work. Winter break was over, and he had to think about launching the new semester. It was his least favorite part of any school year: the paperwork; students pleading with him to be let into classes that were already full; the flood of questions that were transparently designed to determine how little work a student could do while still passing his class; the angry complaints from students who hadn't attended the first week of classes but were outraged at having been dropped.

As much as he usually dreaded all of that, this time, it was something of a relief. The more he had to think about his classes and his students—and even the bureaucratic red tape—the less time he had to think about Sofia.

Not that he actually could accomplish the feat of getting his mind off her.

He did a pretty good job of focusing on work during the school day, but as soon as he got home, everything reminded him of her: a show on television that she'd particularly enjoyed; the box of tea in the pantry that he'd bought because she liked it; the way it felt to lie in his bed alone.

At first, he'd tried avoiding the things that reminded him. When that hadn't worked, he decided to take the opposite approach: he threw himself into his memories of her.

He had set aside the poetry he'd been writing for her, but now he was working on it again. She might never read it now, but that wasn't the point. Patrick had always best understood his own feelings when he saw them in writing. The images, the couplets, the very flavor of the words on his tongue when he spoke them aloud helped him to process everything that had happened.

He wouldn't die without her—that was part of what he came to understand as he crafted each line. The feelings he had for her were sweet and painful and gorgeous in their intensity, and that, alone, was a thing worth experiencing, whether she chose to come back to him or not.

But he really hoped she would.

He was following Bianca's advice because she knew Sofia even better than he did, and she seemed to be on his side in this. He was letting Sofia process things in her own time.

But he didn't know how much longer he could stay away. What if Bianca was wrong? What if Sofia interpreted his silence as indifference? What if she thought his primary emotion wasn't sadness or love, but anger? What if she thought he was through with her?

"Maybe I'm doing this wrong," he told Ramon one day when they met for coffee after his midmorning class. "Maybe I should go over there and make her listen to me."

"Maybe." Ramon was unusually subdued. Where was his easy confidence that he had all the answers?

"That's all you have to say about it? 'Maybe'?"

"If you'd asked me for advice before, I'd have told you not to put anything in a ring box except a ring. But now? I've got nothing."

According to Sofia's sisters, her default mode in any uncomfortable situation was to ignore and avoid whatever was bothering her.

Maybe they were right. She knew she needed to be working through whatever she needed to work through, but she didn't know how to start, and it was so much easier not to face it at all.

As a result, Sofia had exactly three priorities in the days and weeks following Christmas:

1. Don't think about Patrick.

2. Don't talk about Patrick.

3. Don't let anyone else think or talk about Patrick.

The first two were hard enough to accomplish, but the last one was impossible. Bianca, in particular, proved stubborn on the matter.

"When are you going to talk to him?" she asked one Tuesday in January while the office was closed for lunch.

"Talk to who?" Sofia asked. Of course, she was being intentionally dense to annoy her sister.

"It's *whom*," Bianca said. "And you know exactly who I'm talking about."

"Didn't you mean to say *about whom I'm talking*?" Sofia was unable to resist the taunt.

"Shut up. You're being an ass. He doesn't deserve this."

Bianca was right. Patrick didn't deserve this. He deserved much better than an emotionally stunted woman who couldn't express her feelings, who couldn't even properly grieve her parents.

A week later, when Sofia still hadn't talked about it, Bianca came to her at the medical office and slapped a piece of paper onto the desk in front of her. It was a flyer advertising a grief support group.

"You need to go to this." Her big-sister voice shut down any possibility of an argument.

Sofia tried arguing anyway. "Whatever's going on between me and Patrick is none of your—"

"This isn't about Patrick," Bianca said. "It's about you. This has gone on long enough. You need to go."

Then she'd gone into her office and closed the door.

Sofia's impulse was to crumple up the flyer and throw it into the wastebasket. Instead, she made herself look at it. The group met at a church in San Luis Obispo on Wednesday evenings.

She didn't want to go.

If she went, she'd be expected to talk about her feelings. Talking about them would feed them, and they would come roaring to life, uncontrollable, destructive and threatening.

Was it possible, though, that it might not work that way? Was it possible that the opposite might be true?

She didn't go the next night, and she didn't go the Wednesday after that. But she didn't throw the flyer away.

"Have you thought about it?" Bianca asked one night at dinner. She didn't have to say what she was talking about.

"I'm considering it."

Bianca's eyes widened in surprise. "Are you? Well, that's something."

~

THE WEDNESDAY she finally decided to go, all three of her sisters offered to go with her for moral support. They'd been through the same grief Sofia had, they reasoned. Maybe the group would have something to offer them, too.

But Sofia turned them down. Having them there would make her too self-conscious. Besides, their grief wasn't the same as hers. Yes, it had been just as devastating. But the three of them were models for how to handle their sorrow. All of them had cried, talked, shared their feelings. And they'd continued to function normally.

Sofia was the only one who seemed to be stunted by her loss. She was the only one who couldn't seem to accept love in the wake of her parents' deaths. It was probably time to find out why, but that didn't mean she needed her sisters hovering over her as she did it.

"I'll be fine," she told them on a Wednesday in late January when she finally got up the nerve to attend the group. "Don't worry. I can do this."

It sounded good, but privately, she didn't know if she believed it. Maybe she wasn't up to it. Maybe she was too broken to recover.

THE GROUP GATHERED in a church meeting room, a bland, utilitarian space with folding tables and molded plastic chairs. The tables had been shoved against the wall, and the chairs had been arranged in a circle in the center of the room. An urn of coffee stood on a counter next to a plate of grocery store cookies.

She told them her name—that was all. They invited her to talk, but she didn't. She couldn't. But she didn't flee, and that was something. She stayed until the end, then left as soon as the meeting broke up so she wouldn't have to field any questions.

Afterward, she was a little bit ashamed of herself. Why hadn't she been able to talk? Why couldn't she have at least said the minimum— that she'd lost her parents, and that, as a result, she'd deliberately sabotaged the most promising romantic relationship she'd ever had?

Baby steps, she reminded herself. And then she went back the next week.

32

Patrick still had the necklace, and he wasn't sure what to do with it. He could return it to the store. He could sell it on eBay. He'd hoped to simply hold it until he and Sofia got back together, but he was growing increasingly pessimistic about that happening.

He was giving her space, the way she'd asked him to do. He'd been waiting patiently. But the waiting was, more and more, starting to feel like giving up.

Patrick knew he should return the necklace, stop thinking about Sofia, and move on. But he didn't want to move on.

Moving on sucked.

Alone in his cottage after work, as the sun fell in the sky and the shadows lengthened, he found the little, wrapped box in the bottom of his sock drawer and took it out. He looked at it and thought about how Christmas should have been: He should have given her the gift, and she should have opened it. They should have kissed. It should have been the first of many holidays they would spend together, spanning years, decades. A lifetime.

He wouldn't have any of that, maybe, but Sofia could still have this one gift he'd selected for her, this one thing he'd chosen with his heart.

Maybe giving her the gift wasn't waiting, the way he was supposed to do. Maybe it wasn't giving her space. But he wanted her to have it. And, if he were being honest, that was an excuse. He just needed to see her face again, even if it was for the last time.

HE THOUGHT about going to her house to do it. But the risk in that scenario was high. If all three of Sofia's sisters thought he needed to wait quietly for her to come back to him, any one of them was likely to stop him at the front door and turn him away. And even if they didn't, they were certainly going to ask him to leave at the first sign that Sofia didn't want to see him.

The other option was to catch her as she was leaving work. Yes, Bianca would be there. But if they didn't leave the office together, then he might catch Sofia alone. And even if they did leave together, dealing with one sister was better than dealing with three.

He drove to the medical park at 4:45, because the website said Bianca's office closed at five. He saw Sofia's motorcycle in the parking lot—that was a good sign. He positioned his car in a spot behind a tree so he could be inconspicuous if Bianca came out first.

He waited, feeling like a private investigator or maybe a stalker, as five o'clock came and went. Patients and their parents came out and went to their cars. A woman Patrick recognized as Bianca's nurse emerged, got into a Honda Civic, and drove away.

Bianca came out at about 5:10. He was grateful that she didn't notice him.

Patrick was just starting to wonder whether Sofia had even worked that day, and whether it was someone else's bike he'd seen, when she came out of the building and started walking across the parking lot.

He wasn't prepared for seeing her again after so long. It felt like a hard punch to the gut—the knowledge that she was it for him and there was no moving on. Not now, not ever. He would wait for her forever if he had to. It was impossible to do anything else.

But, God, he hoped he wouldn't have to wait forever.

He was so stunned with love that he almost forgot to get out of the car. But at the last minute, as she was getting ready to put on her helmet, he got out and walked toward her, his heart pounding.

"Sofia."

She looked up in surprise, and the expression on her face broke his heart: a combination of love, joy, fear, and sorrow. He could see it all in the way her eyes grew wide, in the set of her chin. She still wanted him. She just didn't know how to be with him.

"Patrick." In the space of a second she gathered herself and shut down. "I was just leaving."

"I'll only take a minute." He pulled the gift out of his pocket and held it out to her. "I didn't know what to do with this. I bought it for you, so ... I want you to have it."

"Patrick ..."

"In retrospect, I can see why you thought it might be a ring. The box size ... I should have seen that coming. If I'd known what would happen, I would have bought you something big. A refrigerator, maybe, or a large-screen TV." His attempt at humor sounded lame even to himself. He swallowed hard. "Just ... please, take it."

She took the package from him and looked at it but made no move to open it.

"All right, well ... I'll just go." He turned and started to walk to his car.

"Patrick."

He paused and waited.

"I'm trying," she said. "I'm working on this. On myself."

He felt a surge of reckless hope. "What are you saying?"

"I'm saying ... don't give up on me yet."

"Never," he said. And he meant it. As long as there was a chance, he would hold onto it as though he were clinging to his own life. Because that felt like what he was doing, exactly.

❧

IT WASN'T the support group meeting itself that made a difference for Sofia. It was what happened after the meetings.

She still hadn't talked to the group, but she'd stopped fleeing immediately after the meeting broke up, and she'd begun to make a habit of staying afterward for coffee and cookies, chatting a little with members of the group, excusing herself when it began to get personal.

One week, she was approached by an older blond woman she'd seen a few times. The woman's name was Debra, she recalled, though Sofia couldn't remember any details of why she was here.

They held cookies sprinkled in green sugar and Styrofoam cups of substandard coffee and chatted about the weather, a new grocery store that had opened in Morro Bay, the best place to get a good pizza with just the right amount of cheese.

Then, just as Sofia was preparing to excuse herself, the woman leaned forward and said, "You're doing fine, you know. It seems like a little thing—just showing up every week—but it's not a little thing. You'll talk about it when you're ready, sweetie."

That bit of validation shouldn't have been a big deal, but for some reason, it was. Sofia's eyes felt hot, though no tears came.

She excused herself and left before anything more could be said, but the next Wednesday, she sought out the same woman again.

"Thank you for what you said last week," Sofia told her.

"Oh, well." Debra shrugged. "Sometimes you just have to hear that what you're doing is enough."

They chatted for a while about something in the news—a storm that was due to hit in a few days—and then Debra looked ruefully into her coffee cup and said, "You know, this stuff is crap. You want to go get some decent coffee?"

Much to her own surprise, Sofia said yes, she'd like that very much.

～

MAYBE IT WAS the fact that Debra didn't ask any questions. Maybe it was the fact that she was a relative stranger who had no expectations, no preconceived notions about Sofia and her family. Maybe it was the fact that the woman reminded Sofia a little bit of her mom.

Whatever it was, Sofia found herself sitting at a café table across from the woman and talking—really talking—about her parents.

She'd never said more than she had to about her parents' deaths —not to Patrick, not even to her sisters. But here she was, talking to this soft-looking fiftysomething woman with her long, acrylic nails, her bleached hair, and her cheap sweater, telling her more than she'd ever said to anyone.

"Bianca and Benny think my father's death was suicide, and Martina thinks it was an accident that happened because he was exhausted," Sofia said, wrapping up that part of the story. She hadn't yet touched on her problems with Patrick.

"And what do you think?"

"I don't know." Sofia looked down into her coffee to avoid Debra's eyes.

"But you've got an idea," Debra said. "What do you think?"

Sofia couldn't say what she was really thinking. She'd never said it, possibly never would say it. The words were locked inside her mind in some dark passageway with no exit to the outside world. What she did say was this:

"I think ... I think I was the last person to talk to him before he died."

Sudden comprehension dawned on Debra's face. "Oh, honey. You think he did it on purpose, and you think you could have said something to change his mind. Don't you?"

Sofia didn't answer.

"You're wrong, Sofia. The first part, who knows? Maybe no one will ever know why it happened. But the second part? It wasn't your fault. He didn't do it because of you. No part of it was your fault."

How could she know that, though? Sofia had clashed with her father often, and she'd done it again that day. She'd been angry because her mother had chosen to stop treatment when it became clear that the cancer was terminal. How had he let her do it? Why hadn't he insisted that she keep fighting?

She'd never said Carmela's death was his fault—not in so many words. But when he'd insisted that there had been no other choice, she hadn't answered him. Then, when he'd said he loved her before hanging up the phone, she hadn't said she loved him, too. She'd simply said goodbye.

Nobody knew about that—not her sisters, not anyone. If they knew, they might hate her the way she hated herself.

"I lost my son to suicide." Debra reached out and put her hand over Sofia's on the table. "I have to believe it wasn't my fault, no matter what I might have said or forgotten to say."

Sofia felt sudden shame that she hadn't even asked—she hadn't even thought about what kind of pain the older woman might have been experiencing. She'd been too focused on her own.

"I'm so sorry." Tears shimmered in Sofia's eyes, and they were the first tears—the very first—since her mother's death. They weren't the cry she knew she needed to have—the big, full-bodied weeping that she suspected would finally make her feel better—but they were something.

33

It wasn't until after her conversation with Debra that Sofia could bring herself to open Patrick's gift. She opened it alone in her room late that night. She untied the ribbon, tore the paper, and opened the tiny box.

She took out the gold chain and draped it over her hand so she could get a good look at the pendant. It was simple, classic, and lovely.

Sofia imagined Patrick choosing it for her, trying to find just the right thing. She imagined him selecting it with care. And with love.

And what had she done? She refused it and ran away. He hadn't deserved that from her. He'd deserved so much better.

She opened the tiny clasp and put on the necklace, then looked at herself in the mirror, at the way the gold disc lay against her olive-hued skin.

Sofia sat down on the bed, picked up her cell phone from the side table, and called him.

"Thank you," she said when he answered. "I opened your gift. It's lovely."

"Oh. I'm glad. You're welcome."

She'd wondered if she would hear anger or irritation in his voice because she'd waited so long to call him, but she heard none of that. Instead, he sounded surprised and happy to hear from her.

"I'm sorry for the way I left. For how I acted. I should have just talked to you."

"Well," he said, "that would have been an option."

Warmth spread through her at the sound of his voice. Suddenly, she couldn't remember why she'd waited so long—why she'd insisted on staying away.

"We could try it," she said. "Just to see."

"We could," he agreed. "Just to see."

She wanted to see him now, this moment, but it was late. "Maybe tomorrow?"

"I'll see if I can clear my schedule." He was teasing her, and she smiled.

THEY MET at Jitters after Patrick finished with his classes. Technically, Sofia should have been at work, but when Bianca had heard that she was planning to see Patrick, she'd shooed her out of the office, claiming they could get along without her for the last couple of hours of the day. Sofia had protested, but Bianca had practically shoved her out the door.

Actually, Sofia was pleased with the way it was working out. Seeing Patrick for an afternoon coffee date was so much less pressure than seeing him in the evening, for dinner or for whatever might come after dinner. Her relationship with him had gone so far off the rails that she had to ease her way back into it.

At least, that's what she told herself. But a big part of her didn't want to ease back into anything. That part of her wanted to leap back into things—especially his bed. She hadn't realized how much she missed him until she made plans to see him again. Now, she was nearly giddy with anticipation. She just hoped she hadn't waited too long.

She hoped it wasn't too late.

He was waiting for her at a table near the back of the room when she arrived at the coffee house. It was raining, and the place smelled of fresh-ground coffee and wet shoes. Patrick was still wearing his jacket, which was speckled with raindrops. She wondered if he'd kept it on because he was planning to make a quick exit.

He stood up when he saw her. The look on his face made the butterflies in her stomach flap their tiny wings. He looked nervous, excited—and lovestruck.

"Sofia. Hi." He pulled out a chair for her, and they both sat.

Two steaming cups already sat on the table: a latte for him, and a mocha—her favorite—for her.

"I already ordered for you." He nodded toward her cup. "But if you want something different ..."

"No. This is great. Thank you."

An awkward silence fell between them, and Sofia began to think this wasn't going to be as easy as she'd hoped.

"I wondered," she said, "that is, I thought ..." She wrapped her hands around her mug, looking into the puff of whipped cream on her mocha and not at him. "Maybe we could try again. Or, really, I would be the one trying. Because you didn't do anything wrong. It was all me, and I—"

"Sofia."

She stopped talking and looked at him, and what she saw in his face scared her.

"Please don't say no." Her voice broke a little when she said it.

"I'm not saying no." He reached out and took her hand. "I'm saying we have to talk. Because something upset you at Christmas, and I know some of what that was, but I don't know all of it. And I don't know if it's going to happen again."

Sofia nodded. "That's fair."

"So? Will you talk to me? Will you tell me what happened to make you run out of there the way you did?"

She tried, but the words didn't come.

"I want to," she told him. "But ... it's not what I do. It's not how I deal with things. I ... I haven't had a lot of practice."

"So, that's it, then? You won't talk about it?" He looked so sad, and she didn't like to see him looking sad.

"I didn't say I won't. What I'm saying is … it's hard."

"All right." He nodded. "Hard's not the same as impossible. We can deal with hard."

SHE TOLD him the story of her parents' deaths. He already knew—he'd heard it from Bianca—but this was the first time he'd heard it from Sofia. They sat in the warm, dry café and sipped their drinks, and she talked while he listened.

That was as far as it went; just the story of how they'd died. Sofia didn't talk about how she felt about it. She didn't entirely know how she felt. Just telling him what had happened—without embellishment—made her feel a tight weight on her chest that made it hard to breathe. But it was a first step.

After she stopped talking, he took a moment to absorb what she'd told him. "I can understand why Christmas was hard for you. I mean … my God. But what was it about the gift in particular that made you run out of there? I know you thought it was a ring, but … why did that upset you so much? Is the idea of marrying me completely off the table?"

Was it? She hadn't considered the question in exactly that way. Did she want to marry him someday, at some point? Or *was* it completely off the table? If it was, he deserved to know. But how could she ever tell him that, knowing what it would mean? Knowing that he'd be wise to move on and find someone else who did want a life with him?

The thought of him moving on, finding someone else, and springing a tiny box on her that actually did contain a ring made Sofia sick with despair.

"It's … it's not completely off the table."

He visibly relaxed, his shoulders falling from where they'd been hovering up near his ears. "Okay. Good. That's … that's very good."

~

OF COURSE, Patrick could wait for marriage. Their relationship was relatively new, and Sofia obviously wasn't ready. But when he looked at her, he saw it all: a house, kids, a dog. The two of them easing into old age together, the family gatherings, the anniversaries. And he wanted it. He wanted everything.

If she'd said it was off the table, he didn't know if he'd have been able to walk away. He was in this too deep. But it would have gutted him. It would have tormented him.

"But if it's not a hard no, then ..." He left the question out there: Why had she run? Why had the possibility of a ring caused her to flee across the country just to avoid it?

Sofia grasped his hands on the tabletop. "Could we maybe leave it for now? I know you deserve an answer, but I just can't. Telling you what I've told you ... It's all I can do right now."

She was pleading with him. He could see that she was desperate for this conversation to be over.

So he changed the subject. Sofia's relief was palpable, but Patrick didn't know how to feel. They'd made progress, yes. But there was still so much she couldn't, or wouldn't, tell him. There was still a big, dark, important part of her she wouldn't let him know.

They could let it go for now, but they couldn't let it go forever. This would have to be resolved. Either she would let him in, or their relationship would remain stalled here, right where it was.

It wasn't enough for Patrick to be kept locked on the other side of a door from Sofia's most closely held emotions.

He wanted to be let in.

~

"SO, she told me that much, but then she just shut down. As though that was all she could do. Honestly, I don't know where that leaves us." Patrick and Ramon were hiking on a strikingly clear Saturday morning at Fiscalini Ranch, with the smell of the ocean in the air and the sky a blue so crisp and bright it could have been painted on.

"But she said marriage isn't off the table," Ramon pointed out. "So that's good."

"Yeah, I don't know about that." Patrick rubbed the back of his neck with his hand. "It's clearly not *on* the table, either. And she still won't tell me what she's thinking. She told me the history—the facts about what happened to whom and when—but not a word about how she feels."

Ramon made a scoffing sound. "Talking about feelings is overrated. I think you're looking at this all wrong. Ask nine out of ten guys, they'll tell you that having a relationship with a woman who doesn't talk about feelings is like winning the freaking lottery."

"Well ... I'm the tenth guy," Patrick said.

"Yeah. You are. And that's your problem."

They'd climbed the hill from the bluffs and were heading into the forest at the top of the rise. Patrick had continued working out since he'd met Sofia, and he was breathing easily, a light sheen of sweat on his skin. Four months ago, he'd have been near collapse. Just one of the many ways his relationship with Sofia had enriched his life.

"It's not a relationship if we don't really know each other," Patrick concluded as they emerged onto a trail that wound through a stand of towering pines. "And right now, I feel like I don't really know her."

"But you said she doesn't talk to her sisters about this stuff either, right?" Ramon asked.

"Well ... that's true."

"Dude. She's closer to her sisters than she is to anybody else in the world."

"That's true," Patrick said again.

"Seems to me you might be low on patience and high on expectations."

It was a surprisingly insightful observation, coming from Ramon. Patrick resolved to think about whether he might be right.

"So?" Benny had Sofia cornered in the hallway, where she couldn't get away. "How did things go with Patrick? Are you two okay?"

"I don't know."

Benny scowled. "Oh, for God's sake, Sof, you won't even tell me that much? For the love of—"

"I'm not being evasive. I really don't know." Sofia had just come out of the shower, and she was wearing a fluffy bathrobe, her hair wrapped in a towel. Her feet were bare on the cool hardwood floor.

"Oh. How can you not know?"

Sofia shrugged. She'd been going over the same question in her mind—whether she and Patrick were okay—and she kept coming up with different interpretations of what had happened. They'd talked, and that was good. But she'd been unable to really open up to him, and that was bad. He'd asked if marriage was on the table—someday —and that was good. But she'd been visibly uncomfortable when he'd asked, and that was bad.

"There are issues," Sofia said, as though that explained everything.

"Of course there are issues. There are always issues." Benny waved her hands around impatiently. "The question is whether they're issues you can deal with."

Sofia wasn't sure whether they were. Patrick wanted the kind of woman who could open up about her feelings, pour them all out so he could understand and dissect them. She wasn't that kind of woman, and she wasn't sure she could become one. She didn't think there was anything wrong with that kind of openness, that kind of free exchange of thoughts and emotions. But she didn't know if she could do it, even for him.

"God, Benny. I just don't know. I don't know if I can give him what he wants."

"Kinky sex?" Benny said knowingly. "Maybe if you try a safe word—"

"Stop joking. This isn't funny."

"I know it's not." Benny put a soothing hand on Sofia's arm. "If it's any comfort, I know what the issues are. We've had those same issues with you since you learned to talk, and we still love you."

Sofia swallowed hard. What would she do without her sisters? Who would she be?

"But," Benny went on, "you might consider the idea that letting people into your little world might feel better than shutting them out. It's gotta get lonely in there sometimes."

34

It *was* getting lonely in there—very lonely—and Sofia was relieved when she and Patrick started seeing each other again. They started slowly—a dinner here, a lunch there.

Sofia was starting to despair, because it was clear Patrick was holding back. He took her home at the end of every date and chose not to come inside with her—even though she invited him in. When she asked to come back to his place, he made excuses about being tired or having to work the next day.

She knew he was protecting himself in case it didn't work, in case she ran again. So she tried to be patient and let him take his time.

At least, that was her intention. But the patience wore thin one night after they had dinner at Robin's. They sat in the garden with white fairy lights over their heads, and he barely spoke. He was polite—gentlemanly to a fault—but the tension between them was undeniable.

When he drove her home and walked her to the door, she turned to him and said, "Patrick? Are we wasting our time?"

"I don't know what you mean."

It was a lie, and it offended her. Because no matter how much she didn't say to him and he didn't say to her, he'd never lied to her.

"I'm talking about the silence!" she said. "I'm talking about the ... the *politeness*! And how you take me out but you don't want to be alone with me. Patrick ... is it over? Is that what's happening here?"

His eyes widened, and he paled a little in the porch light. "God, no. No! Is that what you thought?"

"I don't know what to think." Her heart was pounding, and her face felt hot. "All I know is that I'm lonely and I want you back. I want us back."

He looked away from her into the darkened yard. "I'm just not sure how much of an *us* there is, Sofia." He shoved his hands in his pockets, and the muscles in his jaw flexed. "There's you, and then there's me out here trying to get through a brick wall."

She wanted to be close to him, if not in the way he wanted her to be, then any way she could. She put her arms around him and pressed her lips to his. He was tense at first.

"Take me home with you," she said softly, her mouth so close to his that she could feel his breath on her cheek. "Please."

She felt it the moment he lost whatever battle he was fighting against himself. She kissed him, and he responded tentatively, holding himself in check. Then he relaxed, put his arms around her, and devoured her. The way he returned the kiss was ravenous, desperate.

"Please," she said again.

He took her hand, led her off of the porch and to his car, and took her home with him.

PATRICK HAD MEANT to keep things casual—keep Sofia at a distance—until she worked through whatever it was she needed to work through. They would date, they would talk, they would be together, but he would protect his heart until he knew which way this thing was going to go.

All of that had been shot to hell the moment she'd said *please*.

He'd have given her anything she wanted from him. When the thing she wanted was him, he didn't have a prayer of resisting.

As he drove toward his place with her hand resting lightly on his thigh, he wondered if he was making a mistake. He wondered if he would regret his inability to hold his ground. Maybe. But regrets would be for tomorrow. Today, he needed to be with her and forget everything that had gone wrong between them.

He parked, and they were out of the car when it had barely come to a stop. They rushed up the porch steps, and he pressed her against the front door and kissed her, his body pushed against her, his fingers entwined in hers.

No words passed between them—nothing since *please*—just electric heat. He pulled away from her long enough to unlock the door, then they were inside and on each other in a tangle of limbs and grasping hands and discarded clothes.

He had never wanted anyone the way he wanted Sofia. He hadn't known he could. Now that he did know, he feared that he'd lost all power to say no to her, even if it was right, even if it was what might save him.

He pushed her onto the bed in the dark room and let himself have everything he'd been denying himself, everything he'd been wanting. He touched her soft, smooth skin and tasted her, longing to possess every part of her.

His Sofia.

But she wasn't his, was she? She never would be until she decided to let him in. And what if she never did? What if she always kept him on the other side of some impenetrable wall?

Later. He would think of that later. Now, he only wanted this.

WHILE THEY WERE MAKING LOVE, Sofia let herself believe that this meant everything was okay again. Being with him felt as right as it ever had. Wasn't it possible that everything else about the two of them had been put right, too?

But afterward, when they were both lying amid a tangle of sheets, sated and breathless, he was too still and quiet, and she knew that nothing had been resolved.

She put her hand on his chest, but he didn't look at her. He stared at the ceiling, one arm folded behind his head.

"Patrick? Are you all right?"

"Of course."

"Are you sure?"

"Yes."

At that moment, if she could have said the things he needed her to say, she would have. But how could she explain things she didn't understand herself? How could she lay bare the emotions she hadn't yet excavated?

"Maybe I should go," she said.

"No." Now he did look at her, finally, in the dim moonlight filtering through the window. "No, I want you to stay." He lifted a hand and caressed her shoulder.

She curled her body up next to his and let him hold her, feeling uneasy, as though some unnamed damage had been done that was too late to repair.

IN THE MORNING, Patrick went to work while Sofia was still sleeping. He showered and dressed, then slipped out as quietly as he could so he wouldn't disturb her.

He thought about her as he drove to the university, as he stood in front of his classroom, as he worked in his office.

He wanted to tell himself that it was complicated, but it wasn't. Something simple had happened between himself and Sofia the night before. And that simple thing was that he'd surrendered.

He'd given up trying to distance himself from her. He'd given up trying to protect himself. He'd lost the battle to be all right without her, and he'd finally waved the white flag.

"You look like hell," Ramon told him when they passed each

other in the halls after Patrick's afternoon class. "Did something happen with you and Sofia?"

"We're fine," he said. "We're good."

Because what else could he say? Was he supposed to tell Ramon that he'd decided he didn't need a complete, emotionally intimate relationship after all? That he was so weak, so helpless when it came to her, that he'd settled for whatever scraps of herself she was willing to give him?

"You sure, man?" Ramon peered at him with concern. "Because if this is what you look like when you're good, I'd hate to see what happens when your dog dies."

"I don't have a dog."

"Small favors."

"Look, I've got to go," Patrick said. "I've got a meeting in ten."

He didn't have a meeting, but it seemed expedient to say so.

"Do you know how rare it is to find a man who actually wants to know about your feelings?" Debra shook her head and laughed. "Honey, he's not one in a million. He's probably one in ten million. What are you pushing him away for?"

Sofia and Debra had come to an all-night diner after the support group meeting ended, and they were seated in a booth with steaming mugs of coffee (Debra) and hot cocoa (Sofia). It was still early, so the place was busy with everything from couples to groups of teenagers getting endless refills of their soft drinks. Rain was pelting the windows, and the world outside shone with reflections of headlights on black pavement.

"I'm not pushing him away. Anymore, at least. I mean, yes, I was, but I'm past that now."

"Well, does he know that?"

Sofia's eyebrows rose. "Of course he does. What do you mean?"

"I mean, if you never really talked about what made you run away from him at Christmas, how can he be sure you're not going to do it again?"

Sofia's shoulders fell. "That's a valid point."

"If you feel like he's partially checked out, it's probably because he thinks you might sprint for the door again at a moment's notice, and he doesn't want to be squashed like a bug when you do." Debra stirred her coffee carefully with her spoon.

"At this point, it's almost harder to be with him than not to be, because I can tell he's unhappy." Sofia fixed her gaze on the Formica tabletop.

Debra took a noisy slurp of her coffee and put the mug back down. "Well, he's a grownup, so you're not responsible for his happiness. But you are responsible for yours."

For Sofia, it was starting to feel like pretty much the same thing.

"The interesting question," Debra went on, "is why you're more comfortable talking to me about these things than you are talking to him—or to your sisters, for that matter."

That one wasn't hard for Sofia to figure out. She could talk to Debra because the stakes were so low. She didn't live with this woman, didn't have any friends in common, and wasn't planning to someday—maybe—build a life with her. If Debra judged Sofia, there would be no consequences for either of them. But Sofia cared intensely about what her sisters and Patrick thought of her, and the idea that they might conclude that she was somehow damaged—or, worse, a bad person—was intolerable.

Which raised an important question: why didn't she trust them to love her?

It was the first time she'd thought of it in just that way, and the revelation made her blink like a baby bird first emerging from its protective shell.

"Uh oh," Debra said. "There's something going on in that head of yours."

"It's ... something good, I think," Sofia told her. "Important, even."

Debra nodded crisply, a whisper of a smile on her lips. "Well, there you go, then. Glad I could be of help."

THE NEXT TIME Sofia saw Patrick, she was ready. She'd worked up two important things to tell him, and she blurted them out the moment she got into his car.

"Okay. One: I'm pretty sure my father died thinking I hated him. And two: I can't imagine getting married when my parents are no longer living. It's just ... I try to picture it, and I can't. So, that's why I ran when I thought you were giving me a ring."

"Oh." Patrick gaped at her in surprise. Then his features softened, and he leaned forward to kiss her. "Thank you for telling me that. About your father—"

"I don't want you to tell me it's not true, because how could you know? You don't have to make me feel better about it, because I'm not going to. I just wanted to tell you."

They didn't talk about it any further, but she could feel a significant thaw between them. He was a little more relaxed, a little warmer. A little less tense and distant.

It was progress.

35

Patrick had continued working on his poetry, and he'd been even more productive with it since his problems with Sofia began. Now, the whole suite of poems was starting to take shape. He wasn't a poet—not really—but there was something here, in the words he'd written. He felt that he'd managed to communicate some essential truth about his feelings, apart from whatever artistry might or might not exist in his work.

Sitting in his cottage with his laptop, a mug of tea beside him and a fire burning in the fireplace, he thought about what to do with the poems.

They weren't good enough to be published, unless he went the self-publishing route, which he didn't think he would do. But they deserved better than to sit unread on his computer. Writing was an act of communication, after all, and communication required someone on both ends. His work could never truly *be* if no one read it —or heard it.

Besides, how could he expect Sofia to express herself if he wasn't willing to do the same? When he plunged into the ocean on the day he met her, he'd been brave enough to risk his life. Surely he could be brave enough to send his poetry out into the world.

He went online looking for an open mic poetry night, and it wasn't long before he found one coming up at a café in San Luis Obispo. There were a lot of them, actually—not surprising in an artsy university town.

Now all he had to do was screw up his courage enough to follow through.

～

PATRICK DECIDED his best bet was to stack the audience with people who might be sympathetic to him. So he invited not just Sofia, but also her sisters and Ramon and Lucy. With that many people he knew in the café, he figured he could count on a decent amount of polite applause even if he failed spectacularly.

And there was a very real chance that he might fail spectacularly.

He thought about practicing at home in front of a mirror, but he decided that would make him more nervous. Better to just show up and read his own words from the heart. Nobody would expect him to be a polished performer. This was a local open mic, not nationally televised prime-time programming.

Still, no number of internal pep talks could make him relax completely. He had the sense that a lot was at stake. Not just his own validation as a writer—though that did matter to him—but the expression of his true feelings to Sofia. How would she react when she heard everything that he really felt about her, himself, and their relationship? Because the poems didn't hold back. It was all in there: the love, the longing, the pain, the fear.

Speaking of fear, as the day of his reading drew closer, he began to grow more and more nervous until simple things like sleeping and eating became difficult.

Ramon stopped him in the college library the day before the big event as Patrick was on his way out.

"You ready for tomorrow? Any stage fright?" Ramon asked.

"Stage fright? No. More like outright terror."

Ramon scoffed. "What for? You talk in front of rooms full of people every day."

"Right. But I'm usually talking about other people's writing, not my own. And"—he cleared his throat—"I don't know how Sofia's going to react since the poetry's all about … well … basically, her."

"She doesn't know?" Ramon's eyebrows shot up.

"Well, no. I thought … I wanted to surprise her." That was one way to put it. He'd kept it a surprise because he'd feared that if she knew what he was going to say, she wouldn't want to come.

"Oh, boy," Ramon said.

"Yeah."

When he considered it, he didn't know what he was afraid of. He'd risked his life going kayaking just to meet her. He wasn't likely to die reciting his poetry—barring some unforeseen event like sudden cardiac arrest or the roof of the venue falling on top of him.

Still, risking his life was one thing. But the risk of losing Sofia's love? That was something else entirely.

SOFIA WAS DRESSED and ready for the poetry reading with plenty of time to spare. She couldn't say the same about her sisters.

Part of the problem was that there were four of them and only two bathrooms. And the other part was that both Bianca and Benny had just gotten home and were scurrying around trying to get themselves together so none of them would be late.

"Are you guys ready yet?" Sofia called down the hall toward Benny and Bianca's rooms. "God, hurry up. It's not prom night, it's a poetry reading. Nobody dresses up for a poetry reading!"

Sofia was wearing jeans, a sweater, and a black leather motorcycle jacket, with a pair of boots Patrick especially liked. She'd put on a little makeup and had brushed out her thick, wavy hair, but she hadn't gone to any special trouble.

Bianca and Benny, however, had been at it awhile. Benny was never particularly fussy in terms of her appearance, but she'd had to shower and change. Bianca had been bled on, puked on, and peed on by her various tiny patients, so obviously a certain amount of personal maintenance was in order before she could go out.

"Keep your pants on," Benny called to her. "This kind of magnificence takes time!"

"My pants are on!" Sofia yelled back. "They've been on for a good half hour now, which is more than I can say for you and yours."

She hadn't thought she was nervous, but she was beginning to realize that she was. She wanted Patrick's reading to go well. She knew he was worried about it, and that worry had spilled over onto her, making her feel it, too.

They'd agreed to go to the café separately so that Sofia could bring her sisters. Since it was an open mic format, it didn't matter if they were exactly on time; Patrick could just delay going on until they got there. Still, she didn't want him to have to do that. She didn't want him to sit there obsessing over where she was. He had enough on his mind already.

Martina, bless her, had been ready for twenty minutes. She was wearing a long, floaty dress, Birkenstock sandals, and some kind of head wrap she'd made herself out of hand-painted silk. So, that was one sister accounted for.

Benny came out of her room, finally, and Sofia herded her into the living room before she could reconsider her hair or her choice of T-shirt.

"Bianca!" she yelled. "We're all waiting for you!"

"Sorry. Sorry." Bianca came out of the bathroom fully dressed, with fresh makeup and newly blow-dried hair. She ducked into her room to grab her purse, then hurried out to join the rest of them. "I'm ready. Are we late?"

"Not yet." Sofia checked the time on her phone. "But we'd better get out of here, or we will be. I don't want him to get there before us and worry about where we are."

"Aww," Martina said. "You're nervous for your man! That's really cute."

"Shut up," Sofia said.

"It is kind of cute," Benny put in. "She's not wrong."

As much as she usually enjoyed being patronized, Sofia hustled everybody out to Bianca's car before they could dissect her behavior any further.

"Come on, come on," she told them. "Buckle up. I don't have all day."

"Cute," Bianca said, agreeing with the others.

THE CAFÉ WAS MAINLY a coffee place, but the last thing Patrick needed at the moment was caffeine. The place also had a few types of craft beer, though, and Patrick let Ramon talk him into having a pint, even though he rarely drank.

Anything that might relax him had to be a good thing.

"They're not here yet." Patrick looked at the door. He, Ramon, and Lucy were seated at a big table off to the side of the room, near the stage. They'd saved four seats for the Russos, and he was anxiously watching for their arrival.

"They'll be here," Ramon said.

"But it's already 7:05, and—"

"Believe me." Lucy interrupted him. "A woman doesn't want to miss her boo reciting poetry. Especially when he wrote it himself."

Normally, he might have launched into a conversation about whether the word *boo* was appropriate to use in terms unrelated to cartoon ghosts, but this wasn't the time for that. He was holding himself together by pure grit and determination.

"There you go," Ramon said as Sofia, Benny, Bianca, and Martina walked in the door in a burst of color and that special female magic they all seemed to have. Patrick looked over and his entire body and soul seemed to sigh in relief.

"Oh, boy," Lucy said.

"I ... what?" Patrick tore his gaze away from Sofia to address Lucy.

"The way you were looking at her. Just ... oh, boy."

SOFIA SAW IT, too—the way he was looking at her when she came into the room. He had the look of someone who was utterly and hopelessly drowning in love.

The thought that he felt that way for her, despite the way she'd held him at a distance, humbled her. She didn't deserve to be the one who'd put that look in his eyes. She hoped that one day, she would.

Ramon was the one who got up from the table and ushered them to the seats that had been saved for them. Patrick would have done it, under normal circumstances, but today it was all he could do just to handle his nerves.

Sofia went to him and gave him a quick kiss. "How are you doing?"

"Ah ... okay, I guess. No major coronary malfunction yet, so that's good."

Sofia's sisters called out their greetings to him before choosing their seats. They ordered drinks and settled in. The café had a pretty good crowd, and the mood was festive. If Patrick hadn't looked like he might faint, Sofia would have thought it had all the makings of a fun night out. Maybe it did anyway. Surely he'd settle down after his reading, when the pressure was gone.

"Are you sure you're okay?" Sofia leaned toward Patrick and took his hand. He squeezed hers and nodded.

"Yes. I'm fine. I'm ... yes."

He clearly wasn't, but there was nothing to do about it but wait for his turn on the stage. They drank and talked and listened to random people read their poetry, with mixed results.

Finally, about an hour after they arrived, it was Patrick's turn. He got up, looking shaky, gathered the note cards he'd brought, and took the stage—actually, a wooden platform that had been set up at one side of the café with a microphone on a stand.

Sofia didn't know what his poems were about, because he'd refused to tell her. She'd asked—had wanted to read them, in fact—but he had said they weren't ready. She had imagined that one or two might have veiled references to her, but when he actually read the words, when the rhymes and metaphors and the imagery sank in, she was stunned senseless.

It was all about her.

Every word, every syllable.

"Oh, my God," she said under her breath.

Bianca reached out and grabbed Sofia's hand.

AT FIRST, he was so nervous that the words wouldn't come. He opened his mouth to speak but nothing came out. But he tried again and began to find his voice. He sounded shaky at first to his own ears, but as he read the lines he'd worked so hard on for the past months, he began to feel better, stronger. More steady.

As he read, the words he'd been so worried about, concerned that they were weak or wrong or somehow inadequate, began to feel exactly right. The truth in them pushed through his nerves, through his insecurity, and filled the room with his own pure feeling.

The first couple of poems were simple, with imagery about longing, loneliness, and the initial spark of desire that built into a consuming flame when they met.

Then, like the movements of a symphony, the mood changed. The words about love and destiny mingled with imagery about pain and loss and the torture of unfulfilled need.

It was everything he needed to say to her, and he hoped she was listening.

WAS this how she'd made him feel? The surprise of that hit Sofia like a slap.

Of course she'd known that she'd hurt him when she'd run away at Christmas, and especially when she'd stayed away, holding him apart from her for so long. But knowing that was one thing. *Feeling* it the way his poetry made her feel it—that made her almost breathless with regret.

The final poem, titled "The World is Not Mine," was what finally undid her. In it, he wove together bits of imagery about his feelings for Sofia and about grief: his own over his inability to fully connect with her, and hers over the loss of her parents. It began with the soaring emotion of love and commitment and the contentment of belonging, then crashed to earth with the devastation of irrevocable loss.

Halfway through, Sofia's first tear fell.

She hadn't known she was still capable of crying, because if she hadn't managed it when she'd lost her parents, then what in her life could ever inspire such a thing again?

The sensation was so unfamiliar to her that she barely recognized it when it happened. A heat behind her eyes, a swell of emotion, then that first tear sliding down her cheek.

Once it began, there was no stopping it.

More tears came, then Sofia began to sniffle. Then, before she knew what was happening, she was heaving great, choking sobs. She felt someone's hand on her shoulder—maybe Bianca's—and she was aware that people were looking at her. She got up from the table and walked to the ladies' room. It was an effort not to run.

The bathroom was a one-person affair with no stalls, so she locked the door behind her and sat down on the closed lid of the toilet, her shoulders heaving, tears racking her.

She wasn't crying about one thing, but about everything. Her mother and father, and how much she missed them. Patrick, and how she'd hurt him. Her sisters, and how she'd shut them out when she should have been turning to them for comfort and support.

Those last, awful words she'd said to her father.

As she sat there and let all of her pent-up fears and sorrows and frustrations go, a surprising thing happened. The huge tide of her emotion should have drowned her, but instead, it began to wash her clean.

The relief was both immense and unexpected.

She felt as though some dark beast had been living silently inside her, and now it was leaving—with a fair amount of storm and noise, but leaving nonetheless.

She heard a knock on the door and worried that it might be some unfortunate café patron who needed to use the facilities. Then she heard Bianca calling to her.

"Sof? Are you okay? Let me in, all right?"

Before, her instinct would have been to ignore Bianca and continue to close her out. Instead, she got up on shaky legs and went to unlock the door.

"Well." Sofia let Bianca in and wiped at her eyes, taking in a shaky breath. "He can really write, can't he?"

"I guess so. And whoever he wrote all of that about, she's a lucky woman," Bianca said. "I just wish we knew who it was."

Sofia let out a laugh and smacked her sister on the arm. "Shut up."

Bianca grinned and pulled Sofia into a hug. For the first time in more than a year, Sofia let her do it.

"This is good, you know?" Bianca held onto Sofia fiercely. "You letting all of this out. It's good."

"I know." Sofia pulled away, grabbed some tissue from the roll, and blew her nose noisily. "I know it is."

"And, Sofia? Whatever you've been punishing yourself for, it's time to let it go."

"I know that, too. I just really hope it's not too late. With Patrick, I mean."

Bianca scoffed. "He's in it so deep, I doubt there's any such thing as too late."

Sofia hoped she was right.

36

Patrick had gotten so caught up in his reading that he didn't notice the effect it was having on Sofia until she fled the room in tears.

Now, he wondered if he'd miscalculated. He'd known that some of what he'd written—especially the parts about his own pain and fear regarding their relationship—might hurt her. But his intention had been to let her into his heart, for better or worse. He hadn't intended to make her break down.

The last poem—the one about grief—had been a step too far, he could see it now. He should have known it was too much. He should have left that one out. He should have—

"You've got some skills there, son," Ramon said as Patrick, stunned, came back to the table.

"If she doesn't want you, I sure as hell do," Lucy said.

"Hey!" Ramon protested.

"I'm just saying." Lucy shrugged.

"That last poem might have been too much," Patrick said. Sofia's sisters had all gathered at the ladies' room—Benny and Martina just outside the door, and Bianca in with Sofia—so it was just the three of them.

"No, it wasn't," Lucy said.

"But—"

"It wasn't too much, Patrick," Lucy insisted. "It was exactly enough."

As he considered it, he knew that he agreed with Lucy. If he lost Sofia over this, it would be a tragedy, one he wouldn't get past quickly. He would miss her so much he'd feel it like an injury, like a lost limb or a serious illness. But he wanted her to love *him*, all of him, and that included his true feelings. He wanted her to love who he really was, not who he presented himself to be. There were things worse than loneliness, and being inauthentic was one of them.

"I should go in there," he said.

"Dude, it's the ladies' room," Ramon pointed out.

Still. This seemed like a pivotal moment, and one got so few of those. He had to handle it correctly.

He went into the hallway where the bathrooms were, squeezed in outside the ladies' room door next to Benny and Martina, and knocked.

"Sofia? Let me in."

When the door unlocked and cracked open, Bianca was there, not Sofia. She pushed the door open a little farther to let him in and put a hand on his arm. "Good luck," she said, and went out into the hallway with her sisters.

He didn't want to have this conversation in a café bathroom, but one had to adapt to circumstances.

"Are you all right?" It was on the tip of his tongue to apologize for upsetting her, but he didn't. Honesty wasn't something a person should regret.

"Yeah." She let in a shaky breath and wiped her eyes with her fingertips. "Yeah, I am." She went to him, and he held her.

"I thought people might be bored." He stroked her hair and

pressed a gentle kiss to the top of her head. "At least that didn't happen."

HE'D WONDERED if she might not want to come home with him after the way he had upset her. He'd wondered, in fact, if she might not want to be with him ever again. But, to his delight, she took his hand and led him out the door of the café and toward his car.

"Take me home," she said.

"Okay. Your home or mine?"

"Yours. Definitely yours."

That was as positive a sign as he could have hoped for. But that wasn't the only thing that gave him optimism. Sofia seemed different, more relaxed, as though the tension between them had drained out of her with her tears.

"You're an amazing writer," she told him as he drove. She held his free hand while he used the other to navigate the curving roads of Leimert.

He supposed his writing must have been better than fair if it had this effect on her.

Creativity had its rewards.

SOFIA HAD a lot to say to Patrick, and for the first time, she believed she would be able to say it. Something had been released in her, and somehow, she was no longer afraid.

But that was for later. Now, she just wanted to be with him.

He parked in front of his house, and she led him by the hand up the front walk, into the cottage, and to his bedroom.

This time, there was no rush, no frenzy of desire and need. This time, she moved slowly and carefully. She savored him.

She turned on the bedside light—she wanted to see him—and began to unbutton his shirt, one button and then another, taking her time. He didn't try to take over, didn't try to rush her or take the lead. He simply stood there watching her, his breath slow and even, his arms relaxed at his sides.

"I worked on those poems for months," he said. "If I'd known they would be so effective, I'd have written faster."

"*Ssh.*" She hushed him with a kiss, then returned to her work. She slid his shirt off of his shoulders and let it fall to the floor. She kissed his chest, savoring the taste of him.

Then she went to work on his belt, sliding it slowly out of the buckle.

They made love as though they had to make it last forever, as though this would be their last night, their last moments. But Sofia knew that wasn't true. They would have time. Because she was ready now, ready to let him in completely. She was ready to give him everything he'd been waiting for.

And she was starting here, now.

She would tell him everything, but that would be later. Now, she wanted to show him everything he meant to her. And she had all night—and then a lifetime—to do it.

AFTERWARD, when they were lying under his comforter, relaxed and relieved at having found each other again, she told him everything. She told him how hard it had been for her after her parents' deaths; the guilt she'd felt over her father and the way she'd blamed herself; her feeling that she didn't deserve to move on and be happy when they couldn't; and the reason she'd fled when she'd thought he was giving her a ring.

"It's hard to think about getting married when I know they won't be there to see it," she told him. "Not that you were actually giving me a ring, of course. I didn't mean ..."

"I'd have given you one if I'd thought you were ready for it." As loaded as the conversation was, he said it as though he were telling her what he planned to have for dinner.

She turned in his arms and propped herself up on her forearms to look at him. "Really? You would have?"

"Sure." He reached out and caressed her hair.

"It's just a lot, you know? My mother used to talk about what kinds of weddings the four of us would have. She was excited about it. Said it was one of the best parts about having girls. And she never got to see even one of us get married." A tear slid down Sofia's face. Now that she'd learned how to cry again, it was hard to turn it off.

"Well, that leaves us with an issue," he said. "Because I do want to marry you—eventually—and it's true that your parents won't be there to see it. I wish they could be, but they can't. So, what will we do?"

"Let me think about it." She kissed him and lay back in his arms.

PATRICK HAD KNOWN that there were many and varied rewards to being a writer. But when he'd imagined those rewards—possible fame and fortune, professional recognition, the joy of personal expression—he'd never thought it would lead to this.

Sex? Well ... what male writer didn't think that a well-turned phrase might bring him attention from women? But Patrick had never dreamed his words might save the love of his life from the painful emotions that had ensnared her.

It would be naïve to think that Sofia's grief was over just because she'd talked about it and she'd cried. And Patrick wasn't naïve. But this was a step, there was no denying it.

In the morning, he sang in the shower, got dressed, drove Sofia to work, then kissed her goodbye before heading to the college.

He hadn't gotten much sleep the night before, but to hell with sleep. It was going to be a great day.

37

———

The day after the reading, Sofia arrived at work smiling. Naturally, Bianca noticed—it had been a long time since that sort of thing had happened.

"I'm guessing you had a good night." Bianca watched as Sofia settled in behind the reception desk. "Either that or you snapped last night in the ladies' room, and you've completely lost your mind."

"I haven't lost my mind."

"Oh, good." Bianca rubbed her hands together in excitement. "Then dish."

"A lady doesn't tell what happens between herself and her man in private," Sofia said.

"Since when are you a lady?"

Sofia just smiled.

"Oh, come on." Bianca planted her fists on her hips. "Give me something. I haven't had a date in five months, and I need to live vicariously through you."

Sofia thought to brush her sister off, but she reconsidered in the interests of openness. "Okay. He wants to marry me."

"No shit." Bianca's delivery was deadpan.

"Bianca ..."

"I mean, really, no shit. I knew that. Benny and Martina knew that. You knew that. The cat who lives next door knew that."

"I suppose." Sofia turned on the computer and logged in, preparing to organize Bianca's schedule for the day.

"He actually said it in those words?" Bianca prompted her.

"Yes."

"But the last time the issue came up, you freaked, fled more than two thousand miles, and nearly broke up with him just to avoid it."

"I did." Sofia turned to look at Bianca. "It's different now."

Bianca's eyebrows rose. "Is it?"

Sofia considered her words carefully before she spoke. "I'm still scared. And I'm still … I still have issues. Obviously. But I want this. I want it to work, and I want to deal with things."

"Oh, Sof." Bianca bent over to hug her. "That's so great. I'm so happy for you. I've been worried."

"I know you have been. I was, too."

"So you want to marry him?"

"I do want that," Sofia said. "The thing is … I couldn't think about doing it without Mom and Dad there, you know?" Here were those damned tears again. She wiped them away. "And that's not going to change."

"We'll figure something out." Bianca squeezed Sofia's shoulder.

Sofia still had a lot of crying and thinking and talking to do to make up for more than a year of refusing to do any of those things. Starting was the hardest part, it turned out, so the words and the tears —and acknowledging the feelings—came easier now.

She kept going to the grief support group, and she stood up and talked for the first time. She continued meeting with Debra, who was rapidly becoming a friend she could rely on. She talked to her sisters when things got hard. And she talked to Patrick.

The more she thought about it, the more she realized that she hadn't talked to him before because she hadn't wanted him to think badly of her. If he thought she was damaged—or, even worse, if he thought she'd caused her father's death—how could he want her?

She was coming to realize that everyone was damaged in some way, and her personal brand of disrepair was no worse than anyone else's.

She was progressing nicely, she thought, but there was still a big, black void in her thoughts whenever she considered the subject of marriage—or, more specifically, a wedding. The idea of marrying Patrick was an appealing one, and she wanted that. But picturing it actually happening—Sofia walking down an aisle in a church and taking vows before God? She simply couldn't imagine it without her parents.

Sofia was about to conclude that she and Patrick should scrap the ceremony and sign some papers at the county government office when Bianca brought up the subject one morning at work.

"I have an idea," she said.

"About what?"

"About your Patrick problem."

"My Patrick problem?"

"Specifically," Bianca said, "your how-am-I-going-to-face-a-wedding-without-parents question."

"Oh." Sofia sat up straighter. "Well, hit me with your idea. I'm listening."

"You should have my wedding," Bianca said, as though it were the obvious solution.

"Your wedding?"

"Exactly. The one I didn't have."

Confused, Sofia rubbed her forehead with her fingertips. "Not to state the obvious, Bianca, but since you didn't have it, it's, you know, not a thing. How can I have a wedding that doesn't exist?"

"You can have it because it was all planned. By Mom. It's the wedding Mom would have planned for you—for any of us, really—if she were here."

Sofia's jaw fell. "You planned a wedding with Mom? When? And why? You were never engaged."

Bianca pulled up a wheeled office chair and sat down next to Sofia behind the reception desk. The office wasn't scheduled to open for another ten minutes.

"You remember when I was in love with Troy Davenport in my junior year?" Bianca said.

"Ugh, Troy Davenport." Sofia rolled her eyes. "That guy was a stiff. That haircut. Jeez."

"Yes, well, nonetheless, I was in love with him. And I told Mom I was going to marry him. So we planned the wedding."

"You were what, sixteen?"

"About that."

"And you planned a wedding? You only went out with him once before he dumped you for Penny DeLuca."

"Thank you for bringing back that painful memory," Bianca said. "Yes. I planned the wedding, and Mom helped me. It was a kind of game, or exercise, or ... You know how some girls write out their imaginary married name on their notebook over and over?"

"Sure, but—"

"I didn't do that. I selected a dress and a cake and a venue, and flowers and the hors d'oeuvres. I think Mom got into it partly because it was a way of bonding with me when I was in the middle of my teen angst phase, and partly because she'd always imagined her girls getting married." Bianca's eyes grew shiny, and she blinked a few times to clear the unshed tears.

"Okay, but ..." Sofia's nose crinkled. "You planned this wedding when you were sixteen? Do I have to have the Backstreet Boys at the reception?"

Bianca raised one eyebrow at her sister. "What do you take me for? I had taste even at sixteen."

It was true. "Okay, but ..."

"And it wasn't just me. Mom and I did it together. It was a bonding thing. It was fun. We really got into it."

"Huh." Sofia considered it.

"Let me dig out the notebooks," Bianca said.

"There are notebooks? Plural?"

Bianca grinned. "You'll see."

WHEN THEY GOT HOME that night, Bianca disappeared into her walk-in closet, rummaged around for a while, and emerged with a stack of three-ring binders half as high as she was.

She plunked the pile onto her bed and said triumphantly, "Here you go. Everything you need to plan the wedding Mom always wanted for one of us."

Martina poked her head into the room to see what they were up to. "Oh, my God. Sofia, you're engaged?"

"No," Sofia said.

"Then what ..."

"Sofia wants to get engaged, but she has to solve the Mom problem first," Bianca summarized. She waved toward the binders as though she were Vanna White. "Behold, the solution to the Mom problem."

"Ooh," Martina said.

Sofia picked up a binder and opened it. Inside were scrapbook pages filled with magazine clippings, photos, sketches, and notes. Some of the notes were in the round, looping handwriting of a sixteen-year-old Bianca, and some were in their mother's more sophisticated script.

Each of the binders covered a different subject: dress, decorations, food, beverages, entertainment, flowers, music, ceremony. There was even one for the ring.

The one Sofia was holding was the dress binder. As she leafed through it, she found pictures of dresses cut from magazines along with notes on each one: *too flouncy,* or *too simple,* or *the skirt on this one is right, but the bodice has the wrong silhouette.*

One dress at the front of the book had been circled in red with the notation, *This is the one!!!* It was exactly the dress Sofia would have picked for herself: ivory color, off-the-shoulder boat neck, half-length lace sleeves, voluminous organza skirt. Pretty, feminine, and elegant.

"Oh, boy." Sofia ran her fingers over the photo. She looked at Bianca. "But this was supposed to be *your* wedding."

"Are you kidding? It was supposed to be me planning it, but this is mostly Mom. When the time came, I wasn't sure how to tell her that I didn't want it. If it suits you, Sof, it's yours."

Sofia looked through one binder after another, feeling her mother in each page. Her mother's handwriting, crisp and clear; her mother's taste in every choice; her mother's desire to create the perfect day for her daughter. It was almost as though Carmela was speaking to her through the pictures and the notes.

A lot of the selections were just what Sofia would have chosen, but even those that weren't were so thoroughly Carmela that she could feel her mother's presence as she looked at them.

"Are you sure?" Sofia asked Bianca.

"Absolutely." She gestured toward the books. "This was never me, and it was never really meant to be—it was just a fun thing I did with Mom. If this helps you break through your Patrick block, you're welcome to it."

My Patrick block. Sofia hadn't thought of it that way, but she supposed that was apt enough—like writer's block, but with romance.

If she had this in front of her—this detailed plan laid out by her mother, a plan created out of Carmela's love for her daughters—then maybe she would have some clear vision to hold onto when she thought of her wedding instead of the empty void she'd had before.

Maybe this could work.

～

SOFIA AND PATRICK were sleeping in the same bed almost every night now—about half the time at his place, and half the time at hers. But she wasn't ready to tell him about the binders yet. She was turning all of it over in her mind, processing it.

One night when he was out at a university event with Ramon, Sofia spread the binders over the coffee table in the living room of her house. She and her sisters had just finished dinner—Bianca had made pasta, garlic bread, and a big salad—and they were sitting around by the big stone fireplace as rain pattered on the roof.

Sofia, wearing sweatpants and a T-shirt, her hair up in a ponytail, sat cross-legged on the sofa with one of the binders in her lap.

"How come I never knew about these?" she asked the others. "Did everyone else know but me?"

Benny was sitting on the rug with her back propped against the sofa. "I didn't know about them, but I'm not surprised. Mom was crazy about weddings."

That was true, but Sofia hadn't realized she was so crazy about them that she'd planned one for someone who wasn't even getting married.

"Well ... how come she only planned Bianca's?" Sofia asked. "Where's my wedding plan?"

"She tried to do mine," Martina put in. The three of them stared at her.

"She did?" Benny asked.

"Yeah, but ..." Martina shrugged. "She didn't exactly have the same taste as I do. We fought over the very first item. The cake." She shuddered. "She wanted this giant five-tiered monstrosity with gold and white flowers and these gold curlicue things at the bottom. It was what you'd get if Liberace competed on *Cake Wars*."

Sofia leaned over and sorted through the binders, then pulled one out and flipped through the pages.

"This one?" She held up a picture for Martina to see.

Martina peered at the page from across the room. "Oh, God. That's the one. You don't have to have that one if you do Mom's wedding, do you?"

"No, thank goodness. Looks like that one didn't make the cut."

"Oh, she tried to sell me on that one," Bianca said. "I put my foot down. I might have been sixteen, but I knew if I didn't assert myself early I'd be wearing Princess Diana's dress and standing at the altar with ten bridesmaids."

It didn't take a lot of imagination to know why Carmela had not attempted to plan a wedding for Benny. Even now, Benny was wearing a Mr. Spock T-shirt with a tattoo peeking out from beneath one sleeve. Ripped jeans and a pair of Doc Martens boots completed the look. Her eyeliner was thick and dark.

When Benny one day got married, Sofia imagined it would be in front of a guy dressed as Elvis at a drive-through chapel in Vegas. If Benny and Carmela had talked weddings, one of them would have been screaming and the other would have been throwing things—and there was no telling which would be doing which.

Sofia was glad Bianca had been so accommodating and that their mother had been able to plan at least one daughter's future nuptials. But at the same time, a voice nagged at her. Why hadn't Sofia's mother done this with her? Why hadn't they had that time together? Why had she chosen Bianca and Martina instead?

A couple of months ago, Sofia would have kept the question locked inside herself, letting it simmer. But she'd come a long way.

"Why you two?" Sofia asked. "Why not me?"

"Dad made her stop," Martina said.

This was news to all of the other three, so they turned to focus on her.

"What? Why?" Bianca asked.

"It was the fight about the cake. She and I really got into it. Mom sent me to my room, then Dad told her that the wedding planning had to stop until somebody actually got engaged."

"How do you know what they talked about if you were in your room?" Benny wanted to know.

"I said she *sent* me to my room. I didn't say I actually went."

That made sense, and hearing the story made Sofia relax a little.

"You're actually talking about Mom," Martina said to Sofia. "I don't think I've heard you talk about her this much since she died."

Sofia clutched a binder to her chest. "Well … it was time."

"It was," Bianca agreed. "I'm proud of you."

Sofia could feel her face reddening. "Shut up."

38

____

Patrick was happy with how things were going with Sofia, except for one thing: he had an itch regarding her, a persistent, nagging need that wouldn't seem to let him go no matter how hard he tried to ignore it.

The itch was specific in nature. He wanted—no, _needed_—to get down on one knee, present her with the ring she'd thought she was getting on Christmas morning, and declare his desire to spend the rest of his life with her, forever, until death did they part.

He'd said he would back off until she was ready. But wasn't it possible that she was ready now? She'd certainly come a long way—he'd seen some major breakthroughs in her emotionally. She was talking openly to him now about her feelings, and she really did seem to be dealing with her grief over her parents.

Wasn't it conceivable that all of that progress had prepared her to make a real commitment to him?

He knew he should be patient. He knew he should wait. But things felt so good with her that he wanted it to last forever. Wanted to declare in front of a room full of people—before God, even—that he would do whatever it took to make it last.

And he wanted to hear those same words from her.

"I think I'm going to do it," he told Fiona on the phone on a morning in early spring, a clear, blue-skied day with birds singing in the trees and a soft wind blowing in off the ocean. "I think it's time. I'm going to propose."

"Oh, jeez." Fiona's voice filled with dread. "Are you sure you want to do that?"

"I know she made a bad impression at Christmas, but she was dealing with a lot of things, and—"

"That's not what I meant. Patrick, it's not that I disapprove of her. I don't know her well enough to disapprove. It's just that I worry you're going to get hurt again. The last time she got the smallest inkling that you were going to propose—even though you weren't—she flew all the way across the country to get away from you."

"Okay, fair point. But things have changed." He was sitting in a patio chair on his front porch, the sun slanting brightly through the branches of a big oak tree in the yard. About twenty yards away, a tabby cat was stalking a squirrel. Patrick stepped down into the yard, snatched up a pinecone, and threw it in the squirrel's direction to warn it.

"It's great that things are going well," Fiona said, "but isn't that even more reason to be patient and let things be? You're happy. Maybe you should just ... you know ... sit there and be happy."

"But if we can be even happier, why not do that?" The argument seemed reasonable enough to him.

"You've got to do what you've got to do, I guess," Fiona said. "Just ... go easy, okay?"

"Sure." He went back onto the porch and sat down again. "What about Mom?"

"What about her?"

"Is she going to be okay, you think? With an engagement, if it happens. When it happens. Because after what happened at Christmas ..."

"Mom will be fine. You know her. Whatever's going to get her more grandkids is all right by her. She's pretty much given up on Sean ever adopting, and I'm done having kids, so that leaves you."

The idea of having kids with Sofia—plump little toddlers with her dark hair and espresso-brown eyes—had occurred to him more than once, but now he was almost overwhelmed by the image. He wanted it. He wanted it all.

"Do you really think it's a mistake?" he asked.

"I don't know. And, hell, what do I know about it, anyway? You're the one who's there in the relationship every day. You're the one who's got to make the call."

"Right." A surge of nerves shot through him.

"Whatever you decide to do, good luck," Fiona told him. "I hope it works out the way you want it to."

And if it didn't? He pushed the thought out of his mind.

It just had to.

~

"Which one? We should have brought Lucy." Patrick and Ramon were browsing the engagement rings in a jewelry store in San Luis Obispo, perusing the diamond solitaires and, as an alternative, the colorful gemstones.

They'd come here instead of looking at a jewelry store in Cambria because it was near work, and because Cambria was such a small town that if he'd shopped there, word would have gotten to Sofia within a day. Not only would that have ruined the surprise, in the worst case scenario, it also might have sent her into some kind of self-styled witness protection program complete with a fake name and forged documents.

That wouldn't do. When he presented her with the ring, he had to be ready to do instant damage control if it turned out he'd read the situation wrong and she really wasn't ready.

"You can never go wrong with simple and elegant." The employee behind the counter, an impeccably groomed middle-aged woman who smelled lightly of lilacs, pulled a one-carat diamond solitaire out of a case and handed it to Patrick.

He turned it this way and that, and the overhead lights sparkled in the facets.

"Lucy would tell you to get that one," Ramon remarked.

"You think so?" Patrick stared at the ring.

"Let's find out." Ramon pulled out his phone, snapped a picture of the ring, and sent it to Lucy with a text message asking whether she thought Sofia would like it.

The answer came back almost immediately:

She'd be crazy not to!!!

Patrick asked the price, and he nearly flinched when he heard it. An associate professor's salary at a state university wasn't nearly as much as people thought it was. He had money saved, but this would take a big chunk of it.

And it wasn't just the money. The idea that he was really doing this—putting himself out there completely, whatever might come—made him feel a little shaky and weak-kneed.

"Let me think about it." He handed the ring back to the saleswoman.

By the following day, he'd just about decided to go back and buy the ring when he received a package from FedEx that required his signature. He didn't know what it could be; he wasn't expecting anything.

He opened the package and found a small box enclosed along with a note from his mother.

Fiona told me what you were planning to do, and I thought you might want this. It belonged to your grandmother. Good luck, sweetheart.

He opened the box and found a gold ring with an emerald cut diamond in the center. Surrounding it was a delicate design of tiny diamonds framing the larger one. The band was studded with more miniscule diamonds in two side-by-side rows.

Had he ever seen this ring on his grandmother's hand? He

supposed he must have. It seemed very much like her, and he was struck by a flood of memories.

But what struck him even more was the fact that his mother had sent the ring to him. He'd worried that she would disapprove, after everything that had happened at Christmas. He didn't need his mother's approval—he would marry Sofia, if she would have him, with or without it—but he was nearly overwhelmed by gratitude that she had given him her blessing.

Giving Sofia this ring felt so much more right than giving her some generic solitaire from a jewelry store.

He had everything he needed now. All he had to do was gather his courage and ask the question.

PATRICK HELD onto the ring for a while as he worked on a plan for asking Sofia to marry him. Should he take her to a nice restaurant and do it there? Ask her quietly in private, maybe at his place? Maybe a flash mob on Main Street?

After much consideration, he decided that doing it at her house, with her sisters there, was the best plan. Sofia was inseparable from her sisters, and he thought it might be special for her to have them present if she said yes. And if she didn't say yes—if she had some hard emotions like she'd had at Christmas—it would be good to have them there to support her.

He hoped that emotional support would not be necessary. This was supposed to be a happy occasion that called for celebration, and he was banking on the idea that it would be. He'd spent a fair amount of time judging Sofia's emotional readiness, and he felt good about it.

He thought she was ready.

He didn't like to think about what might happen if he was wrong, but he also didn't want to play it safe. Playing it safe rarely resulted in the kind of life that made a person swoon with gratitude for each new day.

That was the kind of life he wanted for himself and for Sofia. And he felt certain that it was just within their grasp. All they had to do was reach out and take it.

HE'D BEEN CARRYING the ring around in his pocket just in case the perfect opportunity might happen to coincide with an adequate amount of his own courage. The two elements converged on a Sunday evening in April when he was at Sofia's house having dinner with her and her sisters.

Bianca had made the kind of big Italian dinner that Patrick had once thought was a false Italian stereotype, but wasn't. They'd had a first course of pasta followed by a course of braised veal and roasted vegetables. A basket of fresh bread sat in the middle of the table, and they all drank glasses of dark red Chianti.

The first time he'd seen them do this as a regular Sunday dinner —no guests, no special occasion—he'd been awed. Martina had explained that their mother had brought the tradition with her from Italy. While the sisters didn't observe the practice every Sunday the way their parents had, they did it from time to time as a way of remembering how things had been. Before.

While all of the sisters had some cooking skills, Bianca had a gift, and so she was the one who usually did the honors for the big Sunday meals. She simmered sauce on the stove for hours, carefully braised the meat, and sometimes even baked her own rolls for the table.

It was after one of those meals, when Patrick was feeling happily full and slightly buzzed on red wine, that he decided to make his move.

They'd just finished eating, and Sofia had gotten up to start clearing the table. Normally, Patrick would have helped her, but today, he took her hand and said, "Let's do that in a minute. I have something I want to talk to you about."

"Oops. Should we give you two some privacy?" Bianca asked.

"No, actually. I'd like it if you all stayed."

"Patrick, what's this about?" Sofia's eyebrows drew together as she looked at him.

"Just … let's go sit down." Still holding her hand, he drew her into the living room and motioned for her to sit on the sofa in front of the fire.

"Are you sure you want us to stay?" Benny asked uncertainly. "Because we could just—"

"No. Stay. Please." Patrick had imagined that he might be shaking with nerves at this moment, but he wasn't. He was steady. He was sure.

When everyone was settled, he took Sofia's hand and began the speech he'd rehearsed.

"Sofia, you know how much I love you. At Christmas, you thought I was giving you a ring and getting ready to propose. And that was hard for you. I didn't understand why at the time, but I do now. We've come so far since then. *You've* come so far. And while I didn't have a ring for you then, I did already know that I wanted to spend the rest of my life with you. Even though I wasn't asking the question then, the way you thought I was, I knew that someday I would. Someday when I thought you were ready."

He got up from his seat on the sofa and lowered himself to one knee.

"Oh, my God," Bianca said.

"Oh, jeez, Patrick," Benny put in.

Sofia didn't say a thing as Patrick reached into his pocket and pulled out a little square box.

"The idea of a wedding probably still isn't easy for you," he said. "So here's what I propose: you and I will go to the county government building in SLO, apply for a marriage certificate, and then get married in front of a justice of the peace or a judge or whoever it is who does that sort of thing. Then, if you want to, we can have a party or go on a trip, or do something to commemorate the occasion. Or we won't. We could just go on with our lives together without any of that. It doesn't matter. All that matters is that we're together."

He opened the box, took out the ring, and offered it to her.

"Sofia, will you marry me in a low-key civil ceremony?"

She stared at him, frozen, while everyone in the room waited. Patrick appeared calm, but his heart was pounding.

"No," she said.

"Oh, shit," Benny muttered.

"No?" Patrick said.

Sofia got up and rushed out of the room. She went into her bedroom and closed the door.

"Oh, God," Patrick moaned. "I'm sorry. I thought ... I thought she was ready. I thought ..."

Before he could say any more, Sofia's door opened and she came out of the room with her arms loaded with three-ring binders.

"What's all that?" he asked, bewildered.

Sofia set everything down on the coffee table, then took the ring he was still holding and slipped it onto her finger.

"It's beautiful," she said, then kissed him long and deeply. Still wrapped in his arms, she said, "I meant no to the second part, not the first part. I do want to marry you. But ... is it okay if we have Bianca's wedding? I have some binders for you to look through...."

Patrick didn't know what she meant by Bianca's wedding. He didn't know what was in the binders. But his future sisters-in-law were hugging him and kissing him on the cheek and welcoming him to the family.

And Sofia wasn't running—she was right here.

He felt like he was exactly where he belonged, in exactly the right place with exactly the right people.

He couldn't wait to see what might happen next.

GET A FREE LINDA SEED SHORT STORY

Sign up for Linda's e-mail newsletter and get "Jacks Are Wild," a Main Street Merchants short story available only to subscribers. Claim the story at the following web address: https://claims.prolificworks.com/free/TFPZoP8q

www.ingramcontent.com/pod-product-compliance
Lightning Source LLC
Chambersburg PA
CBHW021116110726
47900CB00007B/2209